The
PEACOCK
ROOM

Also by Merryn Corcoran

The Silent Village
The Paris Inheritance

MERRYN CORCORAN

The
PEACOCK ROOM

RedDoor

Published by RedDoor
www.reddoorpublishing.com

© 2019 Merryn Corcoran

The right of Merryn Corcoran to be identified as author of this
Work has been asserted by her in accordance with sections 77
and 78 of the Copyright, Designs and Patents Act 1988

ISBN 978-1-910453-81-0

A CIP catalogue record for this book is available
from the British Library

Cover design: Patrick Knowles
www.patrickknowlesdesign.co.uk

Typesetting: Tutis Innovative E-Solutions Pte. Ltd

Printed and bound in Denmark by Nørhaven

Dedicated to the memory of
Michelle Amass and Clark Boustridge

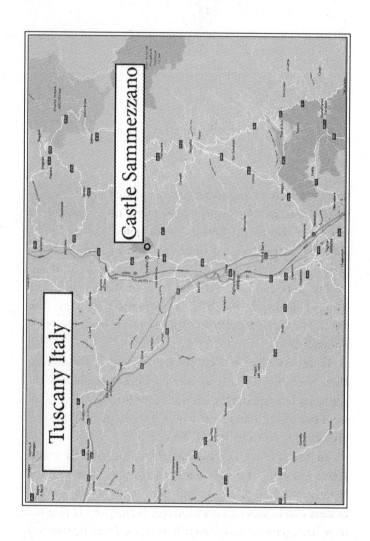

Tuscany Italy

Castle Sammezzano

Prologue

It is my nature to appear arrogant, and I can confirm I am ostentatious and take great enjoyment in displaying my splendour. However, there is documented reason for my conceit. It has been an honour to be hailed as a symbol of good fortune. Throughout history I have been associated with royalty, glory and resurrection. Early Christians believed my blood could dispel evil spirits. The ancients believed my flesh did not decay after death, and so I also became a symbol of immortality.

In ancient Greece I was the patron bird of the goddess Hera. She believed the 'eyes' on my plumage symbolised all-seeing knowledge and the wisdom of the heavens – that if you wove one of my plumes into a necklace of amethyst, it would protect you from witches and sorcerers.

To invite me to take residence in your garden will enhance your estate with the aura of luxury and wealth. I have appeared in the grounds of palaces in India, castles in England, and in chateaus and castles all over Europe. Images of my plumage have been painted and woven into fabrics, and my name is always associated with objects of outstanding beauty.

Whilst you may have one of my exquisite plumes as your personal talisman, it is imperative you never put my actual feathers on display within your four walls. As the king of all birds, I, the Peacock, the most regal and powerful totem of all my kind, decree you leave my poignant, silken, colourful feathers as they were found.

One

It appeared to be one of those rare perfect days when Allegra had the opportunity to be self-indulgent; both children had left for school without any of the usual teenage angst or guilt-fuelled parental torment. She had also cleaned and groomed the house to the minimalist standard that her husband Hugo expected. Making the most of her unaccompanied day, she pulled on her much-loved colourful Bibi vintage dress and slipped into a pair of comfortable flat black pumps.

The Wallace Collection beckoned. The preserved eighteenth-century stately home in Manchester Square just off Oxford Street was a special place where Allegra loved to lose herself. The inspirational mansion offered charisma, beauty and mystery of what had gone before. She appreciated the manner in which the rich furnishings framed the massive rooms; the opulence of the furniture and lavish paintings, encased in their luxuriant frames, always reignited her love of art from the past.

As she locked her front door the fragrance of the potted lemon grass nudged Allegra's deliberations over lunch. The delicate smoked salmon they served in the conservatory café, a modern addition to The Wallace Collection, was one of her favourites. Then she remembered the dry cleaning. *Hugo's suit! Shit, he'll be mad if I forget that again!* She rushed back up the stairs and grabbed the suit along with her Missoni silk dress. As she walked out to the car, she instinctively checked through the suit trousers and jacket pockets and was about to discard what looked like a scrappy receipt when she spotted 'Hilton Hotel' on the crumpled paper.

Throwing the clothes onto the back seat of the car, Allegra clasped the paper as she sat down at the wheel. It was clear a room had been paid for on March 12 at the Hilton Hotel, Park Lane. The itemised list showed the customer had a room service dinner for two, as well as an in-house adult film and room service breakfast, also for two. There was no doubting the recipient. Hugo O'Brien's name leapt out from the paper where he had swiped his Amex card.

Allegra reached for a tissue and wiped her forehead then took the battered leather Filofax from her handbag. Her hands trembled as she frantically flicked the pages back to March, hoping like mad this was all some mistake and it wouldn't be one of those nights her Hugo had been away on business. There it was, written clearly in blue pen. *H. away in Birmingham.*

Rushing back inside, she just made it to the downstairs cloakroom before she fell onto her knees on the cold tiled floor and vomited into the loo. After rinsing her mouth, she caught her reflection in the mirror. Her mascara had run. There were grey flecks showing in her jet-black wavy hair. Hugo had always said alongside her wide, brown Italian eyes that her hair was her best feature. Both those attributes seemed to have abandoned her. Her weight gain probably hadn't helped, either. She was ugly. Past it. By the time she reached the landing at the top of the stairs, she was sure her heart would break.

Clutching her head in her hands, she sat on the edge of the bed, their bed, the one she had shared with Hugo for twenty-two years. Home had always been under Hugo's roof. She had never once considered being with another man. The children, Kirsty and Harry, gave her all the happiness she expected. Had that all not been enough for Hugo?

A numbness set in. Her instinct was to call her best friend, Julia, but realising she'd be at work, it would have to be second choice – her mother.

All thoughts of her day out abandoned, Allegra barely registered the road as she drove the short distance to her mother's house.

'Allegra, I wasn't expecting you. I have to be at my yoga class soon. Why are you crying? What's happened?' Her mother put down her coffee cup and embraced her daughter.

'It's Hugo. He's having an affair.'

'What? Hugo! Are you sure?'

'I'm sure, Mum. Look at this.' Allegra handed her the receipt.

'The bastard! All the support you've given him, and all you gave up for his career, not to mention your two beautiful children—'

Allegra stopped her.

'Mum, I know all that, but clearly I'm not getting it right. I think maybe I've let myself go. Maybe it's my fault.' Her eyes welled up again.

'Well, yes, the weight is becoming a bit of an issue and your hair definitely needs updating.'

Allegra let out a huge sob.

'Oh, sorry, my darling, that came out all wrong. I know you think I'm vain and spend too much time and money on myself, but I do have my admirers!' Her mother smoothed her hair, sucked in her cheeks and widened her eyes as she caught her reflection in the window. 'However, a lapse in grooming is no excuse for Hugo to go off and shag someone else.'

Maria, Allegra's mother, gave birth to her only child aged nineteen after a shotgun wedding. Allegra's father passed away when Allegra was only twelve, so she was familiar with her mother's need to be seen in a youthful light. With the aid of Botox, a great hairdresser and a disciplined exercise regime, as well as inheriting some wonderful Italian genes, Maria was confident she safely passed for a woman in her early fifties.

Their conversation was interrupted by a bell ringing.

'Oh, I do hope Grandpapa didn't hear me!' Allegra sniffed and wiped her eyes.

'He's so deaf these days, he won't have even heard our voices,' Maria said as they followed the sound of the bell up the stairs to his bedroom.

'Look who's here, Papa. It's Allegra come to say hello.' Maria exaggerated her condescending tone as she entered the room and straightened the rug on her father's lap.

The ancient, stooped man with his grey moustache and wiry hair motioned for his granddaughter to sit on the chair next to him and offered her a toothless grin. At ninety-nine, he had lost most of his teeth and couldn't walk, but he still occasionally spoke a few words. Grandpapa wore his days like a faded suit – an empty man whose passion arose from thoughts of a magical folly he knew many years ago. A rather tatty peacock feather lay on his lap. It had been his talisman ever since Allegra was a tiny girl, when he would enchant her with stories of the Peacock Room in a faraway Italian castle.

As Allegra planted a kiss on her grandpapa's unshaven cheek, she inhaled the familiar scent of Novella Melograno cologne. Her mother at least allowed him that indulgence, and would visit the Santa Maria fragrance boutique in Walton Street every few months and buy him a bottle.

Grandpapa viewed Allegra through his thick-lensed spectacles with an intense stare. She recalled that he had always played the major parenting role in her life. Her mother was mostly preoccupied with some new man and her social life. When Allegra was at university, Grandpapa would happily spend time listening to her latest view of interiors and the use of colour in the fourteenth century.

He waited till his daughter had left the room before he spoke. 'My precious *Bellisima* Allegra, every day you grow more like my Mama Cosima. For someone with only a quarter of Italian blood in your veins, I can see all the passion and artistic temperament of a full-blooded Italian woman from Donnini.' He touched his constant companion, the peacock feather, with his wrinkled hand and looked intently at his granddaughter. 'Why have you tears in your eyes, my sweet Allegra?'

'Oh, Grandpapa, I feel so betrayed. Hugo has been cheating on me.' Allegra took the old man's free hand as tears rolled down her cheeks.

'I'm so sorry, my precious girl… But let me tell you something. We all have it in us to let others down. I chose to marry your grandmama against the advice of my own mama. She was right. It was a terrible marriage, but I wanted to get as far away from Italy as I could, and marriage to an Englishwoman was my passage.' He put his hand back on his lap and sighed.

'But why did you want to leave so much, when now all you speak about is your village of Donnini and Florence?' Allegra asked.

He lapsed into Italian babble. '*Il Pavone*, the magic *castello*. My papa...the Peacock Room.' This was what occurred most times. He would appear perfectly lucid, then the dementia would take over and although his words made little sense to Allegra, they were clearly full of regret.

After a minute or so, Grandpapa's eyes flickered shut. The peacock feather dropped to the floor and she placed it back in his wrinkled hand before she quietly left the room.

'So, did the silly old man say anything useful?' Maria asked as Allegra walked into the kitchen.

'No, just the usual about how I look like his Mama Cosima, and the romantic Peacock Room in the magical castle.'

She took a sip of the coffee Maria handed her. 'So now I guess I have to go home and confront Hugo.'

'Will you forgive him?'

'I have no idea. I want to hear what he has to say first, I suppose.' Allegra sighed, kissed her mother, and drove home to face her new reality.

Two

It was apparent both her children were home as Allegra opened the front door. Harry's coat had been thrown in the vague direction of the hallway coat hooks, and Kirsty's trainers were tossed on the floor underneath.

'Mum, is that you?' her daughter called from the kitchen.

As Allegra walked in, Kirsty's face lit up. Allegra called it the 'Mum, I want something' smile.

'Mum, there's an alt-J concert on and everyone's going. Could you just sub me till the end of the month? It's only fifty quid.'

Apart from her rich nut-coloured, shiny long hair, eighteen-year-old Kirsty looked her usual grungy self: ripped jeans, a tight T-shirt, and chipped green toe-nail polish highlighting her bare feet.

Allegra didn't reply. She took a bottle of white wine from the fridge, poured herself a glass, and sat down heavily at the kitchen table.

'Shit, Mum, what's happened to you? You look like crap! Did you have another row with Gran?' Kirsty sat down opposite her mother.

Allegra took a sip of the wine. 'No, I didn't have a row with your grandmother. And no, I won't sub you, as you never pay me back. The whole idea of us giving you an allowance is so you can learn how to manage your money. You have told us you're saving for this gap year you want so much. New Zealand is an expensive option.'

'Well, fuck you too Mum!' Kirsty shoved back her chair, stormed out of the kitchen, and slammed the door.

Allegra hung her head defeated as she subconsciously surveyed the sterile-looking kitchen. It reeked of Hugo's white minimalist touch. When they first met, he was attracted to her creative, artistic personality and her anti-war stance, but after twenty years of working in an ad agency, he viewed his house on a purely commercial, contrived level.

'Hi, Mum. Another Kirsty-the-bitch drama?' Harry commented as he kissed his mother's cheek and sat in the chair his sister had just vacated.

'Yes. Yet another one. But I didn't deal with it very well either...' Allegra drained her glass.

'I'm real hungry, Mum. What's for supper?' Harry said as he opened the fridge door.

Allegra wiped her eyes and looked directly at her son. At sixteen years old, Harry was almost the opposite of his sister. He favoured basic Gap trousers, Converse trainers, and a short haircut that highlighted his weird glasses and completed his geek look. His entire life appeared to revolve around what he could summon on his computer screen.

'Take the mincemeat out, will you?' Allegra sighed. 'I can't really be bothered, so I'll just do spaghetti bolognaise.'

'Call me when it's ready,' he sang out as he left the room.

The familiar sound of the front door slamming unleashed a fresh wave of anxiety in Allegra. Would Hugo know straight away that she knew? Would he deny it, beg for forgiveness? Cry?

'Honey, what's for supper? I'm famished!' Allegra's husband walked up to her from behind and gently kissed the top of her head.

She didn't turn. Instead, she stiffened and kept stirring the boiling spaghetti.

'Oh, what's this – a bad mood! Another row with your mother?'

That did it. Wielding the wooden spoon, she abruptly swung around, unwittingly flicking hot water in Hugo's face.

'Shit, Allegra, watch my face!'

'No, not my mother! You – you unfaithful prick!'

The colour drained from his face.

'Whaa...what do you mean?' he said, uttering a rare stammer.

'What I mean is, for starters, March 12 at the Hilton Hotel!' She threw the spoon down and wrung her hands, furiously attempting to halt her own tears.

'Um, Mum, is the spaghetti ready yet?' Harry walked in behind them.

'Harry, go to your room. Your mother and I are having a discussion!' Hugo barked at his son, who took one look at them both and scurried out of the kitchen.

In a bid to conceal her sobs, Allegra began chopping the fresh onions. A prolonged silence fell over the room as Hugo poured himself a drink, then sighed and sat down.

'We can't avoid this conversation now, Allegra. So...I want to leave you. I'm in love with someone else,' he stated without looking up, and then took a large gulp from his glass.

Allegra continued stirring the onions in with the mincemeat and tomatoes. Shock engulfed her. What was there to say?

'Oh, great, food's ready! Dad, can you sub me fifty quid? I just have to go to the alt-J concert. Everyone's going.' Kirsty bounced into the kitchen and joined her father at the table.

'Call your brother down, please,' Allegra said, still with her back to them.

She swiftly clattered three dishes of the spaghetti on the table, and left the room.

The upstairs bathroom was her refuge.

At university, Allegra had studied European interior architecture specific to the fourteenth-to-eighteenth centuries. This room – and only this room in the house – was entirely hers. Using a fourteenth-century Italian pattern, she had tiled the floor in a Florentine mosaic style. The walls were marble, and the vintage-style bath and basin had cost a small fortune. They looked as if they had been designed specially to complement the astounding floor. The mirror, which lorded over the basin, had been cut to fit the gold ornate frame Allegra had found in an antique shop on Portobello Road. She had extended the size of the room by engulfing what had previously been a linen cupboard and strategically placed a brocade-upholstered antique chair in the space. Hugo had been against the whole concept, but it was the one battle in their marriage she had won.

After ten minutes of weeping fully-clothed in the marble bathtub, she heard nervous rustles outside.

'Allegra, open the door, please. We need to talk,' Hugo called. She wiped her eyes with the back of her hand, stood herself up, and reluctantly left her sanctuary.

Hugo had removed his shoes and sat on their bed, rubbing his head.

'So, what did you tell the children?' Allegra asked.

'Nothing, they didn't ask. Harry said if I was giving Kirsty the fifty pounds for the concert then he would like fifty as well for something for his computer. They are entirely selfish children. It's probably our fault.'

He sighed, then continued, 'I'm sorry this has happened the way it has. How did you find out?' He attempted to look Allegra in the eye but failed and turned away, busily removing his silk Hermès tie.

She attempted to compose herself, to take her time; she wanted to afford him as much discomfort as possible. 'Well, you can take some comfort in that other than the Hilton receipt, I don't know any of the sordid details. But please show me some respect and tell me who she is and how long it's been going on.' Allegra tugged a strand of her hair around her finger and yanked it aggressively.

'Fair enough. But I don't want to cause you any more pain,' Hugo replied.

'For fuck's sake Hugo, my heart has just been ripped in half. What could be worse? Spare me your pompous bullshit!'

'I've never heard you say "fuck" before… You sound like your potty-mouthed daughter.'

'To be precise, she is *our* potty-mouthed daughter. And I can swear worse than that. Now, tell me, who is this slut?' Allegra's face shone bright red.

'Very well.' He cleared his throat. 'First, I'll have you know she is not a slut. Her name is Brooklyn. She works with me, and it's been going on for six months…' His voice trailed off as he looked down at his feet.

'What…the Brooklyn I met at your work party? But she can't be any older than Kirsty. That's just sick!' Allegra clutched her sides, trying to hold herself upright.

'She's a very mature, intelligent twenty-five-year-old. She turns me on and she fancies me madly, which is more than you do.'

There was a tomb-like moment of silence. Even Hugo appeared a bit shocked at his brutal words.

Allegra lifted her head high. 'You have half an hour to tell our children what you have just told me, pack your things and leave. I never want you in this house again.'

Three

'Oh, please say yes, Allegra. Please. Three days in Florence will do you good and the easyJet fares are so cheap. Besides, Hugo can afford to pay for everything after what the arse has done to you.' Allegra's best friend Julia could be very persistent when she wanted something.

'I just don't think I'd be much company, Julia. Some days, I can't stop crying and most evenings I can't even manage to function without a bottle of wine,' Allegra said.

'Come on, Florence is oozing with fourteenth-century architecture or whatever it is you're obsessed with. Wasn't it your specialty subject? And you are half Italian,' Julia replied.

'Actually, only a quarter.'

'To be honest, Allegra, you would be doing me a favour too... Gerald and I have been having some real problems lately. I just need to get away from him for a bit,' Julia said.

'It sounds like we both need a break from men.' Allegra paused, and then added, 'OK, you're right. If I don't pull myself up out of this, no one else will. Yes, I'll come with you to Florence.'

'Hooray! Oh, I'm so pleased. Thank you, you really are my best friend,' Julia gushed. Allegra barely registered that Julia sounded a bit too relieved.

Four months had passed since the discovery of Hugo's infidelity and his departure from the house. In the first few weeks, Allegra had barely moved from her precious bathroom. At first, she had been entirely broken. The pain, which started out as a debilitating stab in her chest, had now moved on to a dull ache. But the betrayal invaded all her waking hours, and she only managed to sleep with the aid of copious amounts of wine.

As vain and self-serving as Allegra's mother Maria was, she was also fairly perceptive. After the first couple of months of watching Allegra wallow in self-pity, Maria arrived one day unannounced. She removed all the alcohol from the house in an act more symbolic of cleansing than issue of sobriety. She berated her daughter for neglecting her children and her appearance, and then promptly phoned the Michael-John of Mayfair salon, booking Allegra for a complete makeover at Hugo's expense. In fact, if Allegra was being honest with herself, their relationship had greatly improved in the past few weeks.

Allegra was also beginning to find some normality in daily tasks. She was about to knock on her daughter's bedroom door when she smelt a sickly aroma. Assuming Kirsty was burning incense, she opened the door.

'My God, Kirsty, what are you smoking?'

Kirsty hastily shoved the spliff behind her back. 'Just a French cigarette, Mum, nothing to get heated about,' she said in a gasp as she coughed out pungent smoke.

'That's a marijuana joint! I'm not an idiot.'

'I am eighteen years old, Mother, and smoking the odd spliff – or "joint," as you call it – is perfectly normal in my group of friends. It's not like it's bloody cocaine.' She stubbed the spliff out in the makeshift ashtray on her desk.

'You may be eighteen, but you are still entirely dependent on me. This is my house, and in my house, you respect my rules.'

'Gosh, Mum, I didn't know you two were divorced yet. Last time I looked, Dad still had a say in what goes on here. Besides, I bet he smokes a few spliffs with his new girlfriend! Maybe you should try some – it might make you a bit more interesting.'

Kirsty's words cut deep, and Allegra stepped back sharply as though she had been slapped. She swung around and hurried out of the room, remaining deaf to the faint words Kirsty called out, and retreated to the sanctuary of her Italian bathroom.

The following morning at breakfast, Kirsty attempted an apology.

'Mum… What I said last night… I – I guess I'm sorry.'

'You are my daughter and for that reason only, I forgive you. But I won't forget, Kirsty,' Allegra stated coldly. 'Words are powerful and you need to use them more carefully.' Allegra took a deep breath. 'Anyway, I have something to tell you both.' She leant over and placed a piece of fresh toast on Harry's plate. 'Next week, I'm away for a few days with Julia, and after yesterday's drug revelation, I've e-mailed your father and asked him to come and keep an eye on you while I'm gone.'

Harry put down his toast, pushed his chair back, and stood up.

'Shit, Mum, that's not fair. I didn't do anything. And I'm almost seventeen, I'm not a kid anymore. He's not bringing that tart with him, is he?' he asked.

'No, Harry. This is our home, and I know he will respect that.'

'I'd quite like to meet the whore who stuffed up our lives.' Kirsty sniggered.

Allegra suppressed a smile.

'OK, that's enough. It won't be an issue, Harry; you have my word.'

A couple of days before the Florence trip, Allegra printed out a map of Tuscany from her laptop and took it with her to visit her mother.

'For goodness' sake, girl, what planet are you on? No one uses paper maps anymore. You need an iPad and an *apt*.' Allegra's mother scooped up her iPad off the table and expertly pulled up a map of the Tuscany region.

Allegra took the tablet from her mother. 'Gosh, it's so easy! Maybe I will buy Harry one after all, and then I can use it too.'

Maria paused for a moment. 'Look, my darling, I appreciate you want to involve your grandpapa in your Florence visit, but please consider how upset and confused he gets…after all it's me who has to deal with him.'

Allegra fidgeted with her screen. Now was as good a time as any to broach the family history. 'Mum, I've never fully understood why he left Italy and what happened to his relationship with Gran.'

'I'm not fully privy to it, either. My mother discouraged me from asking... It was so painful for him to remember. But apparently, when he first came out here, he wanted nothing to do with his past and set about learning English as best he could. He was a brilliant craftsman. His work with tiles couldn't be matched. I now think my mother sensed early on that she was more of a convenience than the love of his life, so after I was born, that was it. She reacted badly to his indifference towards her. They did not have a happy marriage… It rather put me off long term relationships.'

Maria turned the coffee machine on and then continued. 'Old people often think back to their past. Papa speaks mostly now of his missing father. You know, how his father walked out one day when Papa was a boy and never returned.'

Allegra squeezed her mother's hand, and Maria smiled gratefully. 'Thanks for being honest with me, Mum. But I will feel terribly guilty if I go off to Florence without sharing this with grandpapa. Maybe I can even help find out about his father… Don't worry, I'll be subtle.'

The old man screwed up his nose as Allegra popped her head around the door. She held out the iPad and placed it directly in front of his thick lenses.

'So, Grandpapa, I'm going to Florence.'

He stared at her attentively, as if his brain was grappling for the right words.

'Florence, Grandpapa. You know…'

'I was born in the village of Donnini in Tuscany in 1912,' he forced out in a whisper. Behind his spectacles tears brimmed, but he took a deep breath and continued.

'My beautiful mama would cry for my papa. I can barely remember him now. He disappeared when I was just a *bambino*. Some days, she cursed the *castello*. Other days, she hailed its magic. But every day, she wept.' His voice faded and his eyes flickered. 'The Peacock Room was my favourite, but after Papa disappeared, Mama never took me there again.'

'Grandpapa, what *castello*? What is the Peacock Room?' Allegra asked, hoping the Italian term would help him remember. But he just stared out the window. He was far, far away.

Her mother appeared silently behind her.

'Come on, love. You won't get any more from him now.'

Maria persuaded Allegra to join her in a homemade salad washed down with a half-glass of wine.

'You definitely seem happier, Allegra. How is the job hunting going?' her mother asked.

'I've applied to the Chelsea Art School as a part-time lecturer, also to The Victoria and Albert Museum as a trainee curator in early European ceramics, and to a specialist tile shop on Wandsworth Bridge Road for a sales position. I don't really mind what I do. I just need a job. Without Hugo's income things are going to be tight.' Allegra tugged her hair worriedly.

'My darling, you will eventually pull all your hair out if you keep twisting it like that,' Maria said.

'You've said that forever and it's never happened.' Allegra smiled.

'Well, mothers are always right. In the end.' Maria took a little sip of her wine before she continued. 'I'll send a prayer up that you get the trainee curator position. That was always your passion before you fell so madly in love with Hugo. And you were so talented.' She leaned over and squeezed her daughter's arm.

'Mum… Since we're being so honest… Were you madly in love with my father?'

'For a brief moment, darling. But to be honest, if I hadn't been pregnant with you, I probably wouldn't have married him. After the first couple of years, I realised I'd married a dreamer who was just like my father. And he held me back. I've watched Hugo hold you back, especially when it came to your career. I just don't believe marriage should constrain you like that.' She sighed.

'Having said that, the upside with your father was having you… I know you have your doubts, but *you* are the love of my life, Allegra.' Maria reached over and took Allegra's face in her hands for a moment. Then she tactfully led the conversation on to the subject of her grandchildren.

'Once you have fully recovered from this ordeal and have a steady job, you'll need to think about the children's attitudes. Both you and Hugo are allowing guilt to cloud your judgement on their behaviour. They both should have part-time jobs, like we all did at their age. Especially Kirsty, if she expects to do that gap year in New Zealand.' She paused, anticipating Allegra's usual defence.

Instead, Allegra sighed resignedly. 'I know, Mum, I do agree with you. They are just so wilful. I'm really looking forward to going away. With any luck, the kids will give Hugo the worst time ever!'

Allegra hugged her mother tightly before she left, and as she drove home, mulled over the castle and the peacock from her grandpapa's ramblings.

Four

Allegra smiled as she keenly studied herself in the full-length mirror. The new haircut was brilliant and the very camp stylist had covered all the grey – well worth the two hundred and fifty pounds.

I guess mothers are always right. The haircut made her feel more confident, and after an hour-long demonstration of how to apply make-up in the Mac shop, she'd purchased an entirely new kit.

Allegra considered the break-up with Hugo was akin to grief – it had left a gritty residue of frustration and sorrow, not to mention a labyrinth of imaginings. Had there been anyone else? Would Hugo have more children? But the heartbreak had one positive effect: Allegra had shed over five kilos and now at sixty-five kilos, her five-foot-eight-inch frame looked a lot sexier.

She'd packed what she thought she would need for three days in Florence and on Kirsty's advice, she'd indulged in some new trendy Nike trainers especially for walking the streets.

Allegra also wanted to visit museums – and lots of them. There was one that had previously been a great collector's personal home. Museums wouldn't be Julia's thing – she was purely a shopper. But she would definitely join Julia in the Missoni boutique. Allegra adored their signature zigzag pattern and rich colours… It reminded her of the mosaic tiles in her beautiful bathroom.

The thought of the time interrupted Allegra's planning – it was past 7:00 p.m. and Harry still wasn't home for dinner. This was very unusual as, at his request, she had cooked his favourite meal of roast beef with crispy roast potatoes.

His mobile went straight to voicemail on both attempts. She was just about to try again when the landline rang.

'Hi, Allegra, Harry has had an accident. Don't panic, he's alive, but a bit damaged.'

'What accident? What happened, Hugo, how is he damaged? When did he call you?' Allegra's voice rose to hysterical.

'Calm down… He came off his bike near the ring road. He has a broken leg, that's all. The hospital tried your landline first, and when there was no answer, my mobile was the second port of call,' Hugo attempted to placate. 'He's in a cast now and I'm bringing him home.'

When Hugo arrived at the house with Harry on crutches, the first thing he asked was if she had saved his dinner.

'Oh, my poor boy, how bad is the pain? I'll cancel my holiday. You're going to need help getting about on crutches,' Allegra said, vaguely aware of Hugo who was studying her in an odd way.

'No, Mum, you are going on holiday! Dad and I have talked about it and I want you to go. They gave me a cool injection, so the pain's not that bad. I'll sleep downstairs and Kirsty and Dad can run around after me,' Harry said. Allegra hesitated. But Hugo promised to be an excellent nursemaid – almost overly enthusiastic, she thought – so she finally gave in. It was her first holiday as a singleton in years, now that she thought about it.

The next morning, the taxi pulled up outside at the same time Hugo arrived. Allegra's heart still missed a beat when she had to confront him, but she wasn't sure if it was because she still loved him, or because she hated him.

As he got out of his Mercedes sports car, she felt he didn't look quite his usual groomed self. She hadn't noticed in all the chaos the previous evening. His chinos were rumpled, he had darkish rings under his usually twinkling eyes, which now aged him, and she could swear his bald patch had expanded.

'Allegra, you look amazing!' he said as he gave her a lingering once-over.

Enjoying the surge of justified vengeance, Allegra offered him a generous smile. The fitted black jeans, knee-high boots and bright orange V-neck cashmere sweater had been the perfect choice for this encounter. The ensemble highlighted her revitalised figure.

'Thanks Hugo. To be honest, you look a bit knackered. Clearly, the younger model doesn't favour ironing and early nights!' She smiled again as his eyes lingered on her cleavage. 'Anyway, there's a list on the table of stuff needed to feed our son. Only text or call me in an emergency, please. Bye.' She took a deep, satisfied breath as the cabbie shut the car door and eased away from the house.

At Victoria Station Julia greeted Allegra with a big hug.

'My goodness, you're actually on time!' Allegra quipped.

'Yes, because I'm *so* excited!' Julia stood back and cast a scrutinising look up and down her friend's appearance.

'*Mama mia* as they say where we're going! You look *molto bellissima*. I can see your mother's handiwork, but what a fabulous transformation!'

'You are so full of it, Julia. Come on, we'd better get on this train.' Allegra blushed deeply, swinging an arm around her dearest friend as they walked towards the platform for the Gatwick Express.

The two sat opposite each other in a space meant for four passengers and spread out with the table in between. They had been class chums right through high school, and although diverse in their interests and skills, they had shared all their deepest thoughts and secrets. Julia had chosen not to have children, and she was an exceptionally youthful-looking forty-something. She had a great figure, a head of immaculate blonde highlights, and striking azure-blue eyes that captivated men. Dressed in skinny jeans, flat pumps, and a colourful Chanel tweed jacket, she looked the total epitome of Chelsea chic.

Allegra updated Julia on Harry and Kirsty – she was also Kirsty's godmother – on everything including the marijuana incident.

'Well, at the risk of offending, I think she may have a point. It might do you good to indulge a bit and try a spliff. I know you let loose with the vino, but Hugo was always so controlling of your behaviour and it affected his image – and all the time he was doing his own thing on the side. Perhaps you can suit yourself for a while?' Julia gave a hesitant smile.

'Maybe…but I want to be in control of myself from now on. Since Hugo's been out of my life I've realised he did stop me pursuing my love of design… I've become so enthralled with interiors and architecture again. Did I tell you I applied for that curator trainee position?'

After a comfortable half hour chatting on the train, and a further uncomfortable half hour queuing at the airport, the women finally found their cramped seats and the flight went without any major incident.

As they entered the outskirts of Florence, Allegra peered intently out the taxi window. She wanted to absorb every little detail. It was as if she had left all the hurt of Hugo behind and this was her moment of rebirth. Under the luminous sky, she recognised the outline of the Duomo and the surrounding embellished towers. 'Look, Julia, there's the Ponte Vecchio!'

'I love to see a city through informed eyes. How long has it been since you were here?' Julia asked.

'Not since I was eighteen – Kirsty's age.' She gave a gasp as the taxi pulled up in front of the Grand Hotel Baglioni with its impressive late 1800's facade. The hotel sat in proud splendour on the Piazza Unita Italiana. As they stepped out of the cab, Allegra caught the aroma of fresh coffee and the sweet scent of what she guessed to be her favourite vanilla *panettone* wafting from a nearby coffee shop.

Whilst Julia followed the bellboy to the reception desk, Allegra took a few prolonged moments to digest the interior of the eighteenth-century hotel lobby. Expertly placed rich furnishings perfectly matched the symmetrical, ornate floor tiles.

'I just knew this place would suit you when I saw it online,' Julia said as they followed the bellboy.

Their room on the fourth floor was nothing short of opulent and featured two double beds covered in lush black satin quilted bedspreads. The focus of the room was a wrought iron balcony, fronted by French doors, which overlooked the bustling Piazza.

'Julia, remind me to thank you...repeatedly,' Allegra said happily.

Once they had unpacked and hung up their clothes, Julia took a small bottle of red wine from the minibar and poured the contents into two glasses.

'Look, Allegra, I haven't been quite honest with you.' Julia nervously crossed her legs and ran her finger down the oversized wine glass.

'Aha. I thought there was something... Go on then.' Allegra grimaced.

'Well, you needed to get out of London anyway, and you know looking at architecture isn't my thing. Well, um, I've got a bit of a fling going on. It's not serious, just a bit of fun. So, I'm going to spend tonight and tomorrow morning with him. If that's OK with you?'

Allegra was gobsmacked. 'What? You're having an affair!'

'Well, it's not exactly an affair. You know Gerald and I are considering a separation. He's not up to much sex anymore. This is just sex, and maybe some confidence boosting for me. He's married as well, and at a conference here for two days.' She gulped down the rest of her wine.

'You bloody hypocrite! Slagging off Hugo and doing exactly the same thing yourself. Why couldn't you just tell me from the outset? Oh, piss off, Julia! You've completely manipulated this situation for your own ends.' Allegra stomped into the bathroom.

'Come on, Allegra. You know what I'm like, I can't help myself! And Gerald makes me feel so unattractive... I need this. Don't be mad at me. We don't fly out till quite late on Sunday, so we can go out together tomorrow evening and we'll have all Sunday to shop at the Missoni store. I know you love it there…' Julia called through the bathroom door.

Allegra took her time fiddling with her hair and touching up her make-up behind the closed door. She was fuming. What had started out as a perfect day was now in ruins.

Julia gingerly opened the bathroom door. 'Please, Allegra, forgive me. I didn't think it through properly. Given what Hugo has just done to you.' Julia had the grace to lower her eyes and blush.

Allegra glared at her friend. 'You should have just told me. I had an inkling you had some sort of agenda anyway.'

'And would you still have come?'

'Maybe.'

'Look, we're here now. Let's not fall out. It's only four o'clock. Why don't we go for a walk and look at the beautiful statues?'

Allegra reluctantly nodded and they walked in silence to the elevator.

Once they were outside in the busy piazza, the wonderful fresh sights and sounds of Italian life soothed Allegra's temper. Besides, it seemed it was the way Julia and Gerald's marriage worked – break-ups followed by big make-ups. Florence was just too beautiful a place to waste time being angry or sad, and she was flooded with a welcome sense of freedom at being unshackled from all her London dramas.

As the two friends walked towards the Duomo in relative silence, they gazed into shop windows and Allegra made mental notes as to where they would return on their shopping trip.

Then they turned the corner, and there it stood in all its glory – the largest dome in the world.

'Look… See the panels that clad the walls? They are in fact a new addition, and although I understand why they must use modern materials for preservation purposes, I don't entirely agree with the colours. Look, there's hardly any queue, let's go in.' Allegra found her voice as they reached Florence's famous basilica.

'I'm just sure you know every architectural detail of this church, so I will let you reveal each one. I'm sorry again, dear friend.' Julia hugged Allegra and planted a kiss on her cheek.

'Alright, alright.' Allegra brushed Julia off with a good-natured smile. 'First off, this is not called a church. It is the grand dame of all Italian basilicas, or cathedrals as we call them. It is commonly known as *Il Duomo di Firenze*, but the correct name is *Cattedrale di Santa Maria del Fiore*, which translated means "Saint Mary of the Flower". It is a name which, in my opinion, lends an aura of humility in the presence of God to such a proud structure.' Allegra was in full swing, and an audience of one suited her fine.

'Can you imagine, they commenced building in 1296 and it wasn't completed till nearly a century and a half later, in 1436?' Allegra unconsciously twisted a strand of her hair as she spoke.

'How do you remember all these dates? Why would you want to?' Julia frowned.

'I did a thesis on the Duomo at university. That was why I came to Florence the first time – to bear witness to its rapturous presence,' Allegra replied dreamily.

'I suspect your repressed passion hasn't actually been for Hugo at all!'

Allegra ignored the comment and continued her commentary. 'Now, let me add that the façade was altered in the nineteenth century by a chap called Emilio De Fabris, which I feel was a mistake. He put the "Gothic spin" on it. I would have rather they left it as it was in 1436.' Allegra led

Julia over to the rich wooden pews that sat directly under the massive dome.

'See up there – that fresco depicts a scene called "The Last Judgement".' She pointed up to the artwork embraced by the dome.

'Yes, similar to what I just got!' Julia laughed. Allegra shot her a look.

'Sorry,' Julia mouthed.

Allegra continued, 'The artist who designed the mural was called Vasari, but, as happens nowadays in the design world, it wasn't him who actually painted most of it. It was one of his talented students, a chap called Federico Zuccari.' Allegra relaxed back into the pew and continued gazing upwards.

'As an architectural philistine, I appreciate the lesson Allegra. No one knows as much as you do about Italian art history… But we had better head back – the sun is setting already.' Julia stood up, playfully tugging Allegra's hand.

Once back at the hotel, Allegra propped herself up on the oversized bed. She had opened the curtains and French doors to savour the evening light and enjoy the sounds of the busy Piazza below, as she read up on where she might visit the next day.

Almost an hour later, Julia appeared from the bathroom, exquisitely made up, hair blow-waved to perfection, her ample body squeezed into a desperately expensive Donna Karan black number, with a gust of Chanel No. 5 trailing in her wake. Allegra watched as Julia tightly rolled a silk tunic, a pair of black lacy knickers, and some soft heeled pumps, along with a small toilet purse, into her tote bag.

'See you tomorrow around 5:00 p.m., and then we can have dinner together,' Julia said as she left the room.

Allegra sighed in agreement, and settled back on the enormous pillows.

Five

As dusk finally fell, Allegra stepped into her much-loved multi coloured Missoni silk dress. After some deliberation in front of the mirror, over whether to wear practical flat shoes or heels, she chose the heels. After all, she reasoned, she was a single woman in Florence. She even had a room with a view!

Eyeing herself critically in the full-length mirror, she made a comparison with her friend's appearance before she had departed for her assignation. Then Allegra returned to the bathroom and gave her hair a little more attention, added lip gloss, and straightened her shoulders.

On a small side street about a ten-minute stroll from the hotel, she selected a restaurant with well-positioned outdoor seating and ordered an antipasto platter, followed by the pasta of the day: fresh mushroom tortellini.

Pretending to be engrossed by the street-performing violinist whose melodic music added to the ambience of the evening, Allegra observed her fellow diners. In particular, a man at a nearby table. He was seated alone, swarthy-looking with ink-black, well-cut hair and wearing a stunning powder-blue, high-collared shirt. She thought he was trying to catch her eye. Then just as he looked like he might be about to approach her, the sound of her mobile phone invaded the moment.

'Mum, Dad has invited the whore to our place for dinner tonight!' Kirsty screamed into the phone. 'You have to phone him and ban her. It's our house! Harry and I don't want her here.'

'OK Kirsty, stop shouting. Now tell me, have you asked your father not to bring her over?' Allegra checked her watch. It would be about 7:30 p.m. on Friday evening in London.

'Yes, and he told us we had to get over it and move on. But, Mum, it makes me feel sick. She's not that much older than me.'

Allegra didn't have a ready response. There was nothing she could do, and if she was being honest, she didn't want to do anything about it. It was the anticipated fallout Hugo would suffer with their children, and she figured it was something all three of them would have to face eventually.

'Look, darling, as you keep telling me, you are practically an adult now. You can deal with this. The only thing I would ask is that you show your father some modicum of respect.'

Kirsty snapped. 'Like *that's* going to happen!' She hung up.

By the time Allegra had composed herself, the swarthy would-be admirer had gone. As she walked back to the hotel, she decided she would probably not have had the courage to talk to him anyway.

Then it dawned on her. It was the first time she had ever considered dating someone since her marriage break-up. Hugo had shattered both her self confidence and her life as she knew it, as a wife, and mother. She desperately needed a new dream.

The next morning, over a luxurious breakfast of fresh omelette and perfect coffee in the hotel, Allegra managed to program the map on her mobile phone to lead her to the Stibbert Museum. She had chosen the Stibbert primarily because Frederick Stibbert's father was originally English and Frederick had dedicated his life to collecting eclectic art from across the globe. He had donated his museum, a large villa, and all his art collections to the Italian State when he died in 1906. The museum was in the north of the city, up a hill in Montughi – too high even for hiking in her new trainers, so Allegra decided it was time for a taxi ride.

She was reassured that it was the right choice when she arrived at this almost secret gem of a building. There were no queues of tourists, in fact, there were very few people at all at 9:00 a.m. on this fragrant, enchanting Italian morning.

The building appeared like a grand old residential villa, but Stibbert had actually built it specially to showcase his collection.

On entering, Allegra was amazed to discover it was set in a small park featuring some pretty plantings and an original water well. She was ushered up to the first floor where impressive double wooden doors opened into a sweeping hallway, with clever parquet flooring and white walls showcasing the art.

Stibbert was obsessed with armour and had collected it from all over Europe, as well as Japan, the Middle East, and the Orient. However, he also had some excellent wall panels and a diverse array of complex Italian artworks that adorned the walls. The pieces Allegra was keen to have a closer look at were the ones with an oriental influence.

Allegra admired Frederick Stibbert's tenacity to defy the convention of the day. Instead of taking all these treasures back to England and flaunting them to his peers in some manor house, he chose to bestow them in an appropriate haven in his mother's birth country. Allegra believed she understood his passion. As she moved into the different rooms, she experienced a resurgence of emotion and curiosity for beautiful antiquities that she had repressed for a very long time.

It was 12:00 a.m. by the time she had examined every corner of the museum and viewed the informative video presentation about Frederick Stibbert. She caught a taxi into the city centre and wandered in the direction of the Palazzo Vecchio. As she walked past a large green bus, a tout approached her with a leaflet.

Why not join our free bus trip to the new discount designer outlet village? Just a thirty-five-minute ride from here with buses returning every hour.

Allegra studied the leaflet. It featured Christian Dior, Gucci, Ralph Lauren, and there at the bottom of the list – Missoni. 'Why not?' she said out loud, smiling as she hopped on the bus along with four giggling Japanese girls.

Once the tout had filled the seats, an overweight, thick-set man with a mono-brow heaved himself into the driver seat and the door made a slurping sound as it sealed shut.

Allegra considered that Julia probably would be a little pissed off with her, but they could still go shopping together the following day. A bargain Missoni dress or shirt was so much more enjoyable than one at full price. Besides, Julia was having her own fun, and Allegra would enjoy having something to offer at their debriefing rather than just hearing about her friend's sex life.

A middle-aged American woman took the seat next to Allegra. 'Hi, I'm Dallas.' She extended her sweaty hand to

Allegra, who muttered her name, then attempted to subtly wipe her hand on her jeans.

'You have to be so careful in Italy! I was robbed in the street yesterday. It was so awful,' she drawled.

'Really? I'm so sorry to hear,' Allegra replied, in an attempt to sound interested.

'Yeah. It was lucky I had taken my friend Cindy's advice. I'd put my Amex card and my cell phone in my bra, so the shit only got my cash when he pickpocketed me.'

Once Allegra had listened to the minutiae of the robbery and the town the woman came from in the States, she turned towards the window and pretended to doze whilst Dallas turned her attention to the Italian woman across the aisle.

There was an interesting assortment of tourists taking advantage of the free ride. A couple of Australian women, three immaculately groomed camp men who smelt wonderful as they walked to the back seat, a smattering of Italians, and the verbose Japanese girls who didn't appear to draw breath.

The bus left the motorway and Allegra was delighted as the picture-postcard scenes of classic Tuscany began to flash by. Tall cypress trees punctuated the rolling hills with their sharply-defined edges. On flat land near the road, she was captivated by row upon row of small, decorative trees being cultivated for aspirational private gardens and pretentious hotel foyers. Then the bus slowed down as it took a turn down a small road deeper into the countryside.

'Oh, My Gawd! Where are we going? We're in the middle of nowhere!' The American's voice interrupted Allegra's moment of calm.

Then, as she returned to her moving window view, she caught sight of the word 'Donnini'. The next set of road signs said Leccio and Donnini – her grandpapa's village. She quickly attempted to capture the road sign with her phone's camera, but as she struggled with the settings, the bus picked up speed. All she caught were the rows of vines spread out like plumes, laden with grapes. After they passed through Leccio, Allegra hoped Donnini would be the next village. She felt a swell of excitement which soon turned to disappointment as they sped past the village in the blink of an eye.

The bus hurtled through the main street of the small village so quickly she only caught a glimpse of a small store with its flapping plastic, multi-coloured fly screen covering the central door, and vegetables and fruit stacked either side. Next to it was a bar, a garage repair shop, and further along two old ladies dressed in black, sitting on old cane chairs, positioned to scrutinise any visitors and all the passing traffic. Five minutes later, the obese bus driver appeared to grunt as he pulled on the steering wheel and manoeuvred the bus into the parking lot of a large, ugly, newly-built complex called The Mall.

The structure was completely out of kilter with the surrounding countryside. It consisted of several large, warehouse-type buildings that were made of grey linear iron, with only one central window and the designer name emblazoned on the front.

The Gucci building was the most obvious, with its massive 'Gucci Café' sign across its front wall. Allegra studied the directory board in a bid to locate the Missoni store.

It was not at all what she had anticipated. Most of the pieces on sale were from previous very old collections, and the ones on display were mostly garish colours she wouldn't choose to wear. What irked her most were the people, carrying handfuls of designer bags and shoving as they almost attacked the rails of clothes. Allegra wanted out.

It struck her she hadn't eaten or even had a drink for a few hours so she made her way back to the Gucci building and the bustling café. After battling several massive groups of rude shoppers, she finally settled on a bar stool in the window with her cappuccino and a panini. Looking out beyond the mall's buildings, Allegra could see the steel and asphalt halted quite abruptly at the road edge. Across the other side was a rough fence and the beginning of a green area and, further up, what looked like a gathering of tall trees.

'*Scusa, signora, é libero questo sedile*?' An attractive man motioned to the seat next to Allegra and smiled as he balanced his coffee cup and a Gucci carry bag.

'Yes, this is free. I'm sorry, I don't speak very good Italian,' she replied, and smiled back.

'Oh, you are English?' He sat down and looked directly into her eyes.

'Yes, I'm from London. Just visiting for a few days.'

'I see you have no shopping yet. Have you just arrived?' His accent was sexy.

Allegra caught a whiff of his fragrance, which she recognised as Armani. His neatly cut hair reminded her of George Clooney – salt-and-pepper grey. His fitted, pale lemon shirt looked as if it had been sculpted onto his body, while his tight jeans featured a disquieting bulge at the crotch. Allegra quickly averted her eyes, telling herself it was just the angle he was sitting at, on the awkward stool.

He deluged her with questions about who she was travelling with, where she was staying in Florence and what monuments she had visited. As she answered without inhibition, he continued to look her directly in the eye. With every comment and answer, the depth of his gaze and the rhythm of his voice gave Allegra a sense of almost carnal magnetism.

'You had better finish your panino. May I get you another coffee?' he asked.

Allegra shook her head and took a few bites from her sandwich, but was suddenly embarrassed by stuffing food into her mouth. She also felt a pressing urge to go to the loo.

'Will you excuse me for a moment? I need to find the bathroom,' Allegra said. He smiled and pointed to the far side of the café, adding that he would reserve her seat and her panino. She grabbed her bag and made her way towards the universal sign for toilets.

It was with great relief when her turn finally came in the queue. Then she pushed into a position at the mirror to touch up her make-up. She heard a familiar drawl behind her as Dallas the American was recalling her robbery to yet another unsuspecting victim. Allegra had removed her mobile phone to take out her make-up bag, and as she was applying some fresh lipstick, it buzzed. Hugo's number flashed. 'Are the children OK?' she asked.

'They are being so rude to Brooklyn. They are a disgrace, Allegra. They never used to be this bad. I don't deserve all this grief. I want you to phone Kirsty and pull her into line.'

'I can't believe you're telling me this, Hugo. Their disrespect towards you is entirely your own fault. And has it ever crossed your mind that they are rude to Brooklyn because she is a vile little upstart? Just piss off! I am on holiday until further notice.' She snapped shut her phone and with Dallas almost blocking her path to the door, she tucked the phone into her bra and returned to the distraction of the delicious Italian man still sitting beside her empty stool.

He introduced himself as Silvano. As she told him her name, he gently took her hand, brushed his lips across it, then whispered in a throaty voice, 'Enchanting, Allegra.' A shot of raw desire flashed through her body, and in that moment she felt like the only woman in the room.

'How would you like to forsake your shopping for a while? Come and join me for a walk in the nearby countryside and a jazz cigarette. The shopping afterwards will be much more exciting.' His chocolate-coloured eyes flicked up and down her body.

Allegra's mind clouded in a bout of indecision. Then she thought of the conversation with Hugo and caught a flash of Julia's words: 'Get a bit loose, it will do you good.'

As she rose from the stool, he took her hand and led her out of the café towards the main road.

'Romero, Romero!' A girl about Kirsty's age called out as she hurried towards them on the footpath.

Silvano quickly dropped Allegra's hand as the girl approached, yelling furiously in Italian. Silvano snapped a few words back at her then scooped up Allegra's hand again and kept walking. Allegra slowed down. 'Who was that?' she asked.

'She is mad. She thinks I am someone she knows, but she is mistaken. Come on, let's forget about her.' They had come to the end of the mall's complex and crossed the road. He led her up a shingle path to where several early-model, old cars were parked.

Up above them, Allegra could see what she thought were tall red pine trees. They seemed to be planted in a sequence leading up a track on the hill. 'What's up there?' she asked.

'I don't know, but I do know a beautiful place here, come and see.' He led her through a break in the undergrowth to a secluded grassy spot under a tree. He took what appeared to be a hand-rolled cigarette from his pocket and an impressive slimline lighter. He swiped one end of the roll-up between his lips to moisten it, lit up and inhaled without releasing any smoke. He handed it to Allegra.

Well, this would loosen her up. Feigning confidence, she took the spliff and inhaled deeply, but she coughed and spluttered as the weird-tasting smoke hit her throat on its way to her lungs.

'Careful, my beautiful Allegra. Take your time. Let me talk you through it. This is a jazz cigarette. Just gently suck on it and breathe deeply, let all that jazz float into your lungs and bloodstream. Soon, it will hit the amazing senses in your brain.' She followed his instructions then handed back the joint. They shared it until the last ash had dropped.

Allegra fell back on the soft, mossy ground. Silvano lay beside her and as he stroked her hair, she felt the firm stab of his erect crotch against her thigh. Her mind floated away as the marijuana infiltrated her body. He leant over and gently kissed her, his hand lightly rubbing her breast. Allegra felt her nipples harden beneath her shirt at his touch.

Suddenly, a babble of voices disturbed them.

'Don't worry, it is just teenagers – probably looking for a place to do things,' Silvano said as Allegra sat upright.

In that moment, her confused mind switched from lust back to London and her children. *My God, I'm in bushes with a stranger...*

But Silvano the seducer immediately noticed her mood change. He skillfully deflected it with some irrelevant chat about families, and led her back to the subject of pleasure whilst rubbing the back of her neck and gazing into her eyes. 'Does my special cigarette make you feel good all over?'

Allegra smiled, back to the simple delight of being the centre of someone else's world.

'I have something even more exciting. It's very natural and very light but it will make you feel even sexier than you do right now.' He removed a small plastic bag from his back pocket.

'They look like dried mushrooms,' Allegra said as she struggled to see through the haze that had settled in her vision.

'They *are* mushrooms – magic mushrooms! Open your mouth.' Before she had time to resist, he put a couple of the dried fungi on his tongue then leaned forward, crudely pulling her to him, and thrusting his tongue into her mouth.

Whaa..? What have I done? What's going to happen? The mushrooms left an earthy taste in her mouth. Her mood swung wildly back again, a renewed wave of fear sweeping through her. His face seemed to have altered somehow. The warmth from his eyes had disappeared and they were now black and cold. His smile had become a smirk of indifference as he roughly thrust his hand down between her legs. Allegra jumped up instinctively, and out of the corner of her eye, caught him scooping her wallet out of her handbag and into his back pocket.

'What are you doing, Silvano? Please give that back to me!' Her words were slurred, her steps faltering.

He glared straight at her. She could still see the outline of his erection under his skin-tight jeans. 'Well, what do you think will happen? You stupid woman. I steal your wallet. And now we have sex.' He made a grab for her.

Terrified, Allegra hurtled clumsily through the gap in the bushes, leaving her handbag where Silvano had dropped it, and bolted up the nearest track.

He gave chase but soon appeared to give up, and after what seemed like an age, she was forced to stop running uphill and catch her breath. She turned and looked back. Nothing.

Allegra found herself all alone amongst the giant red pine trees.

Six

Allegra leaned against one of the pine trees, too frightened to go back down the hill in case Silvano was still there. Drawing in a few deep breaths, she turned and took a long view of the track. It didn't seem like anyone was following her. She could hear the birdsong and the hum of insects – everything was quiet and still. It was as if the animals were singing just for her and she could hear the distinct individual tune of each bird. Maybe it was the effects of the jazz cigarette, but it was beautiful anyway... Forgetting about her handbag, and about Silvano, she pursued the birdsong, up the track and between the giant trees.

She wandered on endlessly. Strangely, she felt neither tiredness nor sensation – it was as if her legs were the only conscious part of her body. She felt as if she could walk upwards for eternity. Pockets of sunlight radiated down between the heavily laden green branches, announcing her path and encouraging her to walk higher and further.

Whilst the forest around the giant trees was dense and lush, Allegra could now make out the bones of a once-structured park, one that offered pockets of grassy knolls. It would once have been a very beautiful garden, perhaps an entrance to an estate, or a grand Italian palazzo.

Now the haze had lifted from her eyes, she saw everything as if through a magnifying glass. The details were amazing – the effects of the mushrooms must have kicked in. She paused to look closely at a spider that had spun its web between the branches of a shrub. It seemed so real…so three-dimensional – like a woven, floating cloud of fluffy cotton wool, crawling with tiny babies.

She called out goodbye to the engaging spider and walked further up the track. The line of giant trees dwindled and a smallish structure appeared surrounded by crumbling bricks. There was a turret in sight, with a smaller building behind it.

As Allegra walked closer to the crumbling wall, the ivy appeared to move and wave. It was fascinating. She stood very still and watched wide-eyed as the shiny green leaves wove up and down the wall. Was she hallucinating?

She then turned her attention to the turret. The shutters on it were all closed, and she could now see it was a gatehouse possibly to something larger and more exciting further along the wall.

Perhaps she could buy some water there – her tongue was so dry. *It must be what those mushrooms do – they fry your tongue.* Just as the thought shuttled through her brain, she felt a large raindrop moisten her cheek. It was like magic – to think a thought and have the heavens respond. She opened her mouth, tilting her head upwards to sip the raindrops. The drops morphed into a deluge, and while the sensation of moisture offered her dry body a sense of relief, Allegra quickly looked around for shelter.

As she ran through the gateway in the wall, the rain seemed to be beating words. *Faster, faster.* She followed another pathway and there across a patchy lawn stood an impressive building. In her befuddled mind, she could tell it was old, but she simply couldn't date it. It wasn't what she would call beautiful, but it felt…compelling somehow. It wasn't quite a castle, but she felt whoever built it would have believed that it was. It had a tall centre piece of what looked like five stories, encompassing a large decorative clock, and a Moorish arch that shaded the front doors. There was a wing on either side, but she couldn't get a sense of the depth of the building.

'I *am* hallucinating – it must be the mushrooms,' she spoke aloud to herself. The rain continued to pour and she started to shiver. Instinctively, she ran across the lawn towards the castle, the mud squishing under her feet. The front doors grew taller as she approached them. They were bolted fast. She banged loudly with a closed fist, shouting, 'Is anybody there? It's pouring with rain out here!'

But there was no response, just the sound of beating rain on the grey cobbles.

Seven

Allegra scurried to the side of the building, where she spotted a lesser doorway, then down a couple of steps to what looked like a lower-ground floor. Again, she knocked and called out. A new type of silence presided – an enticing silence. She shoved the rickety door and without much effort it fell open into a musty-smelling abandoned kitchen. 'Circa 1980, I'd say,' she muttered wearily.

There was just enough natural light for Allegra to see, and spotting a towel hanging by the cooker, she briskly rubbed the excess water from her shirt and jeans. Then she rubbed her hair. *Wow! I feel like I've had a cold bath.* A renewed invigorating buzz swept over her body.

Discarding the towel, she surveyed the kitchen and walked over to a large door at the back, which in turn led to a staircase. Allegra was immediately drawn to the elaborate Moorish wallpaper accompanying the upward stone stairs. As she moved closer, she could see that it wasn't actually wallpaper, but beautiful tiles. Stroking the slippery colourful porcelain with her hands, she felt compelled to follow the stairs. The rich colours were calling her.

She flicked the light switch but to no avail – the electricity must have been cut some time ago. She carefully negotiated the steps whilst sliding her hand along the furrowed tiles for balance. As she reached the top of the stairs, lack of light was no longer an issue as the rain had ceased, allowing the sun's weak rays to pour into the space in front.

She couldn't believe her eyes. It must be a dream.

The interior design of this room wasn't Italian at all. It was entirely Moorish! The room was swathed from floor to ceiling in the most magnificent tiles. The most prominent colour in the mosaic floors was terracotta, interspersed with sharp blacks and browns. The walls featured an array of blues in all shades of turquoise and aqua. An intricate frieze a third of the way up from the floor, introduced a key line of pink, followed by bordered areas of a design similar to *fleur de lis*. The final section that connected the wall to the ceiling featured rows of diamond-shaped tiles.

Allegra rubbed her eyes. *Was she in a film set? Was she still hallucinating?* As that thought rested in her brain, her eyes were drawn to the doorway on the far side of the room. It sat perfectly, a classic half-moon Moorish shape with porcelain pillars incorporated into the structure.

She stepped through the doorway to a new room – there were no hallways, only doors leading into adjoining rooms. This one gave off a sense of purity in all shades of white. The Moorish influence had been intense. The fully tiled walls were embellished with intricately carved flourishes as they reached up to a mezzanine floor. The room had four grand entrances, each announced by a group of tall pillars.

Allegra lay down on the floor so she could take in every part of this architectural masterpiece. The pillars were repeated on the mezzanine level, where smart, colourful, lead-light windows had been built to allow a drenching of natural light down into both levels. After some time – minutes, maybe hours – she hauled herself up. It seemed a massive decision as to which door to go through next. Her legs made the decision for her as she lightly stepped through the right-hand side.

The abundance of light had been cleverly harnessed to shine through the tall stained-glass windows. She rubbed her eyes in disbelief. *My God. I'm in my grandpapa's place. This is the Peacock Room!*

From the vaulted ceiling, down to the polished floors, there was a vast array of mosaic tiles, painstakingly and strategically laid in the colours of an enormous peacock. The hallucination was overwhelming.

Allegra again dropped to the floor. She lay out flat and attempted to comprehend what lay before her eyes. Did drugs exaggerate existing fantasies? She could see that this first floor room was on the back wall of the surreal building, and the windows were lead-lighted and high. The peacock-coloured tiles were arranged in the shape of fans, to show the peacock's tail on full display. She stood up, her legs suddenly feeling heavy. She wanted to speak, but the words couldn't reach her lips; like sugar in water, they simply dissolved into a distant part of her brain.

She decided to follow the light and looked out the window to the distinct vista of Tuscany, where she had arrived on a bus only a few hours before. Outside appeared normal but inside was her Grandpapa's dream.

The urge to venture through one of the doors at either end of the Peacock Room propelled Allegra forward. But what if the room disappeared? If it really was a hallucination then it would vanish, along with her memory of it.

Allegra felt a light stab at her breast. Her phone! She had forgotten that it was tucked it into her bra. She could take a photo of her dream for her grandpapa, although she knew it could well be blank once she woke up.

After struggling with her befuddled mind to operate the camera, and taking a clumsy snap, she turned to the doorways. Carefully selecting the one that felt like it led further inside the building, she found a smaller, more personal room. An ornate altar was the centrepiece. It was enhanced with rich cobalt-blue-and-gold adornment. Allegra felt a flourish of spiritual love as she reached out and reverently touched the brass crucifix that sat on a Russian-inspired base. The crucifix was accompanied by The Star of David and the star and crescent symbol of the Muslim faith which were painted onto the altar. She had never been particularly religious but in this dream, she believed that God had designed these rooms especially for her. He had taken all the beautiful colours in the world and condensed them into these rooms in Tuscany, just for her.

Allegra's spiritual high was suddenly disturbed as, out of the corner of her eye, she caught sight of something moving through the next doorway.

'Hello?' she called, and walked towards the passing shadow. It was a bit of a blur, but she could just make out an old man. For an old man, he was walking fast, she thought.

Something about his demeanour offered her a sense of warmth. *Perhaps he's a little deaf, like Grandpapa.*

'*Buongiorno!*' she shouted, her voice reverberating through the empty rooms. She picked up speed as she followed him through door after door, each room more magnificent than the last. But there wasn't time to take it all in, and all of a sudden, he was gone.

Allegra was confused. Where had he gone? She had so many questions and she wanted to find out what he knew about these beautiful rooms.

She took a breath and looked around her. She was now in a room of white and cream tiles interspersed with tiny mirrors. It was like a fairy tale of *Arabian Nights* proportions.

The last of the afternoon sun was catching the mirrors and they twinkled like sunset stars. One of the doors within this twinkling room led up another beautifully tiled staircase. Perhaps the old man had gone up there? The staircase was dark, so Allegra trod carefully. As she stepped out into what she assumed was the third floor, she experienced another colour explosion.

Missoni! Surely all things Missoni had been born here? The walls were tiled in lines of diverse but strangely complementary colours, all in a distinctive zigzag pattern – the Missoni family's design statement. Allegra reeled from the sheer magnificence of the space.

At the front of this room, coloured lead-lighted doors opened out onto a balcony. Allegra pushed the doors open and the crisp air refreshed her face. She looked out over the front lawn of the castle – everything appeared perfectly normal. The sun had gone down and the evening was still. The rhythm of her slow breathing was the only sound that disturbed the monotonous silence. Allegra scoured the lawn and surrounding trees, hoping to get a glimpse of the old man again. Perhaps he was the caretaker and lived in the gatehouse? The silence was broken only by a single bird's song and a ripple of wind through the trees.

She felt a little chilled and walked back into the Missoni room. She clicked at her phone a few more times, but wasn't sure the camera was working as there was no flash. An overwhelming sense of tiredness consumed her. It was growing dark; perhaps she would rest for a bit. Every room had been void of any furniture so far, but she could make her way back to the basement level, where the kitchen was located. Surely there would be a chair there.

She took the staircase back down but didn't arrive in the *Arabian Nights* room like she expected. Instead, she found herself in yet another room of impressive proportions, one which featured a dramatic, ornate fireplace. Unsure which way to go, she chose a door to the left where she was confronted by a large, oval-shaped stone bath set in the centre of a marble-tiled room. There was only one door here, so she left the same way she came in. The doors and rooms seemed to go on forever.

Finally, she found another small downward staircase. With the sun now gone, the rooms were dark and the stairs were pitch-black. Using the light from her phone, she managed to navigate her way down to the kitchen. Thankfully in the next room she found some chairs and even a sofa. Allegra fought to keep her eyes open, but sleep beckoned. She grabbed a musty throw from one of the chairs, lay down on the sofa and closed her eyes.

Eight

Allegra felt something digging into her back. *Strange – the hotel bed was so comfortable last night.* Then the smell hit her, a musty smell that made her sneeze. She opened her eyes.

'Shit! Where am I?' She sat bolt upright. She was in a ramshackle sitting room with ugly flocked wallpaper. Through an opening was an industrial-looking kitchen. She madly attempted to focus. What happened? The bus trip to the mall…the Italian… Yes! She had run away from him. *Oh, my God, the jazz cigarette.* How could she have done that? *And the mushrooms…* Then the colours of her dream flooded her consciousness. The Peacock Room, the Missoni design, the *Arabian Nights…*

Allegra glanced at her watch. *Double shit! It's 7:00 a.m. I should be at the hotel with Julia.* She dialled Julia's number, but there was no reception.

Crap, where am I? She walked through the kitchen and pushed the door open. The morning light stung her eyes. She stalked around to the front of the building, keeping her eyes on her phone. Finally, she could see a few bars of reception. Allegra redialled Julia's number.

The call was answered immediately. 'Where the hell are you, Allegra? I've been absolutely frantic!'

Allegra suddenly felt confused and stupid. 'Oh, Julia, I don't know where I am. I smoked a joint with some Italian man. He robbed me and was about to do more, so I ran away and have just spent the night on a filthy sofa in some abandoned castle.' She burst into tears.

'What? OK, OK, calm down. At least you're alive. Let's work this through logically. How did you get to the castle? With the Italian man?'

'No, I took a bus to a discount designer village called The Mall. It's near a village called Donnini – I remember because that's where my grandpapa came from.' Allegra wiped her nose on her sleeve.

'Hold it, let me write this down. Can you walk back to the village?' Julia asked.

'Not sure. Now that I think about it, I walked up a hill – for quite a long time – and was surrounded by very tall trees. That was after the man stole my wallet.' Allegra blushed with embarrassment.

'Here's what I'm going to do. I'll get hotel reception to look up this Donnini village as well as The Mall, and ask them to phone the local police and see if they will come and find you.' Julia sounded calm and in control.

'Will you call me back?' Allegra started crying again.

'Of course, just give me a few minutes. Don't go back inside the castle, stay in the open. Is there anyone else there?'

'I think there may be a caretaker...an old man...but he didn't hear me. He must have gone back to the gatehouse. Maybe I'll walk down towards that? I think it's on the way back down the hill.' Allegra sniffed again.

'That's a good idea. Walk away from the castle – you don't know who owns it, or if it's safe. Call you back soon.' Then Julia hung up.

Allegra looked back at the castle. To think, just the night before, she had such psychedelic dreams. They were so real. She longed to go back up the stairs and check the rooms once more. But her foolish behaviour was enough to make her blush with shame, and her lack of memory was nothing short of terrifying. As Julia said, better to leave the place straightaway.

As she followed the path down through the wall to the turret gatehouse, it became apparent there was no one inside. The shutters appeared as if they had been bolted shut for a very long time and on closer inspection, the front door was padlocked.

How strange – just the day before, the ivy had been moving. Waving at her. Now it simply glistened with the still morning dew. Allegra sighed as the phone shrilled in her hand.

'OK, all sorted. The hotel has been really helpful. They had a policeman phone me, and he speaks excellent English, thank God. His family are local so he knows exactly where you are. He said to tell you to follow the main path down the hill between the giant trees and by the time you arrive at the bottom near the gate, he will be waiting for you. Are you all right with that?'

'Yes, thank you, Julia. I'm so sorry for all this.' Allegra let out another sob.

'Don't worry about it, just get back here and then you can tell me everything.'

She proceeded cautiously down the hill. In contrast to the sunny, magical journey upwards, a pervasive grey chill hung over the morning and the rich colours from yesterday had bled into the green of the trees. Allegra had the worst headache ever and she could only walk very slowly with the pain stabbing her forehead repeatedly. She struggled to demist her brain and recall the past seventeen or so hours since she hopped on the bus in Florence. As she walked, memories began to return to her in bursts.

A rush of relief swept through her as a policeman in a very smart uniform came into focus down the track. He walked towards her, smiling. Once he was close and she had acknowledged him, he respectfully removed his cap to reveal a mop of jet-black hair.

'*Buongiorno, Signora*. I am Massimo Rossi from the Florence police force. I happened to be in the area when the call came in. I spoke with your friend, *Signora* Julia, at the Grand Hotel Baglioni.' His eyes were full of concern. 'Are you hurt? Are you in any pain?'

'No. I have a terrible headache, but I'm sure it will pass. I just feel such a fool,' Allegra replied, hanging her head as low as it could possibly go.

'Come and sit in my car. I have some water.' He motioned her to his squad car that was parked close to the entrance to the park.

'Is that gun real?' she asked, seeing his holster as he turned around.

'Yes, does it bother you?' he replied.

Allegra nodded. 'A bit.'

He opened the passenger door for her and removed his gun, placing it in the glove compartment.

She sank into the passenger seat and sipped the bottle of mineral water he handed her.

'I'm sorry, but I must ask you some questions. Is that all right?' Massimo opened the car windows. 'First of all, were you robbed?'

Allegra told him the entire story, from when the man called Silvano picked her up in the café. He listened intently.

'Did he make sexual advances to you?'

'I think so, but he didn't get far. After we smoked the joint, the mood changed and I realised I'd put myself in a compromising position.' Allegra blushed.

'Well, if it makes you feel any better, you're not the first female tourist this has happened to in the past five months. You are in fact the fourth reported case. And sadly, if it is the same man, he raped one of those women. He also gave them hallucinogenic mushrooms...' His tone was raised almost in question.

Allegra remained silent for a moment, then reluctantly replied, 'Yes, I think he gave me those, as well. I had some very weird dreams last night up in that castle. Well, they must have been dreams.'

'I can see this is a struggle for you. I will drive you back to your hotel and after you have eaten and had a rest, we can talk some more.' He leant over and fastened her seatbelt. As they passed through Donnini, she was aware he gave a friendly wave to a couple of people, but she was so dozy that she soon fell asleep. The next thing she knew, they were pulling up in front of the hotel, and the policeman escorted her to her room.

Julia embraced Allegra, and simultaneously managed to raise her eyebrow in the direction of the attractive rescuer.

'It's good to see you too, Julia,' Allegra said firmly.

'*Signora* Allegra needs to eat and rest now. I will return tomorrow to formally interview her.' He offered the two friends a smile.

'Well, that's tricky because we are booked to fly back to the UK this evening,' Julia responded with a flirtatious smile.

'Oh my! I can't possibly go back today and face the children in this state.' Allegra grabbed a tissue and loudly blew her nose.

'Well, I have to work tomorrow.' Julia was suddenly all serious. 'Would you be OK here on your own? Maybe we can change your ticket?'

'I guess so.' Allegra sniffed.

'May I offer some assistance?' Massimo paused and gave a reassuring smile. 'Why don't I go and talk to the hotel reception? I'm sure they can stretch this room for one, maybe two nights. I can reassure you the effect of the drugs will pass. Let *Signora* Julia change your flight booking, and I promise, we will look after you.' Massimo gently patted Allegra's hand.

Julia nodded in agreement and promptly phoned the airline. 'I can only get you on an easyJet flight on Wednesday morning. Will three extra nights suffice?' Julia asked. Allegra nodded.

Massimo returned and informed them that the hotel management were very sorry that she had such a bad experience in Florence and that she could have the room for three more days, at half price. He then wrote down his mobile number and handed it to her.

'Please, call me anytime if you are worried. I will call to interview you at 9:00 a.m. tomorrow, downstairs in the foyer. Your memory will have returned by then.' He put his cap on and left.

Julia did not waste any time. 'Wow! He's rather gorgeous. But I guess that's neither here nor there. What on earth happened, Allegra?'

'I haven't eaten a thing since lunchtime yesterday. Please feed me something, and then I'll talk.'

Once Allegra had devoured the room service steak, fries and salad, and was propped up on the bed with a hot cup of soothing tea, she went over the whole sordid tale.

'Well, I did say you should loosen up a little, but dope and magic mushrooms in the bushes in the middle of nowhere with a stranger is taking it to the extreme!' Julia responded. When Allegra started to fiddle with her hair, Julia said more gently, 'The castle sounds amazing, though. Was it for real, do you think?'

'I don't know. It seemed real in a way, but from the outside, and looking back as I left, things just didn't add up. Maybe Massimo will be able to tell me more about it tomorrow. He is local after all. But listen Julia – I've lost everything in my handbag… my credit cards and my driver's licence,' Allegra said.

'We will ring the bank, and they'll cancel all your cards, and you can go online to the DVLA and report your stolen licence and apply for a new one. Your ticket is sorted. I've put the difference on my card. Here's five hundred euros.' Julia opened her purse and handed her the cash. 'I can get out some more if you think you'll need it?'

Allegra kissed Julia's cheek. 'Thank you. I don't know what I would have done without you. I'll be OK once I've thought of something to tell the children… And now we are even. You messed up my first day with your love tryst, and I messed up your shopping day with my crazy drug-taking!' Allegra smiled. 'You haven't even told me the details of your night of passion?'

'Let me just say it was absolutely nothing in the excitement stakes compared to yours.'

Allegra fought to keep her eyes open as Julia chatted on about her lover. The next thing she knew, Julia was shaking her awake.

'Wake up. I left you to it, but it's been five hours since you fell asleep and I need to be heading out to the airport.'

'It must be the after-effects of the drugs. I feel like I only shut my eyes for a moment.'

'Right then, my friend! Keep me posted, and call me if you need anything. Though I daresay the sexy policeman will look after you well enough!' Julia laughed, then kissed Allegra goodbye.

Nine

As Allegra lay in her luxurious hotel room bed, snacking on yet another room service meal, and with CNN busily humming in her orbit, her thoughts kept drifting back to the past twenty-four hours. Primarily, to the interior of the top three floors of the castle.

She popped down to the guest computer in reception and googled 'magic mushrooms'. From reading about people's hallucinations, it seemed that visions were only distorted – or adjusted – by the drug's influence. So, there must have been some original Moorish architecture within that castle. On the other hand, you couldn't believe everything you read on the Internet, and it's not like you could run legitimate tests on magic mushroom users either.

She suddenly remembered the photos and scrambled to retrieve them from her phone. But there was nothing there. Maybe she pressed the wrong button? In all the drama she wasn't quite sure if the policeman had told her the name of the castle, and even if he did, she had no memory of it.

Unable to take this chain of thought any further, she turned her attention to London. Allegra recalled the short conversation she'd had with Hugo and the children. He sounded pissed off that he had to stay another couple of days without Brooklyn. But reassuringly, Harry and Kirsty expressed little interest in her 'flu' which was lucky, given that Allegra was excited to be seeing the impressive Massimo again in the morning.

She had brought only a limited wardrobe, but Julia had left her some black leggings and her beautiful silk tunic, *just in case*. After Allegra had given the tunic a press, she moisturised her legs, then slipped on her kitten-heel shoes. As she checked herself in the mirror, she felt reassured that the finished product was a vast improvement on what Massimo had seen the day before.

He was waiting in the foyer holding a folder when Allegra exited the lift. '*Buongiorno, Signora* Allegra. You look much more rested this morning. How do you feel?'

'I am much better than I thought I'd be, thank you. I haven't had breakfast yet – would you join me for coffee?' Allegra asked him as she moved towards the hotel café.

'With pleasure.' He offered a warm smile.

After an appropriate social pause whilst they ordered their espresso, and once the effeminate waiter had finally left, Massimo began his serious line of questioning.

'I realise yesterday you were in a state of shock, and perhaps, understandably embarrassed. But I implore you to be honest with me *Signora* Allegra. This Silvano's real name is Romero, and he is a predatory criminal that we need to catch and lock up. You must tell me if he acted inappropriately towards you.' He hesitated, then continued. 'Also, would you be comfortable looking at some photos to see if you recognise him?' He tapped the A4 folder he had placed on the table.

'Yes, of course. If I can help at all, I'd be happy to look at the photos... And although I'm ashamed about what happened yesterday, I can tell you in all honesty that he did not rape me, if that's what you mean. I agreed to go with him to smoke the joint, so I know that was a reckless choice on my part.' Allegra shifted uncomfortably in her seat.

Massimo nodded and opened the folder.

She rifled through about ten mugshots of swarthy-looking men, some clean-shaven but most with shaded beards. Then she saw him. She picked up the photo, keenly studied it, and then placed it down in front of Massimo.

'Without any doubt, this is the man I met at The Mall who stole my wallet.' She breathed out and leant back in her chair.

Massimo closed the folder. 'Excellent. That is most helpful *Signora*.'

'Sir? Um, Massimo? May I ask you some questions about the castle?' Allegra asked. As he turned to face her, Allegra noticed a long scar on his face, running from ear to jaw.

'You may, of course. But just now I need to get to the station to file my report. We have enough to apprehend this man. May I suggest instead that you join me for dinner this evening? I will be off-duty, so not bound by police restrictions. You can ask me anything you like.' He smiled as he pushed his chair back, placed his cap under his arm and collected the folder.

'Thank you, I'd be delighted,' Allegra replied, hoping she wasn't too obvious in her excitement.

Once back in her room, she tried on every combination of the limited clothes she had. 'Bugger. Just when I really need a credit card, I don't have one,' she said out loud. At that very moment, her phone rang.

'Hi, it's me. How did your police interview go?' Julia said.

'Well, his first concern was whether I had been raped.'

Julia interrupted her with a gasp. 'Oh, Allegra, you weren't, were you?'

'No. I could have been, but I think ultimately he was more interested in the wallet than me.'

'Thank goodness,' Julia said.

'The con man is actually called Romero and apparently he has done this before.' Allegra went on to tell her about the 'date' with Massimo. 'I'm sure he just intends to answer my questions about the castle. Anyway, I'm too old for him. And another thing,' she carried on as Julia started to protest, 'he carries a gun. You know how I feel about violence.'

'Just because you are anti-guns you don't have to be anti-hero! And he's at least forty anyway, with no wedding ring. Why don't you wear the Missoni dress? It looks great on you.'

Allegra smiled to herself as she hung up the phone. With the decision about what to wear locked in and an entire afternoon to kill, she decided to spend a hundred of her euros on a visit to a spa. It offered a massage and a facial, followed by a hair wash and blow-dry. She had always been so cautious about spending money on herself when the children were growing up. Hugo seemed to have a knack of making her feel guilty. Well, that was all blown out of the water now. He had chosen the younger, high-maintenance Brooklyn, so he would just have to accept the new, more expensive version of his ex-wife.

In the beautifully fragrant, darkened spa, as the masseuse worked her deft fingers into Allegra's back, any residue of trauma from the day before floated away. A series of delicious immoral thoughts, all involving Massimo, peppered her reflections. These desires were intertwined with the hallucinations of the rooms in the castle. Perhaps, she pondered, the effect of the marijuana and the magic mushrooms had not quite worn off.

It was 7:00 p.m., and it seemed an age since Allegra had been standing nervously in the hotel foyer. But she could clearly see the large clock behind reception – it had only been five minutes.

A tall man smiled at her as he walked through the entrance doors. It took a few seconds for her to register that it was Massimo. God! Out of uniform he looked incredible. He was dressed in perfectly fitting chinos with a pure-white shirt and an impressive, well-cut navy-flecked jacket. As he approached her, his curling smile and the depth of his gaze made her feel quite giddy.

'*Buonasera, Signora* Allegra. You look magnificent this evening. Perhaps you are fully recovered from your ordeal?' he said.

'Yes, I think I am, thank you. Please, will you call me Allegra?' She beamed back at him.

'Of course, if you will call me Massimo?'

Allegra nodded.

'I have taken the liberty of choosing a small restaurant about a ten-minute walk from here, if that is OK with you?' He gestured towards the main doors.

Allegra momentarily considered the heels she was wearing, but then remembered this was the new Allegra. *Think sexy, not practical.*

He was a good five inches taller than her, and when he noticed her falter on the cobbled footpath, leaned downwards slightly and gently offered his arm. He smelt delicious, like fresh lemons and limes. His face was naturally olive and enhanced by a tan. As they walked arm-in-arm, Allegra felt decidedly pale against the sooty night.

'This restaurant is off the tourist trail. It is owned by friends of mine, so I can promise the best food and service.'

Massimo chatted comfortably to her about food, as well as the buildings and lesser monuments they passed en route.

The restaurant was tiny, with only about ten tables. The owners had come out to greet Massimo and to be introduced to Allegra. Then they were ushered down some hidden steps into a basement, where the other tables were closely packed in. The walls were lined with racks full of wine bottles. The room was illuminated with rows of candles which created a shimmering flicker that reflected off the mass of glass.

Massimo assisted Allegra into the seat facing the room at a secluded little table for two. After quizzing her about what wine she preferred, he ordered a bottle of Chianti Classico. Sensing she was out of her depth, he was enthusiastic when she sought his advice on what to order. To begin, he suggested the fresh fig entrée. The fruit was cut into quarters and accompanied with just a smidgen of soft cream cheese, with mint leaves chopped on the top. For main, he recommended a veal chop grilled and drizzled with butter and sage.

Once they had finished the delicious entrée and were settling into their mains, Allegra repeated her question about the castle.

'Its official name is *Castello di Sammezzano*.' He pronounced it slowly for her. 'I have to be honest with you, I have never been inside. In recent years, very few have. However, I talked about it with my mamma today. She lives in our family home in Leccio and was able to confirm some things for me.' He paused and took a bite of his veal before continuing.

'*Castello di Sammezzano* was originally built in the sixteenth century. Then in the eighteenth century, the Marchese Ferdinando Panciatichi Ximenes d'Aragona inherited it. Apparently, he was a very clever but arrogant man. He became disillusioned with Florentine politics and the Italian people, so he retreated to the *Castello di Sammezzano* and spent all his money, and the rest of his life, developing it into his sanctuary. According to what Mamma has heard, it is rumoured there are many rooms of fantasy – one, supposedly, for each day of the year.' He paused again.

'Please, go on. This is just amazing... When I was a student, my fantasy was to have a room for each day of the year.' Allegra's face lit up with excitement.

'I'm not sure what happened when the Marchese died. But what I can tell you is that in the 1990s, an international hotel group purchased the castle. There were efforts to turn it into a hotel, but they were short-lived and after a relatively short period of operation, a government department placed a preservation order on it. Apparently, the hotel group went broke. So now, it is basically abandoned, with a local preservation society keeping an eye on it. I was told they have one day a year where they allow access to one or two VIPs.' He topped up Allegra's glass.

'So, do you know much else about this Marchese? Why did he choose Moorish architecture and not more classic Italian?' Allegra was transfixed.

'From what Mamma indicated, society at that time dismissed him as very odd; what he did was like building Disneyland within an ancient castle. I have not seen it myself... I was studying in England during the short time it was renovated and open to the public.' They were interrupted by the owner, who was desperate to hear that Massimo's beautiful friend was enjoying the food.

Allegra smiled and made all the right noises, but wanted to get back on to *Castello di Sammezzano*.

'Tell me, do you have an Italian heritage? What was your maiden name?' Massimo asked, once they were alone again.

'Well, technically, I'm only a quarter – my mother's papa, my grandpapa, is from Donnini, but he left aged eighteen and married an Englishwoman. My mother hyphenated her name, so I used to be Allegra Mancini-Soames before I married.'

'Are you still married?' he asked.

'I'm in the process of getting divorced,' she replied, looking down at her plate.

'I am very sorry. I didn't mean to pry. And I certainly didn't wish to upset you.'

'I'm OK now. It hurt like hell when it was all happening. But it's in the past now. What about you?' Allegra attempted to sound nonchalant.

'I was married when I was still in my teens to a girl from our village. A big mistake, really. I made the decision to leave her before we ended up having any children. I was ostracised for a while after that, which was my motivation to go to the UK and study English. I worked in London for a while, then decided to join the Florentine police force. So here I am. They sent me out when they received the call about you, because that area is where I grew up and I also speak fluent English. I am very pleased they did, as I wouldn't have met you otherwise.' He reached across and pressed his strong hand on hers.

As Allegra chatted she caught a strand of hair in her fingers and twirled it. He encouraged her to talk about herself. He listened intently as she shared her pre-marriage aspirations in architecture and design. She briefly talked about the children, but didn't give too much away about her situation with Hugo. He was intrigued to hear all about her grandpapa and explained that the villages of Leccio and Donnini were almost side by side, so he would question his mamma further about the *castello* and the Mancini family.

Massimo's words were infused with authority, and the vibrancy of his voice made them resonate, as if they came from a deep well. It was hard not to compare him to the effusive, arrogant man her soon-to-be ex-husband had become.

After a limoncello nightcap and protracted Italian farewells with all the staff, they finally walked out into the crisp Florentine air. Allegra gave an involuntary shiver and Massimo immediately placed a strong arm around her shoulders, drawing her close as they walked.

'Do you need my jacket?' He motioned to remove it.

'No, thanks, your arm around me feels warm enough.' Then she giggled and realised that the Chianti and limoncello were having an effect.

They lingered and looked across the lamp lit Arno River, just catching sight of the Ponte Vecchio in the distance. Allegra felt a reassuring sense of comfort and solace under the arm of her tall companion. His English faltered a little here, probably due to the wine, but this only added charm to his modulated words about Italian history and culture.

The foyer of the hotel was empty when they arrived. Massimo led Allegra across to a secluded spot out of the gaze of the sole receptionist. He held her face in his hands and fervently kissed her lips, before gently letting go.

'Beautiful Allegra, I will say *buonanotte* now. I will call your room first thing in the morning, and if you still feel the same way, I will take the day off and spend it showing you *my* Florence.' He was very precise. Allegra nodded and laid her head on his shoulder. He walked her to the lift, kissed her again and stood watching her until the lift doors had closed.

Allegra fell on her bed fully clothed and kicked off her shoes off. That kiss was something else. She hugged her arms and rocked in delight... It was the best time she'd had in years.

Ten

In her waking haze, Allegra could hear the faintly familiar ring of her mobile phone from somewhere in the room. She finally located it in Julia's borrowed handbag on the chair.

'God, Allegra! What's this rubbish about the flu! You've never had the flu in your life. You should be back here with your children. This is highly inconvenient for me,' Hugo's voice barked out at her.

Allegra glanced at the bedside clock – 8:00 a.m. 'Hugo, can't you cope with your own children?'

'I have a very important meeting this evening which means that I can't return to the house and the children, and I don't trust leaving Kirsty to help Harry, or to be on her own all night. She's been a nightmare!' He sounded frantic.

Allegra smiled to herself. 'What could be so important that you couldn't return to be with your children?'

'Well, if you must know, it's Brooklyn's birthday and I'm already in deep shit over all this. You need to catch a plane this morning. After all, I'm paying for it.'

That did it. Allegra hung up and then turned off her mobile. She was fuming. What did she ever see in Hugo? She couldn't remember. What a jerk he had become.

As she began her shower, the hotel phone shrilled out. Assuming it was Hugo having another pop, she took her time answering it.

'Allegra, I am imagining you look wonderful when you wake up,' Massimo practically purred into the handset.

'Oh, hello,' Allegra replied, savouring the warmth of his voice.

'Would you be happy to spend the day with me? I would so love to show you *my* Florence.'

'I'd love to, but what about your work?'

'It's no problem, I am due some days off. Shall I collect you in about an hour?'

'I'll be waiting in the foyer. See you soon.'

After she hung up, she turned her phone back on and dialled Harry's mobile.

'Hi, Mum, are you OK now? Are you coming home today?'

'I'm OK now. Are you all right?'

'Sure, school has sent me heaps of work and I'm great on the crutches now. It's just Dad is throwing a hissy fit about some date he has tonight. Kirsty and I told him we'll be fine.'

'I'm over the flu now, but I could only get a suitable flight tomorrow, so I'll see you tomorrow afternoon. Say hi to Kirsty for me. Love you.'

Allegra felt home camp was under control – or as much as she wanted it to be – so she could again focus on the trivial thought of what to wear. She was showered, her wavy hair sorted and make-up carefully applied, all in double-quick time. Her policeman was waiting in the foyer when she exited the lift.

She couldn't help but notice some admiring glances as Massimo, in his jeans and blue cashmere sweater, escorted her across the foyer. She felt a little unsure that her black jeans, knee-high boots and orange sweater were conservative enough for the very well-dressed Florentines. It was as if Massimo sensed her insecurity, and as soon as they were outside, he turned to face her, taking both her hands.

'You look *fantastico* in that colour. Sexy, in an English sort of way. Allegra, I feel so proud to walk with you.' His voice sounded close and sensual.

Allegra was too distracted to take in very much of the surroundings as they walked and talked. They eventually arrived at a flourishing piazza where Massimo encouraged Allegra to choose one of the busy outdoor cafés.

Allegra took this as a sort of test. She selected the one that looked the busiest, with customers she assumed were Italian (their conversations appeared more physically animated and the dress code was distinctly chic). Massimo smiled. 'Good choice,' he said, then ordered their coffees.

She listened attentively to what Massimo had planned for the day, and then steered the conversation back to the subject of the castle.

'I have been dwelling on what happened to me up at *Castello di Sammezzano*… I can't help thinking that the Peacock Room that I saw is the one my grandpapa rants about. Although he has dementia, he also has his lucid moments. If you were sincere about asking your *mamma* if she knows anything about the Mancini name, I would be most grateful.' She hesitated as Massimo eyed her with an intent stare.

'I give you my word on that. I go and visit *Mamma* most weekends. Also, I will find out the details of the preservation society of the castle and forward you an e-mail address so you can follow up.' His words were precise and he spoke in a policeman-like manner. Then he sipped his coffee, without taking his eyes off her.

She smiled, and Massimo let out a breath.

'When you smile, Allegra, the sun dances. So be assured I always want to make you smile. I will get you all the information I can. Meantime, let's commence today's tour.'

As they left the café, she looped her arm in his and felt a warm rush of security as he patted her hand.

Their first stop was the Accademia Gallery.

'No visitor as interested in the arts as you, could miss a few minutes with Michelangelo's amazing *David*,' Massimo said as he flashed his Police ID card and they walked in, ignoring the queue.

Allegra was in seventh heaven. Massimo was charming, handsome, and seemed happy to indulge her passion. As they traded views in front of the awesome *David*, a loud, gaudy couple invaded their space. After exchanging a knowing glance, Allegra and Massimo walked towards the exit.

As they departed the gallery, the sun had fully engaged with the day.

'Do you fancy a picnic lunch?' he asked.

'Absolutely!' In a cobbled side street, no more than an alley, Massimo guided her to a wonderful delicatessen. The man serving seemed familiar with Massimo and offered them a little taste of stuffed tiny capsicums, a slice of special home-made salami, and a piece of a wonderful creamy cheese before he packaged it all up in neat paper containers.

'Where are we going?' Allegra enquired.

'Wait and see.'

As they turned the corner, Allegra recognised the distinct Pitti Palace sitting up on a rise in a large semi-circle.

'No, we are not queuing or going inside. I know a special spot in the gardens where we can have our picnic.' Once

71

again, he walked past the queue, flashed his card, and they were ushered straight through.

'Now this is one place I do know something about.' Allegra raised her eyebrows. 'I studied the history and the monuments within these Boboli Gardens as part of my Florentine studies when I came here as a student.'

'I'm very impressed,' Massimo replied, as they arrived at a wrought-iron seat tucked discreetly behind a large bush with a view of a pond.

Allegra enjoyed every morsel of their lunch, especially as Massimo managed to put a humorous Italian spin on the contents of each container they opened. According to him, all Italian food was the 'best in the world'.

'Did you know that in 1656, a father and son team called Giulio and Alfonso Parigi completed the structure of these gardens? They built that stone amphitheatre over there. Back then, it was by far the most impressive outdoor theatre in Florence.' Allegra twisted a strand of hair as she spoke.

'My goodness, Allegra, you speak so knowledgeably. I can even detect some Italian pride in your English words. Maybe you will be a little too *intelligenti* for a poor Italian policeman like me.'

Allegra laughed, and pushed Massimo playfully away. He grabbed her hand, and kissed it.

The day had cooled down, so they decided against any more museums and walked in the direction of Allegra's hotel.

'I don't wish to pressure you, but may I suggest that you visit my apartment this evening and I cook you some humble pasta?' Massimo put Allegra's chilled hand to his warm lips.

Her lips remained fixed, but her eyes gave away the truth. 'Only if it's not too much trouble. I don't want to put you to any bother.'

'Why are you English always so polite? I only invite you because it will be my pleasure. I'll collect you at 7:30 p.m.' Then he kissed her lightly on the lips, and she walked across to the lift.

Eleven

Once Allegra had returned to her hotel room, she switched her mobile phone back on. There was a barrage of beeps indicating voice messages. She also noticed the hotel phone message light was flashing. Reluctantly, she dialled her message service. The first message was a torrent of frustration from Hugo, still demanding she fly back on the next available plane. The second was from Julia, who said she would try the hotel line, and the third was from her mother.

Shit! She had forgotten completely to tell her mother she would be two days late coming home. She quickly dialled her number.

'Allegra, thank God! Harry said you had the flu and had to stay in Italy, then Julia was very elusive when I called her, and she cut me short saying she had a meeting. But I know you two! What have you been up to? Do you have an Italian lover?'

Allegra smiled. 'Not yet, Mum, but I may have soon.' She gave her mother a very abridged version of the robbery and the need for the police report.

'Gosh, Allegra, that's terrible. I'm so relieved you are OK... But I also must tell you that Grandpapa is not well. When exactly will you get home?'

'What's wrong? I'm coming back the day after tomorrow and I don't think I can change my flight now, as Julia booked it on her credit card...'

'Now, now! Don't panic! I'm sure he will be with us for a while yet. The doctors have him on all sorts of medication. Just enjoy your time there. Grandpapa would want you to, after all.'

'OK.' Allegra wavered. 'I'll call you as soon as I arrive.'

After Allegra put down the phone, loving memories of her grandpapa flooded her thoughts. Should she really be going on a date while he was ill, and so far, away? But it was too late to cancel Massimo now. The time was already 7 p.m.

She selected the only clothes Massimo hadn't yet seen, and the only option left from her limited wardrobe was Julia's black leggings and a long, black, fitted jersey knit top. As she struggled to tie the cobalt-blue silk scarf at her neck, the rich colour evoked memories of her grandpapa and his peacock feather. Since she was a little girl, he would encourage her to choose vibrant colours, at first in her colouring-in books and then later in her clothes. She recalled her overbearing grandmother telling him that his 'Italian' colours weren't appropriate for a child. Allegra felt a pang of regret. She suddenly wished she had given the old man more of her time and asked him more about his past when he was still able to give a coherent answer. Now in this city of history, beauty, and romance, Grandpapa's coded history had begun to feel relevant.

As Allegra had anticipated, Massimo arrived before her. He was waiting in the foyer, the halogen lights highlighting the scar just above his jawline. The scar somehow added an extra dimension to his demeanour, an air of mystery.

As he drew her to him, she inhaled his fresh, now familiar fragrance. He brushed her cheek with his lips and took her hand.

'My Allegra, we need to be quick as I don't have the police car this evening, and I have parked directly outside the door.' As they arrived at the car, the concierge was already writing the number plate down.

'I use my police persona to take liberties. It's just the Italian way, but I was pushing it a bit there.' He laughed as he accelerated away from the hotel.

Within a very short time, they pulled into a parking spot by the river. Allegra followed Massimo as he punched some numbers into a keypad that opened a massive door into a large, imposing building.

'The elevator is ancient and very unreliable, so if you are OK, I suggest we walk the three flights up.'

Allegra took it all in. The marble staircase, the elaborate wrought-iron banister, and the exceptionally high ceilings.

'I'd hazard a guess this was built around 1820?' she said.

'Almost correct – 1838 – before we became a united Italy and when Florentines still had money.' He used two keys to unlock his heavy loft door.

Allegra was reassured at first glance that no woman had recently lived in Massimo's apartment. It smacked of his masculinity. Although the hallway floor appeared to be original black and white marble tiles, the rest was an eclectic mix of antiques and contemporary pieces.

An elongated tiled central hallway led to a sitting room at the end with a bedroom, a study, the kitchen, and bathroom off either side. Allegra followed Massimo to the sitting room, which was dominated by an antique leather sofa and an oversized tapestry armchair that was positioned in front of a wall-mounted flat-screen TV. He had set an oval wooden dining table ready for a meal, complete with several heavy church candles as a centrepiece. Allegra was impressed. There were two Philippe Starck transparent chairs positioned on either side of the table.

'I note your smile – so you like my design statement?'

'Well, I was smiling because I would have thought in spending that sort of money on what are basically plastic chairs, you would have chosen an Italian rather than a French designer. As the Italians are, after all, "the best in the world"!'

Massimo laughed.

'However, I love the contrast and even though he's a modernist, I do appreciate Philippe Starck's genius,' Allegra added.

The meal was simple but delicious. Massimo admitted he'd bought the pasta from a delicatessen, but it was made fresh that afternoon, and he had prepared the pesto sauce himself from his own basil plant. Allegra found herself drinking a lot more red wine than usual and by the time he brought out the cheese and fruit platter, she was quite giggly. When it was apparent Allegra wasn't interested in the cheese, Massimo put on a CD, then poured them both a *grappa* and motioned for her to join him on the sofa.

'Wow! This might be strong enough to start my car!' Allegra screwed up her nose.

'Just sip it slowly. It's an acquired taste.' Massimo pulled her towards him and with the *grappa* wet on his lips, he gently kissed her. 'Maybe it tastes better this way?' Then taking the glass from her hand, he enveloped her in his arms. He kissed her, keeping his hands firmly around her waist and shoulder.

'Allegra, are you ready for this? I don't want to pressure you, but I am desperate to make love to you,' he whispered in her ear.

'Yes,' was all she could manage.

He led her to the bedroom, where he had turned on the bedside lamp; he flicked it off and let the full moon illuminate the room through the oval window. Allegra stood, a little unsure about what to do next. He lifted her arms and removed her top, then kissed her décolletage and whispered quiet endearments in Italian. He guided her to the bed and began to remove his clothes. Allegra quickly removed her leggings and sat in her white underwear.

'*Wow!* You are so beautiful.' He sat down beside her, still wearing his fitted underpants, with an obvious bulge. They lay kissing and stroking as he skilfully undid her bra then slid her knickers off.

Allegra felt a primal instinct kick in. In that moment, she desired nothing else but him. There were no sudden movements. Massimo took things slowly, sensually, touching her, licking her. He timed it perfectly, mounting her, and watching with desire as she writhed in her orgasm. Then he let go and finally joined her in mutual satisfaction.

Afterwards, he rocked her in his arms and continued to croon beautiful Italian words in her ears. She heard the distant ringing of her phone somewhere in her handbag, and couldn't bring herself to find it. But what if something had happened to Harry…

'Grab the dressing gown from behind the door, *Tesoro*,' Massimo called as she scuttled out of the bed. She eventually found her bag by the hall table, but she'd already missed the call. She could see it was Kirsty, but she hadn't left a message so it couldn't have been anything urgent. Scrutinising herself in the hall mirror, she ran her fingers through her tousled hair and wondered who was the woman in the mirror looking back at her. Massimo's lovemaking had given her beauty.

Massimo was propped up on the bed when she returned. His bronze body looked good enough to eat, highlighted by the rays of moonlight against the pure white sheets.

'Drop the gown, *Tesoro*. Let me look at your body.' He smiled.

'I've had two children, Massimo, and this is the first time I've ever been with a man other than their father.' She hugged her arms around her body.

'I am forty-five years old. I don't want to be with a mindless young girl. I prefer a woman.' He turned so Allegra could see his back. The moonlight glinted on two large scars.

'You can see the scar on my face. I also have battle wounds, but I accept they make me who I now am. We have shared our bodies. To share our souls, we must embrace all the components of each other's lives.' He reached out as she dropped the gown and pulled her down beside him.

'You must have girlfriends, Massimo. A handsome man like you, living here in such a romantic city, I bet you have plenty of admirers,' Allegra fished.

'I had a girlfriend for quite a long time, but after my first marriage experience, I was cautious about commitment. She also wanted marriage, so it finished. Yes, I admit there are plenty of women about, but I feel most of them have an agenda. So, it's been a while now since anything serious.' He kissed her cheek and then continued talking.

'When I saw you walking down that path from the *castello*, my heart leapt. You looked so vulnerable, so beautiful. I knew the minute you sat next to me in the squad car and sipped that water that I wanted to spend time with you.' He drew

79

her towards him, stroking her belly and brushing his fingers over her mound. She was instantly aroused. She stroked his reawakening manhood then, as her passion peaked, she guided his stiff member into her body and cried out in ecstasy.

Allegra fell asleep in Massimo's arms and when she awoke alone in the bed, she momentarily forgot where she was. Sitting up and taking in the bedroom in daylight, the evening's memories flooded her heart. She could hear movement and noises from the kitchen. She leapt up, grabbed the dressing gown, and hurriedly went to the bathroom. As she looked in the mirror and attempted to tame her hair, she felt completely alive. Taller, more beautiful, more herself.

'Ah, you are up. I wanted to wake you with my special coffee.' Massimo arrived at the bedroom door at the same time as Allegra. He carried a tray with two cups of coffee and two pastries, and they sat side by side on the dishevelled bed.

'The coffee smells amazing,' Allegra said as she touched the pastry. 'And this is warm! Did you just bake it?'

'Well, I would like to say I did, but no. I sneaked out quickly and bought them from my favourite place. They are delicious – taste!' He broke off a piece and put it to Allegra's lips, then let his fingers linger.

Once she had swallowed the first bite of pastry, he leant over and kissed her lips.

'I want to taste you in the morning, *Tesoro*.' Allegra fell onto her back. He opened her gown and delivered soft, quick kisses from her décolletage down between her breasts. She purred with enjoyment as the kisses increased in intensity, and for the third time in twelve hours, Massimo's love-making evoked sensations of lust and love that had been dormant for so long.

While Massimo was showering, Allegra asked if she could print out her air ticket. He pointed her in the direction of the room he used as a study. She waited patiently for the printer, and looked up at his bookshelves. Spotting two upturned frames under a couple of books, curiosity got the better of her. They were probably photos of girlfriends. She could still hear the shower running so she quickly flipped them over.

They were framed certificates. The first showed he had graduated from the English police academy with distinction. The other was a citation for bravery from the UK police force. Then she heard the shower close off so she hurriedly put them back and replaced the books.

'Are you ready?' Massimo appeared from the bedroom, all fresh in his police uniform.

'I have decided I definitely love a man in uniform!' Allegra grinned.

'That may be so, but this man has to get you to your hotel then to the airport, and then somehow concentrate on his work.' She noticed that he subtly dropped his gun into his small carry bag as they walked out the door. Allegra shuddered. If only he didn't have to have it with him all the time.

On the ride to the airport, Allegra brought the conversation back to *Castello di Sammezzano* and her concerns about her grandpapa's health.

'As soon as I have any new information, I will e-mail you, and God willing, we will work out a way to meet again soon,' he reassured her.

Allegra held back the tears as she kissed her lover one more time before walking through the departure gates. She knew for sure that however this all played out, her life with Hugo was history. From this day onward, everything would be as fresh as lemons and limes. A new future.

Twelve

Allegra finally boarded the cramped budget flight. She was relieved to have a window seat so she could look out the window and avoid any conversation. The pure white clouds reminded her of comforting creamy mashed potato. She mentally drifted back through the amazing events of the past four days. Perhaps that dreadful Silvano, or Romero, or whatever he was called, had done her a favour. Well, there was no other way she would have met Massimo. Maybe this was how middle age was supposed to feel? Free, and yet supported? Hugo had always assumed responsibility for most things in their relationship and their home. In the beginning, she had enjoyed that. He filled in the parts that were missing and that she longed for in a father. But as she got older, it became apparent that on Hugo's part, it was all about control.

And as for *Castello di Sammezzano*... Seeing it had reignited her thirst for the passion and provocation of colour in architecture. She had felt ecstatic wandering though those magical rooms. It wasn't just the drugs, she had sensed a profound connection. Her greatest wish was to find a way to return and understand just how much of what she had seen was real, and how much was the result of the hallucinations. If Massimo was there too, then so much the better.

London appeared bathed in a mellow autumnal light, as her taxi drove down Redcliff Gardens towards Fulham Road. The suburban trees glowed with ruddy russet branches. But any personal glow dissipated the minute Allegra arrived at her home and unlocked the front door.

'Mum, I'm so glad to see you!' Harry called as he scurried to her on his crutches. For a short moment, he was her little lad again.

'Dad's girlfriend is such a *loser*. We had to put up with her for two meals. It was so embarrassing!'

'Come, let me make a cup of tea and then tell me everything.' Allegra dropped her bag at the base of the stairs and slung her arm around Harry as he hobbled to the kitchen.

'Where's Kirsty?' she asked, turning on the kettle.

'Up in her room, I think. Dad said he wouldn't be back today after he left this morning. Boy, was he in a bad mood with you for being sick and not coming home,' Harry said as he manoeuvred himself onto the chair beside his mother.

'Mum, you're home, great!' Kirsty bounced into the kitchen, removed her earbuds, and pulled up a chair.

The children willingly offered Allegra a blow-by-blow account of Brooklyn. How she sulked, how their father spoke to her in a baby voice and how they would make vomiting noises if either Brooklyn or Hugo so much as touched each other. Allegra smiled at their humour.

Then Kirsty suddenly burst out, 'Oh, Mum! Sorry, I forgot to tell you, Gran rang. You must call her immediately, she said. It's about Great-Grandpapa. He's in hospital.'

Allegra's face went pale and she swiftly retrieved her phone from her bag.

'Allegra, darling, the doctors tell me he doesn't have long. They've given him some morphine and said no more visitors for today. But please come first thing tomorrow, OK?'

The next morning, Allegra hurried to get to the hospital, all thoughts of her Italian lover and the castle blasted from her mind.

The Chelsea and Westminster Hospital was only a short drive up Fulham Road. The highly polished floor in the private wing gave off a freshly cleaned, antiseptic fragrance and as Allegra entered her grandpapa's room, she was shocked to see how small he appeared in the pristine, white bed.

The only colour in the room appeared to be the peacock feather he clutched. The rich green, blue, and teal hues seemed so vivid to her, sparking memories of the Peacock Room again. His eyes flickered as she sat down beside him.

'Hello, Grandpapa. I'm back from Italy. I think I visited your magical castle. Is it called Sammezzano?' She spoke directly into his ear.

His eyes opened wide. Without his thick-lensed spectacles, she could see them clearly. The colour might have faded, but they still emanated that same rich warmth she remembered as a child.

He curved his lips into a faint smile, and lifted his hand. Shaking, he endeavoured to pass the peacock feather to her.

Allegra went to stop him. 'Grandpapa, you keep the feather for now. I have seen the Peacock Room and somehow, I will find out all the things you need me to know, I promise.' Allegra felt the slow release of his hand at the same time her mother walked in and quietly joined her at the bedside.

The three sat in silence as the morning sun appeared to fade behind a dark clouded sky. His breaths became laboured.

'He is on his way now, Allegra,' Maria said as she put her arm around her daughter and her other hand, along with Allegra's, on the old man's. They all touched the peacock feather. Grandpapa gave one tired last gasp, and then finally, there was silence.

Thirteen

Allegra moved through the days following her grandpapa's death in a state of disbelief.

She experienced a momentary high when she received a text from Massimo, but told him she must grieve with her family. She wished she knew him better and could offload onto him, as the sadness would have been easier shared. But she needed to stay strong for her mother; whatever their differences, she had also lost her papa.

Her dreams were prolific and peppered with flashes of the visions she had seen in the castle. They mingled with memories of her grandpapa's younger face, when his hair was still a rich brown colour and he wore a neatly trimmed moustache. One dream kept repeating itself – a peacock, lit by sunlight, strutting in front of her, its colourful tail fanned open and swishing about. There was no peahen in sight. It was as if the peacock was trying to attract her attention.

Julia had arranged to meet Allegra at her mother's house the evening before the funeral. They had gone through all the arrangements and were chatting about timing when Allegra's phone beeped. She smiled as she silently read the message.

'Is that from your policeman?' Julia asked.

Allegra raised her eyebrows but didn't respond as she concentrated on her return text.

'What policeman? What have I missed, daughter of mine?' Maria asked.

'Oops! Have I let the cat out of the bag? Sorry,' Julia said.

'No, it's OK, Julia,' Allegra said, then turned her attention to her mother. 'Mum, the policeman who assisted me after the robbery ended up taking me for dinner and, well, we ended up in bed.'

There was a pregnant pause before Maria roared with laughter.

'Well, I never! Wouldn't have placed you with a policeman given your anti-violence stance. Why on earth didn't you tell me?'

'You've had so much on your mind... I just didn't want to talk about my happiness when we haven't even said goodbye to Grandpapa yet.'

'Your grandpapa would have loved to know you had an Italian lover, even if he is a gun-toting policeman,' Maria responded.

Allegra shuddered. 'Well, actually, I'm not sure what kind of policeman he is. I snooped a bit when I was in his office printing out my boarding pass. He has some sort of framed citation for bravery from a UK government department.'

Julia and Maria exchanged glances.

'So, did you ask him about it?' Maria queried.

'No. When we were exchanging notes on our backgrounds, he just said he studied in London. He had placed a couple of books on top of the frame so I assumed for whatever reason, he didn't want to share that history with me just yet.' Allegra played with a strand of hair as she spoke.

'I'm sure you two aren't giving me all the details here. Just because I'm grieving doesn't mean I can't hear all the juicy bits.' Maria looked expectantly at her daughter.

Allegra gave in and recounted the full story of the conman, the robbery, the drugs, and the castle. Maria was transfixed.

'My God! Finally, some excitement in the family. I can't wait to hear what this Massimo has to say, and I'm even more intrigued about the skeletons in his closet. He must have done something extraordinary while he was here.'

They reverted to talk of the sad day they had to face in the morning. Her mother had all the funeral arrangements under control. One week after his death, Luigi Mancini was to be buried in the Brompton Cemetery. Hugo had called twice and seemed intent on attending the funeral with them. Since her time in Florence, for some reason, he had been much more cordial towards her. But Allegra had told him firmly he was not welcome.

'Gosh, Mum, the limo is awesome!' Harry said, peering out the window as the shining black funeral limousine pulled up to collect Allegra and the children. Maria was already ensconced in the back seat. She sat solemnly, appropriately dressed in extravagant black, her blonde hair draped with a dramatic black lace headscarf. The look was punctuated with a slash of bright red lipstick. She had been insistent that they all wear black and that Allegra and Kirsty had something suitable to cover their heads.

Harry and Kirsty took the forward seats and Allegra joined her mother in the back seat.

'Seriously, Grandma, this is all a bit over the top, isn't it? A bit like a scene from *The Godfather...*' Kirsty said. Allegra suppressed a grin.

'For your information, Kirsty, your great-grandpapa was a proud Italian man. He was held back from fully living that life, but in death, I am giving him the respectful farewell he deserved. And as his family, we will all comply with that standard, thank you.' Maria turned abruptly, facing straight ahead as the limo moved out onto Fulham Road.

Allegra touched Maria's black-gloved hand. 'Mother, perhaps you should tell us what will take place at the Mass and afterwards. We three aren't familiar with Catholicism like you are.'

'I thought Gran was a Buddhist!' Harry whispered.

'That was yesterday, after the Kabbalah stage. Today, it's Catholic,' Kirsty whispered back.

Maria placed her hand over her mouth to hide a smile while Allegra made a 'stop' gesture by wagging her finger at her daughter.

'All right, you lot, you've made your point. But I was christened a Catholic, and this is what my father would have wanted.' Maria replied whilst maintaining a straight face.

Their limo pulled in behind the massive hearse as they approached the tiny church that Maria had managed to wrangle for the service. There was a small group of people milling outside, mainly friends of Maria, plus a few old friends of Grandpapa. Allegra was relieved to spot Julia.

'I see your children have added their own spin to the required mourning kit,' she shook her head and whispered as they stepped out of the car.

Allegra considered her small family. She thought they looked quite splendid in their black mourning ensemble. Harry's feet were a little out of kilter, clad in green trainers with his black hired suit and fresh white shirt. Kirsty had 'pimped' her black dress with a large skull pendant, which she deemed relevant. Allegra even had the required black silk scarf in her handbag, just in case her mother got really pushy. Her dress was black and she had acquired the 'Italian funeral chic' look by wearing it with heavier black tights and some very sober suede court shoes.

The family turned from their seats in the front row to watch as the coffin was carried in by the six sombre pall-bearers. Allegra had to wipe her eyes when she saw what her mother had organised. The solitary peacock feather lay on a bed of soft green moss on top of the coffin. Harry took her hand and passed her a tissue as she sniffed back her tears.

The service wasn't the full requiem Mass. Even Maria hadn't been able to persuade the priest of that, given he'd never seen any of the Mancini family at any of his services. But Maria read out the poetic tribute she had prepared. They sang two well-known hymns, and the whole process lasted forty minutes before they were back in the limo heading towards the nearby Brompton cemetery.

Only a few attended the graveside. Once the coffin was ready to be laid in its final place, the funeral director quietly asked if Maria would like the peacock feather. She looked to Allegra who nodded back, and Maria indicated he should hand it directly to her daughter.

After the coffin had been lowered into the ground, the handful of mourners threw in their rose petals as a final act of farewell.

The caterers had begun serving cups of tea to the guests by the time Allegra and the family arrived back at Maria's house. Julia had already arrived and chatted to Harry and Kirsty while Allegra made her way around the room.

'Hello. I assume you are Allegra?' A tall man in a brown suit extended his hand. She nodded.

'I am James Hackney, your grandfather's lawyer,' he stated, with what sounded like a couple of plums stuck in his mouth.

'Oh, I see. I'm pleased to meet you. Thank you for coming.' Allegra was a little taken aback.

'I hope you don't mind me being so forward, but as sole beneficiary of your grandfather's will, I will need to meet with you soon to sort everything out.' As he spoke, Allegra's mother came to join them.

'Good, I see you two have met.' she said.

'Mum, what does he mean sole beneficiary? Of what? And shouldn't anything of Grandpapa's go to you?'

'This is not the time to go into things, Allegra. Your grandpapa was very explicit in his instructions, and I happily agreed with all of them. I'll talk to you about it later.'

Fourteen

Although the funeral was over and Grandpapa laid to rest in South London, Allegra felt a persistent sense of unease. Too much change in too little time. And through it all, she couldn't help but constantly reflect on the castle, and the Peacock Room.

As she sat at the kitchen table and opened her laptop, she was immediately deluged with sixty e-mails dropping into her inbox.

She trawled through and deleted most of them.

Then she opened the one marked 'Interview'. It was from the Victoria and Albert Museum, requesting she fill in the attached form and bring it with her to the interview that had been set for the following week.

Allegra's heart soared. Of the four positions she had applied for, this was the one that had responded – and the one she had cared about most.

Next, she opened the one from Massimo marked '*Tesoro*'. She so wanted to be his darling.

My Allegra,

Although you only spent one precious evening with me in my apartment, your fragrance lingers and it feels lonely without you. I am so sorry to hear of the loss of your beloved grandpapa. However, ninety-nine is a ripe old age to exit this mortal coil.

On a separate note, I have contacted the preservation society for Castello di Sammezzano and a local man called Signor Bazia is the chairman. He confirmed that in the 1990s a prominent hotel group bought the castle and they commenced converting the ground and lower ground floor to a hotel. However, after only two years of operating, they had started to play around with the actual fabric of the upper floors of the building and a zealous preservation society placed an order against them. Then a judge ruled the hotel group could not proceed with their operation so the hotel closed and, while they are still the owners, they have abandoned it.

The current local preservation society is fighting to protect it from vandals. They have a website and a Facebook page to raise money to one day reinstate it, in its original form, as a museum. I won't bore you with the details here in my e-mail, as it is all online, in English. Once you have read it all and if you still want to see the castle again, I may be able to twist Signor Bazia's arm to allow a special visit. I don't wish to invade your mourning, so I will wait for you to text me and tell me when I can call. Sending you my love and much more.

Massimo x

Allegra's pulse quickened as she re-read his words, and her flesh burned at the thought of his hands on her naked body. She would finish answering her e-mails, do her errands, then text him after dinner. Just as she had typed 'Castello di Sammezzano' into Google, she heard someone open the front door.

'Allegra, it's me,' Hugo called as he walked up the hall towards the kitchen.

'Hugo. Perhaps now would be a good time for you to give me your key?' she said, holding her hand out.

'This is still half my house,' he replied. He held a bouquet of white flowers.

'As far as I'm concerned, it's not the half with the doorlock. And besides, how would you feel if I had a key to your and Brooklyn's apartment?'

'Well, it's not like you have a man here, is it,' Hugo snapped back.

Allegra half smiled. 'Well, not just at the moment. What is it you want, Hugo?'

He looked slightly taken aback, and handed her the flowers. 'I didn't come to argue, I came to officially, and sincerely, say how sorry I am about your grandpapa.' He sat down opposite her at the table.

'Thank you,' Allegra said graciously, as she went to the cupboard to find a vase.

'What did you mean "not at the moment"? Do you have a boyfriend?'

Allegra filled the vase with water and proceeded to arrange the flowers.

'Allegra, did you hear me? Do you?'

Allegra looked straight at him and paused before she replied. 'I think at our age, we use the word "lover" rather than "boyfriend", don't you think?' She raised her eyebrows quizzically.

'What? Not an Italian!' He couldn't quite get the words out. 'All the time you said you were sick, and you were with some man!' He stood up abruptly with his hands on his hips. 'I had to endure all that shit from our children and from Brooklyn. They were cruel to her! It may not even last now, because of all that!'

'If I have a lover, Italian or otherwise, it is none of your business. You have chosen your path, and I have just adapted to circumstances. Now, I thank you for the flowers and your condolences, but I'd rather you leave, please, and you can leave the house key on the table. Otherwise, I'll have to have the locks changed and it will be you who pays,' she spoke calmly.

Hugo backtracked. 'I'm sorry, Allegra, that all came out wrong! Look, maybe I have been a bit hasty. Maybe this is just a midlife crisis I will get over.'

Allegra interrupted him. 'No. I don't think so. It's been over for four months and you put me through absolute hell. Just leave the key and get out, please. Now!' She was on her feet, holding open the kitchen door.

'Look, think about the children and what may be best for them. Remember, I still have control of the money.' He paused, and then added, 'Bear that in mind, as well!'

She marched him up the hall.

'No, Hugo, it's my turn now. I'm thinking of what is best for me!'

Once he had stepped outside, she immediately shut the door and quickly turned the inside lock.

Allegra calmed herself down with a strong, hot cup of tea, and then resumed her Google search.

But she couldn't concentrate. Her focus had been distracted by Hugo's final shot about the children. She could see he was having second thoughts about Brooklyn, or rather Brooklyn was having second thoughts about Hugo... Perhaps he wasn't able to keep up with the younger woman's demands. The thought of parting with half of the home and money would be weighing on him too.

Before Allegra's trip to Florence, this would have been a perfect solution – to have her old life and her husband back. But now something sparkled in her heart. Massimo may have been a part of it, but it felt deeper than that. It was as if with Grandpapa's passing, she needed to know more about who he'd been, about his past in Donnini, and the *Castello di Sammezzano*.

As the Google options appeared on her screen, she hit Wikipedia which offered basic information, then moved on to the Preservation Society webpage.

It spoke of the original owner, the Spanish nobleman who built the castle in around 1605. Then she refreshed her memory with what Massimo had previously told her – the Marchese Ferdinando Panciatchi Ximenes d'Aragona, who had inherited it in 1853. He had become disenchanted with Florentine society and decided to add his own legacy to the building. He became both the commissioning party and the architect. She had some understanding of the snobbish opinions of the day. The descriptions in the information talked about a merging of Moorish and Gothic designs, which resurrected Allegra's wild imaginings of the castle. The information in English was scant, and her frustration grew that she hadn't bothered to let Grandpapa teach her Italian.

She was so engrossed in her research that she lost track of the time. Harry was calling out that he was home, and what was for dinner? It was 5:00 p.m. She had been lost in thought about *Castello di Sammezzano* for the past three hours.

'They're changing my cast to a lighter one tomorrow,' Harry announced at the dinner-table.

Kirsty had asked, very politely, if Allegra could lend her thirty pounds to go to yet another concert on the weekend. Because Kirsty had secured a part-time job for the forthcoming holidays to save for her gap year, Allegra agreed to a loan. Anything to conclude the family meal proceedings quickly... Then she could retire to her bedroom for a clandestine phone chat with Massimo.

His response was immediate after she had texted him.

'How are you feeling now, *Tesoro*?' As soon as she heard his voice, her lust returned.

'I have been thinking about you, Massimo. Thank you for the lead on the castle. I've been looking at it today, but a lot of what I need to know is in Italian and the translator on my computer is pretty basic.'

'I'm pleased you've missed me, but I can see perhaps you have missed the ancient *castello* more!' She heard the smile in his voice.

'I'm sorry! I guess I do sound a little obsessed. It just feels so close to Grandpapa, and his history...'

'No, I am sorry, Allegra. I will try to understand. I did ask my *mamma* about the Mancini family in Donnini, and she said she has heard of them. Also, there is a very old lady with the family name of Mancini still alive today. Maybe I could go and chat to her. But I will save this for when you come to visit.'

'I want to come back, soon, but I have a job interview next week and I need to see my grandpapa's lawyer. Give me a week or so, then I'll see what cheap flights I can find' Allegra replied.

They continued to chat about everything, and nothing. The man who had robbed Allegra still hadn't been apprehended and she expanded on what she knew about the job at the museum. Before he hung up, Massimo hinted that if Allegra couldn't make a weekend trip soon, he might even come to London.

That night she went to bed, smiling.

Fifteen

When the lawyer called, he made an appointment for Allegra to visit on Friday afternoon. Allegra rang her mother to ask if she would accompany her and they agreed to meet for lunch beforehand. It was going to be a big day, as she had her first interview with the Victoria and Albert Museum in South Kensington at ten o'clock that morning.

Allegra dressed in what she considered appropriate for a serious interview – a pair of neat black trousers and a smart white shirt. But after scrutinising herself in the hall mirror just before she left the house, she decided black and white was too minimalist… Not her style at all. She rushed back in and threw a hot-pink silk scarf around her neck.

When Allegra was at university she had visited the famous museum numerous times, and the majestic entrance never ceased to make her feel small and insignificant. The amazing Victorian building was engorged with a diverse range of historic items including collections of art, jewellery, furniture, architecture, and conversation pieces collected from every corner of the globe. It was one of the great wonders of Allegra's world.

She was ushered up to the HR office on the fourth floor and after a ten-minute wait, shown to the office of a Mrs Ennor. The short, blonde woman offered no smile or reassurance as she introduced herself; she just motioned for Allegra to sit in the chair opposite her desk. She slowly studied the documents Allegra had handed over.

'You're a little older than I anticipated. I see you actually haven't worked in this field except for one year after your degree.' She raised her well-plucked eyebrows and looked intently at Allegra.

'I've been bringing up a family, but I've kept up my interest and I believe my qualifications are exactly what you specified in the advertisement. Is my age a problem?' Allegra struggled to control her shaking voice.

'Let me be clear, Mrs O'Brien. At the Victoria and Albert, we are not ageist. We select the best person for the position.' She raised her eyebrows, paused again and stared expectantly at Allegra.

'Well, I believe my maturity, along with my passion for this particular area, would be beneficial to the position.' Allegra managed to get the words out steadily this time.

After some more questioning, the stern woman eventually invited Allegra down to the third floor and introduced her to Desmond Tipple. He was of an undetermined age, with pale white skin, a slightly beaky nose and a head of red unruly hair.

Mr Tipple oversaw twelfth-to-nineteenth-century European art, ceramics and architecture. He was charming in an old-fashioned way, in his knitted waistcoat and worn corduroy trousers, and invited Allegra on a tour of his department. She felt privileged to be shown the secrets of such a famous establishment. It was a great relief to have her recent adventure with *Castello di Sammezzano* under her belt, for when Mr Tipple enquired as to what she was currently researching, she could give both an informed and passionate answer. He told her with some pride that he read and spoke fluent Italian. As she left the museum, Allegra offered up a small silent prayer of hope – this would just be the perfect place for her to work.

Maria was waiting for her at their designated café.

'How did it go?' she asked, once Allegra had joined her with an iced coffee.

'Well, the initial interview with the HR woman was excruciating. I did get to meet the chap I'd be working with and, although he didn't give much away, I think I may have impressed him a little.'

As they arrived at the lawyer's office, Allegra stopped short. She had talked so much about the interview that she hadn't asked her mother about the will. Mr Hackney greeted them wearing the ugly brown crumpled suit he had worn to the funeral. His office had a musty smell about it and Allegra was almost compelled to ask him to open a window.

'Now, Mrs O'Brien, or may I call you Allegra?' Mr Hackney asked in his plummy manner.

'Allegra is fine.' She forced a smile.

'Your grandfather first visited me over twenty years ago when he was seventy-nine years old and asked me to keep this box.' He patted a square, battered-looking box that Allegra thought might have been for shoes in a previous incarnation.

'It was quite an unorthodox request, as being a law firm, we don't normally provide storage solutions.' He screwed up his nose as he pronounced the word 'storage'.

'However, Luigi Mancini was a persuasive, determined man, and we agreed to keep it in our safe until his demise.' Mr Hackney made another forced movement with his nose before he continued.

'Mr Mancini was very clear in his instructions that you should have the box. His instruction was that you should read his mother's diary in its entirety to understand what happened "back then", whatever that means.' He offered Maria a glance.

Maria sucked in her cheeks and flicked back her blonde locks as she smiled.

He continued. 'In addition, he left you ten thousand pounds, which with my fee deducted and with compounding interest, is now in the region of fifteen thousand pounds.'

Allegra gasped. 'Where did Grandpapa get that sort of money? Surely, Mum, this should go to you?'

'No, dear, I know all about this. Your grandpapa gave me plenty from his pension as we went along, and he always wanted his savings to go to you.'

'So, if I may proceed?' Mr Hackney interrupted.

Allegra nodded, stunned.

'I will have the funds placed directly into your bank if you would be so kind as to give me your account details. But if I may be so forward, your mother has informed me of the recent separation from your husband. Therefore I would advise you to open a separate account in your own name and not mention this legacy to him.'

With the meeting over, Allegra went to pick up the box. It was very heavy.

Once they were out on the street, they hailed a cab back to Allegra's house.

She could not contain her curiosity a moment longer. 'Mum, where did Grandpapa get all this money? It's crazy!'

'I'm guessing he squirreled away the extra he earned from doing tiling work for friends on weekends and evenings. My mother took all his normal salary to manage the household. Also, I think he received a small amount from the sale of his mother's house.' She patted her daughter's knee. 'Like me, he wanted you to have independence. If you fancy doing something frivolous, you don't need Hugo's permission. This is your money to spend how you wish.'

Maria then opened her purse and handed Allegra a small silver crucifix. On the back of it were the words *Ti amo per sempre. Alessandro*.

'This was on the chain Grandpapa wore. It should be yours, Mum, not mine,' Allegra said.

'I want you to have it. The translation is "I love you forever." Alessandro was my grandpapa, and he and my grandmama gave each other identical crucifixes when they married.' Maria kissed Allegra's cheek.

'They must have been a very romantic couple.'

'They were, my darling. Our family attracts romance,' she said with a wink, and Allegra instantly blushed.

Maria dropped her daughter off at home, and then took the black cab on to her own place.

Allegra found the house pleasingly empty. She switched the kettle on then sat down at the kitchen table, placing Grandpapa's crucifix around her neck.

She moved her attention to the box in front of her. It was made of strong cardboard, a worn brown colour, and about the size of a pair of man's shoes. There was absolutely no writing or branding on it. As she removed the lid, she was met with the same musty smell that inhabited Mr Hackney's office. It must have been twenty-five years since the box was last opened.

Sitting at the top was an envelope, yellow with age, and in Grandpapa's neat writing the name *ALLEGRA* written across its middle. She carefully undid the seal and took out the letter, which was written on lined paper.

My Dearest Allegra,

If you are reading this, I will have passed away, God willing, to join my Italian family in Heaven and perhaps to finally find out why my papa disappeared. You are twenty-two as I write and prepare this box. You visited Florence a couple of years back for your studies, and I so wanted to try and tell you about my upbringing nearby in the village of Donnini in Tuscany. But my wife makes life very difficult for me and says I must leave you to be an English girl and not put my Italian regrets in your pathway. So, I stayed quiet. But I can see you have developed into a very intelligent young woman, with a passion for architecture, history, and colour, and I believe, as you grow older, you may develop an interest in your Italian family history.

I harbour my regrets. I shouldn't have left my mamma when I did. I should have searched for my papa. But back then I had no idea where to start. I just wanted to escape mamma's shame that engulfed our home. My mamma was a skilled writer for her time, and when she died, I discovered her diary. I have kept it for you. Perhaps somehow by reading this, you may solve the mystery of papa's fall from grace and his disappearance. From the moment I write this letter to the moment you

read it, please believe that despite my bitter marriage,
your mamma and you, my bambina Allegra, were the
best things that ever happened to me.

Ti voglio bene per sempre.
Grandpapa Luigi Mancini

Allegra wiped her damp eyes with a paper towel. Then she placed the letter on the table and lifted the leather-bound book from the box.

How wise her grandpapa was. Twenty years on and he was right; she *had* developed an interest in her Italian history. She would find a way to honour his wishes.

As she opened to the first page, the only thing she could read was the date: August 1915, the month and year her grandpapa was born. Her great-grandmother's pregnancy must have been the inspiration to commence her diary. The rest, although written in a beautiful hand in legible ink, was all in Italian. It was a thick diary, the last entry being in 1930. She could see a lump under the last page, as if there was one folded beneath. She carefully turned it. A rich-coloured peacock feather had been cut off just below the feather line and perfectly pressed on the back page – a silent missive from her grandpapa.

Allegra was interrupted as she heard Kirsty open the front door and call out. She quickly put the letter, the diary, and the feather back in the box and placed it out of sight in the broom cupboard.

'I'm so excited about tomorrow's concert. We're all meeting at Sally's and going together, then I'll stay over at hers as it's cheaper just to get one cab back,' Kirsty chatted as she opened the fridge and grabbed a slice of cheese.

Allegra was relieved; Kirsty's upbeat mood would make for a happy weekend for everyone.

After the three of them had finished dinner, Allegra smuggled the box and her laptop up to her bedroom. She started writing.

Dear Massimo,

I have enjoyed such an interesting day. In the morning I went to an interview for a position at the Victoria and Albert Museum, which in some ways was like a dream come true. When I was a student of historic interior architecture, I spent many hours researching and wandering around the vast rooms there. I was always in awe of the scholars who had the foresight to place so much effort into preserving the past so we might understand the present. I would be honoured if they offered me the job.

Then I visited my grandpapa's lawyer and was very surprised that he had bequeathed me his mamma's diary. It is written in an impressive leather-bound book and scripted with a neat hand. But my massive frustration is I can't read it. Oh, how I wish I had shown more interest in my grandpapa's language.

Oh, I've just reread this – sorry, I do go on a bit, don't I? I just wanted to share my day with you and let you know you are in my thoughts before I give in to my drooping eyelids and fall asleep.

Love A x

Sixteen

Allegra woke the following morning with a feeling of purpose. She spotted her laptop light flashing to indicate she had mail. Massimo had replied and, as she expected, he had offered to translate the diary. But only on the condition that Allegra was present so that he could read it aloud to her.

She was starting to think she had the hormones of a lovesick sixteen-year-old, as she read Massimo's endearments and basked in his choice of lavish Italian words. Her life had changed so much... The veil of security she assumed would always be there with the father of her children had been ripped away. On reflection, her past was white and sterile, as if Hugo had scripted it. Well, that script was over. Now Allegra was emerging like a peacock, full of colour and self-belief.

She was so enthused about seeing Massimo again and decided to check whether her mother would 'babysit' the children for a weekend. Kirsty was being exceptionally cooperative at the moment. She had spent all afternoon trying on different combinations of clothes and playing songs by the Foo Fighters, the concert she was so excited about. She had finally chosen a bright red bomber jacket and a pair of strategically ripped jeans, and practically skipped out the door. Allegra kissed her goodbye, and handed her ten pounds towards the taxi fare back to her friend's place later.

Allegra had passed out exhausted whilst watching a DVD. But she was disturbed from her sound sleep by a ringing from somewhere in her dreams. *The home phone.* She scrambled sleepily to pick it up from the bedside table.

'Mrs O'Brien?' a formal male voice asked.

'Yes, I'm Allegra O'Brien. Who is this, please?'

'I'm Sergeant Mark Rennie from the Metropolitan Police. I'm afraid it's about your daughter, Kirsty.'

'My God! What is it? Has there been an accident?'

'No, she hasn't been in an accident, but we have arrested her for being in possession of a Class A drug.' The sergeant paused a moment to allow his words to sink in.

'What? Where is she?' Allegra struggled to compose herself.

'She's in a holding cell at Chelsea Police Station. She is entitled to a phone call and she requested that I call you.'

'I'm on my way right now,' Allegra said, then quickly hung up the phone. As she pulled on her jeans and sweater, her mind flashed to Massimo. She sent him a short text. *Are you awake?*

Then she gently woke Harry and told him she had to pop out, to which he grunted and pulled the covers over his head. Her phone rang as she unlocked her car.

'What's wrong, Allegra? I just received your text,' Massimo sounded drowsy.

'I'm so sorry to wake you, but I didn't want to phone Hugo and I don't know what to do. I'm on my way to Chelsea Police

Station. They told me my daughter has been arrested for possessing a Class A drug. I don't even know what that is.'

There was a pause as Massimo collected his thoughts.

'OK, leave it with me. You carry on to the station, and I'll see what I can find out and call you straight back.' Then he clicked off.

It was three o'clock in the morning, so Allegra made the short drive up the Kings Road and into Sloane Avenue in no time. As she opened the door of the police station, the stench of fresh vomit invaded her nostrils.

'Can I help you, madam?' a ruddy-faced policeman asked from behind a reception desk that was protected by a steel grill.

'I've been told my daughter, Kirsty O'Brien, has been arrested.'

'Ah, yes. You need to take a seat, please. Sergeant Rennie will be out in due course.'

He motioned her to one of three hard, grey plastic seats positioned under a messy pin board. She was about to object when her phone shrilled from her handbag.

'Allegra, I've had a word with the arresting sergeant. I told him that I am a relative and a former Metropolitan policeman. He told me they will be keeping the two girls and one young man for at least one night in the cells. They do this often with first-time offenders as a scare tactic. However, Kirsty may also be charged with supplying, so this needs to be handled correctly from the outset. It will be very difficult for you to make bail for her tonight without a lawyer, so I suggest after you have seen her, go home and get some rest, then call a lawyer in the morning. Don't worry, *Tesoro*, she will be all right. This will be the first of many harsh lessons in her life. I will phone you tomorrow.'

'Thank you,' was all Allegra could manage before he hung up.

Kirsty looked a sight when she was ushered into a cold, windowless room to talk with her mother.

'Mum, I'm so sorry! It was just some E! I only took one tab and Pete asked me to mind his stash in my handbag. The police had an undercover guy standing right beside us at the concert. He was acting as if he was stoned and I thought he was a friend of Pete's, who thought he was a friend of ours. After the concert, the undercover guy asked us if he could buy a tab and Pete gave me the nod to give him one from the stash. I didn't even take the money, Pete did.' Kirsty started to cry.

Allegra reached out to her. 'I've been told I can't bail you out tonight without a lawyer, so you will just have to bear up. I'll call someone first thing in the morning, and we will get you out then.' Allegra tried to sound reassuring.

'Shit, Mum, don't tell Dad, please!' Kirsty managed between sobs.

'Well, I can't promise that. Your father needs to know. But we will have to see what we can sort out with the lawyer.'

They were interrupted by the sergeant. 'OK, your time's up. Back to the cell, young lady.' He motioned for Kirsty to get up and leave.

Allegra squeezed her hand as she passed. 'I love you, darling,' she said as Kirsty disappeared down the hallway.

Seventeen

Allegra dozed restlessly for the couple of hours before the sun joined the day. She decided her mother would be her first port of call, as she would know an appropriate law firm to call on a Sunday. Mr Hackney certainly wouldn't fit the bill and calling Hugo at this stage was not an option.

She drank about three cups of coffee as she watched the kitchen clock tick to 7:30 a.m., the earliest she knew she could safely phone her mother.

Maria immediately agreed to help, then drove straight round to Allegra's house.

'My lawyer has given me the name of an excellent firm that handles these sorts of cases.' Maria handed the number to her daughter.

Allegra wasted no time and soon had stated the full details to the gentleman on the other end of the phone. He listened sympathetically then said he would phone her back after he had spoken to the police.

'What's going on? What are you doing here so early, Gran?' Harry asked as he wandered into the kitchen in his pyjamas. The two women exchanged glances but gave no immediate response.

'Oh right! What has she done now?' he asked, rolling his eyes.

'Your sister is in the cells at the Chelsea Police Station for possessing drugs,' Allegra replied, as she tugged at her hair distractedly.

'What! Does Dad know?'

'No, and don't you say anything to him or any of your friends. No Facebook, no nothing! Do you understand, Harry? This does not leave these four walls.' Allegra wiped her eyes and looked expectantly at her son.

'Yes, Mum. OK, OK, I get the point.'

It was midday and the lawyer hadn't phoned back. Allegra felt panicky, drinking endless cups of coffee and watching the phone. Harry wandered in and out, offering unwelcome scenarios of arrests for similar crimes he was reading about on the Internet.

'You go up and shower and change – you look terrible, Allegra. I'll man the phone,' Maria said. Allegra rushed upstairs and, as she was dressing, the phone rang.

'Mrs O'Brien, after some discussion with the sergeant, I believe it may be in your daughter's best interests to stay in custody another day. From what they have told me, the police are putting pressure on the young man who was arrested with the girls. They are endeavouring to get him to confess to both possessing and supplying the drugs, and if that is the case, the girls will face a lesser charge.' The lawyer paused.

'Oh! What do you think will happen if we pursue bail today?' Allegra asked.

'It will cost a lot of time and money, as there's a legal procedure to follow, and a court appearance. The way I'm suggesting, we have a fifty-fifty chance she may walk away on Monday morning with a fine and a warning,' he replied.

Allegra agreed, and the lawyer informed her that the sergeant would keep her notified whichever way they decided to progress.

'Mum, she is allowed one visit today, so I'll make some sandwiches. I'm sure she'll be starving,' Allegra said to Maria. There was a loud knock at the door.

'I'll get it,' Harry called as he rushed to the front door.

Both women looked a little puzzled as they heard two sets of footsteps walk up the hall.

'Massimo! What on earth are you doing here?' Allegra slapped her hands to her mouth. Maria smiled. Harry looked extremely puzzled.

'I heard you needed some professional support, so I caught the Gatwick-bound plane out of Florence at 8:30 a.m. and here I am. Your own private policeman!' He offered a huge smile.

Allegra gulped then introduced him to her mother and her son, attempting to stay as cool as possible. They made room for him at the table and Allegra served them all some sandwiches and coffee.

She updated Massimo on Kirsty and what the lawyer had said. 'We were just about to visit and take her something to eat when you arrived.'

'My advice would be just for you to go, Allegra. I will accompany you, and in my capacity as a former UK police officer see what I can find out, and what favours I may be able to call in.' As Massimo spoke, Allegra noticed Harry's interest pique.

'So, Massimo, do you carry a gun?' Harry asked.

Massimo smiled. 'Not when I travel in civilian clothes.'

'That's good, 'cause Mum hates guns. So, if you're Italian, how come you were in the UK Police force?' Harry was persistent.

Massimo smiled again, a bit less confident. 'It's a long story, which I'll be happy to share a bit later. But just now we need to see what we can do for your sister's predicament.'

As Massimo dealt with Harry's questions, Allegra turned and pretended to wrap the sandwiches. She tried to control her shaking hands. Then she quickly excused herself and rushed up to her bathroom, where she applied some make-up, a squirt of perfume, and changed her shoes. On her return, Maria gave her a knowing smile and assured her she would stay at the house with Harry till they returned.

'So, *Tesoro*, you put that lipstick and perfume on for me? I'm touched.' Massimo pressed his hand to her leg as she started the car. Once she had backed from the driveway and turned out of the street, he asked her to pull over. He unbuckled his seatbelt, leant over and kissed her.

'Oh, Massimo, thank you so much for coming. I'm sorry if I seem a bit strange, it was just seeing you arrive so unexpectedly.' She kissed him back.

'I had to come. You have gotten under my skin, Allegra. And we Italians are spontaneous. So now that I'm here, let me see what I can do to help this situation.'

Once they arrived at the police station, Massimo took on a whole new persona. Allegra asked to see Kirsty and as she was ushered to the interview room, Massimo disappeared off to an office out of sight.

'Oh, Mum, it's awful in here. I haven't slept, and I have to pee in the room with other women. One of them is a hooker!'

Allegra handed her the sandwiches, which she devoured in a shot. It was a bit of a challenge working out how to tell her daughter that she had an Italian policeman friend assisting, so for now she decided to leave out the more delicate parts of the story.

'I have a friend who used to be a policeman helping us. What may get you out of here without a criminal record is if your friend Pete admits the drugs were his. That he was selling them, and he coerced you to put them in your handbag.'

Kirsty blushed. 'Well, I didn't know he was selling them to others. We paid him for them but thought that he was just covering his costs,' she whispered.

'Hell! You have got to be joking! That's not going to wash then!' Allegra fumed.

'I'm so sorry, Mum, I really am. I feel so ashamed. I hate being in this hole... Do you think this ex-cop friend can really help?'

A policeman opened the door. 'Come on, young lady. We'd like to ask you a few more questions, please.' He motioned for Kirsty to go ahead and then turned to Allegra. 'You may wait in reception if you wish. We have no idea how long this will take.'

Allegra sat waiting in the hard, grey plastic chair. The vomit odour from the previous evening had been replaced with a strong antiseptic smell. In her solitude, she attempted to fathom how her world, in twenty-four short hours, had been turned upside-down yet again.

It was an hour before Massimo appeared from the offices behind the reception.

'Come, let's walk out in the fresh air and find a coffee,' he said as he placed his arm around Allegra and guided her out the door. They sat down in the trendy Conran café around the corner; a stark contrast to the morbid police station.

'I don't really have a right to be as angry as I'd like to be. It would be hypocritical after the mess with drugs I got myself into in Italy. It's just that I worry for my daughter. She thinks she's all grown up, but she's not.'

Massimo leant over and gently removed Allegra's hand from her hair.

'I convinced the arresting sergeant to grant me an interview with this Pete who, incidentally, already has a criminal record for supply. Hopefully, I have persuaded him to admit to everything and acknowledge that the girls, other than paying him for their tablets, were entirely naïve about everything else. The sergeant is going back in now to ask him for a written statement, so fingers crossed.' Massimo spoke in a gentle tone.

They finished their coffee and Allegra relished the comfort he afforded by holding her hand as they walked back. When they arrived at the station, she was aware of a big change in attitude from the reception officer.

'Come through, sir,' he said respectfully to Massimo as he buzzed him into the back offices.

Half an hour later, the sergeant appeared and invited Allegra through to his office, where Massimo and Kirsty were waiting. The sergeant faced them.

'Young lady, you are very fortunate to be leaving here with just a warning. I trust your accommodation overnight may be enough to prevent us seeing you again.' He looked expectantly at Kirsty.

'I promise,' she said, her eyes wide with shock.

'We can see you have a supportive family, and you are lucky to have an Italian uncle who cares so much about you. Stop using drugs and start doing something useful with your life.'

Massimo stepped forward, shook his hand, thanked him, and walked behind Kirsty to the door.

'Thank you, Sergeant, from the bottom of my heart,' Allegra said as she clutched his hand in appreciation.

'He was a very brave man, your relation. I remember the incident well. It's him you need to thank.' The stern sergeant gave her a nod before he shut the office door.

Eighteen

Kirsty sat silently in the back seat of the car. Allegra didn't press her; she was too overwhelmed with relief to say anything.

The aroma of Maria's special Sunday roast chicken welcomed them into the house.

'Thank God!' Maria said as she hugged her granddaughter. Even Harry managed a stiff squeeze for his sister.

'Harry and I have done a quick shop and prepared us a roast chicken dinner. We would like you, Massimo, to be our special guest.' Maria flicked her hair back, batted her eyes, and beamed at Massimo.

'I'd be delighted.' He returned the smile.

Allegra left Massimo in the kitchen chatting to her mother as she accompanied Kirsty upstairs and Harry followed.

'So, what was it like in the clink?' Harry was gagging for details.

Allegra reached out to hush him.

'No, it's all right, Mum, I'll tell him. Bloody awful, little brother! I hated it. I never want to go back, and I'm not going to talk about it ever again. And neither are you!'

Once Kirsty had showered and changed, Maria and Allegra served up the meal. Massimo poured the wine.

Allegra could see Harry was itching to ask questions, but he knew well enough it was his sister's call.

Kirsty was so hungry she had practically inhaled her meal before turning to Massimo.

'I know it's you I have to thank for getting me out of my mess, Massimo – or should I say, "Uncle Massimo"?' She offered a sly smile.

'What! Are you some relative of Great-Grandpapa?' Harry blurted out.

Maria pressed her napkin to her mouth to suppress a grin. Allegra winced, but before either woman could offer an explanation, the Massimo she had first met, Massimo the policeman, emerged with a plausible reply.

'Let me enlighten you. Your mother has been doing some research into her Italian background, and we met when she was in Florence. Our grandparents come from neighbouring villages, so we have been exchanging notes and she has asked me to assist her in a translation of her great-grandmama's diary. I also coincidentally was once a policeman on the force in England.'

Massimo took a sip of his wine and surveyed his audience.

Harry was straight in. 'So, why did you join the UK police when you were an Italian?'

'It was an exchange programme of sorts that they were offering at the time. And, being originally from a small village, much like your grandpapa, I wanted to see the world. However, it got a bit rough for my liking, and I opted to return to Italy and work as a rank-and-file officer in Florence.'

Before Harry could ask another question, Allegra interrupted.

'That's enough for now, Harry. Let's leave Massimo to his dessert.'

Harry and Kirsty eventually left the table whilst the other three finished the bottle of wine.

'I've made up the bed in the spare room, if you need it' Maria said.

'I don't think it would be appropriate for me to stay, thank you. I can slip out and get a hotel. I have a tentative return booking for an 11:00 a.m. flight tomorrow from Gatwick,' Massimo replied.

'No please, I insist. It's perfectly appropriate for my relation to stay over when he has, yet again, rescued a member of this family from a crisis,' Allegra said.

Massimo laughed, and Maria took her cue. 'On that note, I'm off. Thank you again, Massimo, for being so kind to my family.' Maria kissed him on both cheeks, flicked her blonde hair back and afforded Allegra a mischievous smile before she left.

Once they were alone, Allegra ached to ask about Massimo's time on the force in the UK. He must have had a sixth sense, she thought, as he managed to completely divert the conversation.

'Now, how about you show me this diary? We need to add authenticity to our story…cousin!'

Allegra brought down the box and reverently took out the leather-bound book. She placed it open at the first page on the kitchen table in front of Massimo, and he began to read out loud.

I have set about this inventory of my life as so many changes have taken place in such a short time. I find myself expecting a baby; it is the best gift God has ever given me and the best gift I shall ever give my handsome Alessandro. I

was not conceived by my parents, they adopted me because
I was an orphan. But regardless, I enjoyed a wonderful
upbringing and never wanted any other parents...

As Massimo's rich, clear voice began to read the descriptive, colourful words of her great-grandmama's most private thoughts, Allegra was transported back to another time, where life seemed simple. The two most important things to her great-grandmama were her *bellissimo* Luigi Mancini, the most cherished baby in all of Italy, and her husband, the handsome, loving Alessandro Mancini.

After the first twenty pages, Massimo's voice was fading and Allegra touched his hand.

'How can I ever thank you? You have saved my life twice.' She gently kissed his cheek and traced his scar with her finger.

'I will easily find a way, and we will be naked in your bed I think!' he whispered into her ear.

'No Massimo... I need to tell my children about you first... Break the idea of a new man in my life to them gently.' Allegra stumbled over her words.

'It's OK, *Tesoro*, I understand. Please then, show me to my own room for the night.'

He collected his overnight bag from the hall and followed Allegra to the spare room at the back of the house.

'Are all the other bedrooms upstairs?' he asked as he pushed the door closed.

'Yes.' Allegra gave a small gasp as he pulled her forward and kissed her neck. She instantly felt the strain of her erect nipples against her bra. Before she knew what had happened, he had her jeans off and had removed his trousers.

'We must be very quiet!' He placed his hand on Allegra's mouth.

The sex was urgent; he took her over the bed and entered her with hot desire. Once it was over, Allegra giggled as he held her in his arms on top of the neatly-made bed.

'So, I gather you don't really take no for an answer!'

Afterwards, Allegra lay awake upstairs in her own bed; she didn't want to risk the children finding out just yet that she had a lover.

Her thoughts instead lingered on her great-grandmama Cosima's diary. A whole new dimension, an essential part of her past, was revealing itself. So far, Cosima had only spoken of herself, her husband, the pregnancy, and the baby. She wrote, as Allegra imagined she would have spoken, in elongated, florid, drawn-out romantic words. Finally, Allegra gave in to sleep and drifted off to sinful visions of the man in the bedroom below.

Kirsty surprised everyone by rising early. She had made coffee and toast, and was sitting chatting to Massimo when Allegra arrived in the kitchen.

'Gosh, Mum, you look great this morning. You don't usually put your make-up on to see me off to college,' Kirsty said with a silly grin.

Allegra blushed. 'Oh, well, I'm driving Massimo to Victoria to catch the Express and then running a few errands. We will talk this evening.'

They all left the house together and once Allegra had pulled into the car park at the station, Massimo asked her to walk him to the platform.

'Please book your tickets today to come to me, *Tesoro*. I need you, and we need to finish the diaries.' He kissed her and then stepped onto the train.

Nineteen

Three days had passed since Kirsty's incarceration and Massimo's rescue mission. Allegra could hear Harry's chatter with his father as he arrived home from dinner. She was about to scoot up to her bedroom to avoid Hugo, but they intercepted her on the stairs.

'Hi, Mum. Dad took me to The Botanist in Sloane Square. It was so cool!' Harry said as he gave his dad a hug and headed up to his room.

'Do you have a bottle of wine open?' Hugo asked Allegra.

'I don't fancy a drink, thanks. I was just off to read on my bed,' Allegra replied.

'Well, come on, at least have a chat with me.' He walked into the living room.

Allegra shivered; they hardly ever used this formal room and it had a vicious chill about it. Hugo flicked the gas fire on. They sat in the stiff armchairs facing each other.

'You used to say being in front of a flaming fire was so romantic.' He smiled at her, warmly, in a way she hadn't seen for some time.

'Did I? I don't remember.'

'Come on, Allegra. We can be pleasant, can't we?'

'I'm not being unpleasant. It's just I don't actually wish to sit and chat to you, Hugo. So, spit it out. I can see you're about to make an announcement. Your engagement, perhaps?' She eyeballed him.

'No, actually, quite the contrary. I've decided to break up with Brooklyn.' He paused to take a breath before continuing. 'I feel it was all just a big mistake. And I thought maybe you would consider spending some time with me. It's what Harry and Kirsty would want. Maybe we can get things back how they used to be.'

'You are unbelievable, Hugo. You haven't broken up with Brooklyn. I bet she dumped you!' She crossed her legs and folded her arms across her chest.

'It was a mutual decision, if you must know, but she is keeping the apartment. Let's face it, this house is still half-mine and I know you are still in love with me, aren't you, Allegra?'

She stared at him as he carried on.

'Harry told me the only man in your life is some Italian policeman who is helping you with family research. That hardly sounds romantic, and it's not like there's anyone else.'

'Oh, really, is that what our son told you? A great little spin-doctor he is. Actually there *is* someone in my life and the children know nothing about him, as I've been discreet, unlike you.' Allegra took pleasure in the change of expression that passed over her ex-husband's face.

'Well, I'm sure we can both forgive each other these affairs and move on,' Hugo replied.

Allegra was on her feet.

'I've done nothing to be forgiven for! You were living with another woman and had instigated a legal separation; so technically, I am a single woman and may date whomever I please.' She bent down and turned the gas fire off.

'Hugo. I want you to leave, now.' She switched off the light and walked into the hall.

'But Allegra, I've got nowhere–' He attempted to continue the conversation in the hallway.

'Please. Do as I ask, Hugo.'

'OK then fine. I will leave. But Allegra, just agree to think about it. Not for me, but for our children?'

She looked him straight in the eye. 'No. Hugo, I'm sorry, it can't work. I'm not in love with you anymore.'

She finally heard the front door click shut. Clutching her chest, she turned and walked up the stairs.

Allegra woke the next morning with chaos surging through her veins. They had been a happy family before Hugo had the affair with Brooklyn. She had loved him, hadn't she? Or, in later years, had she just loved the *idea* of Hugo? Harry did need him. He was a young man... Was she being selfish? Should she consider Hugo's offer?

'Harry, what did you tell your father about Massimo?' Allegra asked over breakfast.

'Nothing about Kirsty's arrest!'

'What! You little geek shit! Don't tell him anything about me, do you understand?' Kirsty fumed.

'OK, OK, Kirsty, hear me out. I didn't mention your arrest. I knew you'd go mad. Dad just wanted to know if Mum maybe had an Italian boyfriend or something. Because of all that time in Florence... I just told him about Massimo helping her research Grandpapa Luigi's past.' Harry removed his glasses and rubbed his eyes.

'Thank you, Harry. I believe you. And Kirsty – calm down, for goodness sake. Your father won't ever know, I promise you.' Allegra reached across to both sides and patted her hands on her children.

Kirsty usually left with Harry, but that morning she seemed to be lingering.

'Are you still upset about what happened, love? I'm sorry I can't agree to fund the gap year now, after the drugs thing. You'll just have to accept that and find another way to make it happen.'

'Ah, Mum, it's OK. I know Zara will be going to New Zealand without me. Maybe I can go next year instead...' Kirsty shifted from one foot to the other. 'I sort of just need to unload something about Dad, if that's OK?'

'Right. What kind of unload are we talking?' Allegra leaned back in the chair and tugged a piece of hair in her finger.

'Well, I have a friend at college whose mother works at Dad's office, and hears all of Brooklyn's gossip.' She paused and sat down.

'Go on.'

'She says Brooklyn demanded a big apartment in Notting Hill, marriage, and wants a baby this year, or else she will leave Dad.' Kirsty looked nervously at her mother. 'So, I know he's my father and I guess deep down I must love him, but it doesn't feel like it at the moment. Not like I love you, and I know it's not my business what's going on with you and that Massimo bloke, but I saw how happy you were around him.' She paused with her hands clasped nervously.

'Oh, darling, I love you, too. I'll be honest with you. I am at a crossroads with your father and Massimo. Be assured, I will do what I believe is right. But I haven't made any final decisions yet,' Allegra said.

Kirsty interrupted her.

'I don't know what he's told you, Mum, but he's been a bastard, so don't go back to him for our sakes.' A tear formed in the corner of her eye. Allegra reached out and hugged her daughter.

'Thank you for feeling brave enough to talk to me.' Allegra pulled back and smiled, wiping away a tear of her own.

After Kirsty left, Allegra needed to soothe herself. There were so many mixed emotions whirring around: Hugo offering to come back, her feelings for Massimo, and her past, all bound up in the diary.

After a long soak in a hot bath within her sanctuary, she returned to the kitchen and made a strong coffee. Then she placed the diary beside her at the table and opened her laptop.

Tesoro,

I have managed to get us a private visit to the castle accompanied by the chairman of the Preservation Society, as he wants a favour from me in the future. This is how we Italians work. However, it can only be a week on Sunday, so I am suggesting you fly down on Friday and as it is a bank holiday, return on the Monday, or later. I thought we might take a room at a small hotel in

Reggello, which is close to both our family villages and near to Sammezzano.

I must rush.
Love Massimo xx

Allegra smiled as she considered what favour Massimo would have to do in return for helping her. She gently ran her finger across the diary, thinking this was what she had wanted; it was compelling, an inherited bond from her great-grandmama Cosima, that was tugging gently at her soul.

She navigated to the easyJet site and booked her flights.

Twenty

Allegra struggled to place her carry-on bag in the overhead locker. The diary felt as if it weighed a ton. And how much would they achieve with the translation anyway, with only two full days together?

Hugo hadn't attempted to contact her since his last visit, and she had decided to do all in her power to free her mind of him completely over the weekend. She dozed off during the flight and only woke when she heard the pilot announce their preparation for landing.

Allegra's pulse quickened as she spotted Massimo across the crowd in the arrivals hall. He looked so attractive, dressed in a smart blazer and faded jeans.

'I am so happy you're here.' He hugged her then took her wheelie bag and guided her out to the car park.

Allegra's mood brightened further as they drove towards Reggello. Massimo outlined his plans for the weekend. They included dinner that evening at their small hotel, a visit to talk to the old Mancini woman in Donnini the following day, then *Castello di Sammezzano* on Sunday.

Allegra was silent.

'What is it, *Tesoro*? Have I missed something?' Massimo glanced from the wheel.

'No, but I need to tell you... I so appreciate your help, of course, but I also need to feel independent. Like I am contributing my share of the hotel cost and meals. Especially after this split from my ex-husband.'

'But you must understand, Allegra, I am an Italian man. The hotel is not expensive, I got a good deal, and it is not a lot of money.' While his eyes stayed firmly on the road, his tone was quite clear.

'I understand an Italian man's pride, Massimo. I remember my grandpapa. But I have just left a marriage with a very controlling man, so maybe we can compromise on this?'

He didn't get a chance to reply as they had arrived outside a delightful large villa with a sign *Villa al Vento*. A slight woman with wild, blonde hair, and dressed in black, appeared to greet them. She waved a welcome and her mouth arched into an obliging smile.

Allegra stepped out of the car and gasped as two large wolfhounds bounded up beside her.

'*Non ti preoccupare, loro hanno i cuori dei micini,*' their hostess called out. Massimo quickly translated, 'Don't worry, they have the hearts of pussycats,' as the hounds gave Allegra a good sniff.

The owner, *Signora* Barbara Dell'Aquilia, had been recently widowed and was now the sole owner of the small ten-bedroom hotel. Once she had fired rapid questions at Massimo and informed them about dinner, Allegra was relieved to be shown to their room.

They had been assigned the hotel's largest suite, which was attractively decorated in several shades of blue. But as beautiful as it was, Allegra could not forget the unfinished conversation. She was quiet as she unpacked her small bag.

Massimo removed his jacket. 'So, tell me what your compromise might mean. I can't bear for you to be upset. If you talk to me, Allegra, perhaps I can discover a way to swallow some of my Italian pride?' His humour broke through her armoured heart; she finally relented, went over and kissed his cheek.

'I'm sorry I snapped. If I'm being logical about it, you have only been practical in organising everything for me. How about I buy us lunch tomorrow, and then when you come to London to visit, it's all on me?'

'Deal!' He took her in his arms, returned her kiss, then pushed her onto the bed, running his fingers through her hair.

As he gently rubbed her back, Allegra almost purred. It felt as though Massimo offered more – both acceptance and balance. But as he unbuttoned her shirt, all her thoughts reverted to carnal lust.

Signora Barbara continued her energetic hospitality throughout the meal. For Allegra, it bordered on intense, but Massimo discreetly patted her hand and quietly explained that after ten years of marriage, their hostess was just coming to terms with her loneliness as a widow. She was an old family friend, and it was important to have Massimo and his English girlfriend to stay.

Once back in their suite, Massimo picked up the heavy diary from the top of Allegra's case and indicated for her to sit next to him on the bed. He commenced reading from where they had left off.

During the two hours he read to her, they discovered Grandpapa Luigi's papa, who was called Alessandro, was forty years old when Luigi was born. He had worked at *Castello di Sammezzano* since he left school, as did his papa before him. Alessandro was the Marchese Ferdinando's favourite tile maker and, according to his adoring wife, he was also the Marchese's right-hand man.

My husband is a special man, a man who knows how to keep a secret.

'What do you think she means?' Allegra asked.

'We'll see. She finishes there and doesn't make another entry until a month later. *Tesoro*, it's 1:00 a.m. Please, we must go to sleep, my voice is worn out. I promise we will read some more tomorrow.' He closed the diary and they drifted to sleep in each other's arms.

After a few hours of sleep, Massimo rose and opened the heavy brocade curtains to reveal the day. The dawn proclaimed a magnificent morning of Tuscan colour.

They shared a simple breakfast of coffee and a jam-filled croissant on the balcony of their suite, which overlooked the small but perfect pool and shady boughs. Then Massimo gave Allegra some privacy to finish preparing herself for the day and went off to find *Signora* Barbara.

As she brushed her hair, Allegra pondered on what they had read from the diary. It occurred to her that great-grandmama Cosima was extremely literate – even educated – for a woman of that time and married to a humble tiler.

She found Massimo chatting to their hostess with two massive hounds sprawled at their feet in the charming garden, which appeared even more beautiful for its lack of upkeep.

'Barbara said to tell you she apologises for the state of the garden. It was her late husband's domain and she hasn't been able to bring herself to employ a gardener.' He smiled compliantly at both women.

Allegra patted the hounds and made appreciative noises about the garden, but inside was itching to move on to their visit to Donnini. It was just a ten-minute drive away, and Massimo furnished her with a running commentary on almost every house that they passed. Allegra merged his comments with thoughts of her grandpapa and her great-grandparents, trying to imagine what it would have been like to make this journey by carriage, decades, even centuries ago.

Twenty-One

Massimo slowed down the car as they approached Donnini and parked in an appropriate spot close to the café. The small village was a hive of activity, Saturday morning being a cherished social day rather than a work day. A few elderly men stood inside the bar of the café, sipping espresso. The men seated around the two outside tables were drinking something orange alongside their espressos.

'They are having an *Aperol*. It's a digestive, so they say, but if I drank one at 10:00 a.m. I would probably be unable to drive a police vehicle!' Massimo said as he acknowledged the old men.

Further along the street, Allegra recognised the shop with the plastic fly-strips from her bus trip. Two grey-haired old ladies dressed in black were well positioned on plastic white chairs outside. Allegra felt like a curiosity beside Massimo. Everyone knew him, and they seemed to acknowledge him with distinct regard.

He guided her off the main street and up what was more or less an alleyway. The aged *Signora* Mancini was waiting for them, opening the door before they had even knocked.

Allegra immediately sensed the woman's aggression. Her bitterness was embedded in her face, as if it had taken up residence there many years ago. Massimo spoke to her in a tone Allegra hadn't encountered before, hushed and conciliatory; she figured it must've been the one he saved for angry old women.

The woman begrudgingly ushered them into her small sitting room. The sofa and armchairs were covered in protective plastic that she made no attempt to remove. Allegra sat uncomfortably on a slippery chair and studied *Signora* Mancini's face for any sign of family likeness.

Massimo posed a few questions, to which she fired out an assault of answers, whilst madly flinging her hands in the air. She took a breath, screwed up her mouth and pointed to Allegra, and then exploded with another torrent of words. Massimo stayed calm with a distant, fixed smile and listened intently. When the woman paused for breath, he subtly murmured to Allegra that he would translate everything once they had gone.

He continued his gentle probing and the old woman responded again with rapid, aggressive answers. *Signora* Mancini completely blanked Allegra. When they had both thanked her in Italian and said goodbye, she said nothing, simply raised her hand and shut the door behind them.

'Don't ask me anything till we are back in the car. There are eyes and ears everywhere in this small place,' Massimo said as he pitched a fairly quick pace back to the car.

'Well, tell me everything! She was clearly pretty furious,' Allegra said once they were seated in the car.

'First, I'd like to say if you are actually blood related to that witch I hope your moustache doesn't start growing any time soon!'

Allegra laughed. 'Come on be serious, what did we Mancinis ever do to light her fire?'

'I'm not sure it's what you want to hear, and, given her twisted state of mind, I wouldn't be sure it's all true.'

'Massimo, stop being so Italian and eeking this out for drama. Tell me!' Allegra slapped her hands on her knees.

'I asked if she was related to Luigi Mancini. The witch Mancini informed me she is widowed from a man who I gather was your grandpapa's second cousin. It looks like no blood relation, *grazie a Dio*!' He chuckled at his own joke.

Allegra shoved his shoulder to keep him talking.

'According to the witch, your great-grandmama Cosima was born illegitimately. She used a less delicate word than that. Mancini legend says that Cosima was known to give bad luck and she snared Alessandro Mancini, which then sullied a good family's reputation.'

Allegra stared intently at Massimo. 'Are you saying after all these years that this "bad luck" is still remembered?'

'There's a reason for it – Italian pride. Let me tell you what she said, in my own words. As we know, when Luigi was three years old, his papa, Alessandro, disappeared. We also know that prior to his disappearance, the Marchese had died and his daughter had inherited the *Castello di Sammezzano*. Alessandro had been given the position of guardian of the *castello*, a great honour. However, after his disappearance, it came to light that there were several precious art works that couldn't be found. The rumour was that not only was Alessandro married to a bastard, but he was also a thief and a deserter. And you must be tainted by all this, given your family association!' Massimo smiled then leant over and kissed Allegra.

'What a load of old tosh,' she said. 'But the mystery deepens… In addition to my great-grandpapa's disappearance,

I may now have to find out about his unlucky, illegitimate wife.'

They drove up the road for a few kilometres, and Massimo pulled into a small restaurant where they enjoyed an antipasto platter full of delicious cheese and salted ham. After a quick espresso, the next stop was Leccio.

'You are very brave to take me to meet your mamma,' Allegra said as Massimo negotiated the car around the winding roads.

'She would have heard I am in the area by now, and that I'm with an Englishwoman, so my life wouldn't be worth living if I didn't call in.'

'I do appreciate that my status as an almost-divorced Englishwoman with children, is not ideal for an Italian mamma's precious son. I'm a bit nervous...' Allegra grimaced.

Massimo reached over and patted Allegra's knee. 'What's the worst a seventy-year-old can do to us?' He laughed. 'Mamma's not at all like the Mancini witch. She's intelligent enough to know that in our forties we all have baggage. Besides, I'm divorced as well, and she knows I've as much baggage as anyone else.'

The Rossi house had been in the family for four generations. It was located off the main road at the end of a long pebble driveway lined with immaculately groomed cypress trees. The driveway ended at the front door in a circle with a well-worn water feature in the middle. The house was two stories high, built with light-coloured stone and pale lemon shutters in typical Tuscan style.

Massimo opened the front door and called out. Allegra followed nervously. She had never imagined she would be experiencing this type of teen angst at forty-two.

His mamma was nowhere to be seen. At the end of the hallway they entered the kitchen. Huge iron pans were suspended from an iron rail that hung from the ceiling alongside bunches of dried tarragon, sprigs of thyme and wild rosemary, which enveloped the room with an enticing fragrance. There were two large baskets of fresh onions and bright red peppers sitting on the island beneath them. As they moved outside, Allegra could see the wonderful garden it had obviously all come from, with lettuces all in neat lines, a row of corn, and rich red tomatoes coiled around stakes. Massimo called again as they approached a fowl house. They could hear a clucking noise inside, and Allegra distinctly heard a rude Italian word that she had, on occasion, heard her grandpapa use.

'Mamma, watch your language! I have brought a guest with me.'

A plump woman with salt-and-pepper hair swept back into a bun appeared at the door of the fowl house, carrying a basket of feather-strewn eggs. She beamed at her son and kissed him warmly on both cheeks, then swiftly turned her attention to Allegra.

'Chi abbiamo qui?'

Allegra didn't need a translation. She forced a smile as Massimo quickly explained to his *mamma*. The old woman put her basket down, wiped her hands on her apron, and then extended one hand to Allegra. Her handshake felt warm and sincere and Allegra breathed a little easier as they followed her back into the kitchen.

Signora Rossi spoke a smattering of English, which was about as much Italian as Allegra spoke. They muddled along, both wishing to please Massimo with their efforts. He translated where required, though Allegra suspected some editing along the way. Naturally, she wanted them to stay for dinner, and Massimo had his work cut out extracting them without offending her.

'Your *mamma* is delightful! It wasn't nearly as bad as I thought it would be,' Allegra said as they drove back to the hotel.

'I have to agree with you. And she seemed genuinely happy to meet you. We'll see what she has to say after she has dwelt on it for a few days!'

They had an early evening meal of creamy mushroom risotto with grated truffle at the hotel, and settled down to continue reading the diary.

During the next two hours of solid reading, they learnt how the craftsmen who helped renovate the castle had lived on the grounds when the Marchese was alive. Alessandro's father worked there as a tiler till he died, and Alessandro also lived there until he married. The Marchese had given the marriage with Cosima his blessing, despite her illegitimacy. From what Massimo and Allegra could glean, he had also helped them procure their house. Besides that, Cosima wrote about daily life, her feelings for her precious Luigi and her passion for husband Alessandro.

Massimo's voice was waning. They were still in the first year of the diary. They decided to stop for the day and cuddled up in the large carved bed, the open curtains allowing the Tuscan stars to flicker overhead as they slept.

Twenty-Two

Allegra woke around 6:00 a.m. Massimo was sound asleep beside her. It was Sunday, the most exciting Sunday Allegra could imagine. Today she was going to revisit *Castello di Sammezzano*.

'Massimo, have you ever considered the theory of coincidence before? Are situations merely a coincidence, or are they preordained?'

'My! You are prophetic this morning!'

'Well, I've been dwelling on what actually motivated me to catch the bus to The Mall that day in Florence.'

Massimo reached out to her across the bed.

'I think it was the lure of a discount Missoni dress!' He smiled, and continued, 'This is your big day. But you must remember this is an unofficial visit. The castle is actually owned by a company that has only allowed the Preservation Society limited access, so we must show our respect and adhere to the time limits this *Signor* Bazia stipulates.' Massimo sounded very official. Then he pulled Allegra into his arms.

Barbara brought up their breakfast tray at 8:00 a.m. and by nine Allegra was pacing the room.

'Calm down, *Tesoro*! We will leave at ten as I agreed to meet him there at ten-thirty and it's only a short drive.' Massimo patted the chair next to him on the balcony. Allegra sat back down.

'You can't imagine how I feel. The rooms in that castle have been in my thoughts and my dreams since that drug experience. It is the strangest sensation for me. I just can't wait to get back there and see that it was real.'

They arrived at the entrance gate, and Massimo pulled in beside a small blue Fiat. A man with long legs appeared out of the car and, in deference to Allegra, greeted them in English. Allegra shook his hand and thanked him profusely.

'It is possible to drive up to the castle, but today we will walk. The road is unstable in places, and I mustn't do anything that will draw attention to this unauthorised visit. Massimo must believe you are very special, *Signora* Allegra, to convince me to do this,' *Signor* Bazia commented wryly as he opened the gate and they followed him into the park.

As they walked, their host revealed himself to be verbose in Italian and English. Any words he didn't know in English he simply replaced with Italian ones, and the more he spoke the more rapidly his words came out. Allegra struggled to follow some of his commentary, but she managed to capture most of the details. The amazing tall trees she assumed were firs were actually Californian Sequoias. In the one hundred and fifty years since they were planted, the trees had thrived, growing up to fifty metres tall and some as wide as 8.5 meters in diameter. *Signor* Bazia went on to say that the Marchese Ferdinando was a very keen botanist, and had designed most of the park of some four-hundred acres himself.

As they approached the turreted gatehouse, Allegra could see that no one lived there. The man she assumed was a caretaker must have been an interloper like herself, sheltering from the rain. He must have thought he was in trouble when she called out, which would explain why he ran away. She thought better of mentioning this part to *Signor* Bazia...

She laughed to herself as she fingered the rich green ivy that had made its home on the fence around the gatehouse. In its previous incarnation, it had grown and moved in front of her eyes.

'Why are you smiling, *Tesoro*?'

Allegra was so absorbed in her thoughts that she hadn't registered any of her companions' chatter for the last few minutes.

'Oh, I'm just remembering some of the crazy 'hallucinations' that day – you really wouldn't believe what this ivy is capable of.'

They talked as they walked, and finally approached the tree-lined track that led to the lawn in front of the castle. A heady mix of anticipation and trepidation hit Allegra. This was it. Her heritage. Somehow, it was all connected to the castle.

Signor Bazia signalled them to halt. He needed to deliver his speech and impress them with his knowledge before they entered. Massimo offered reverence towards the tall man, standing still with his hands clasped, while Allegra struggled to hide her impatience.

'I'm sure you are already aware that this castle was originally built in 1606, four hundred years ago. Then in the eighteenth century, the Marchese Ferdinando Panciatichi completely remodelled it in a controversial Moorish Arabian style. We know that during World War II, the Germans occupied it as a hospital, looted much from the gardens, and stole a statue of Venus from a special grotto at the rear of the building.' He paused and, to Allegra's relief, took a large key out of his pocket and unlocked the gate as he continued his commentary.

'The hotel that opened here briefly in the 1990s has left an ugly legacy on the ground floor. However, I understand that these floors are not in your interest.' They had arrived at the steps to the large front doors.

'Due to the limited time we have, I suggest we skip the ground floor and go directly up to the more colourful levels.'

Allegra grasped Massimo's hand as they walked in. The entrance hall was very plain, with a terracotta tile floor and pale lemon plaster walls. *Signor* Bazia led them over to a staircase directly to their left and, as there was no electricity, he took a small, powerful torch from his pocket to light the way.

Allegra was still holding Massimo's hand when they came to the first floor. The room had been cleverly designed to harness the sunlight; it streamed in through the stained-glass windows making the room look like a glinting watery rainbow. Allegra's dream was real. Her whole body trembled – it was as if God had opened the door and given her a peek at what lay in wait in Heaven.

She dropped Massimo's hand and stood perfectly still. Her eyes rose upwards to the vaulted ceiling and she then gradually moved them downwards. She absorbed every detail, capturing the strong hues of every possible blue in the colour spectrum. The tiles, along with the niches and corners, were all perfectly blended to create this Arabian-influenced fantasy.

Signor Bazia cleared his throat. Massimo, who hadn't uttered a word, gently tapped her hand.

'*Signora,* if I may commence. I would like to tell you that despite the rumours of 365 rooms in this castle, one for every day of the year, there are in fact a lot less. We only have one hour, so we will get through as many as we can.' He walked through the ornate archway into the next room, indicating that they follow him.

'Allegra, I can now completely understand your obsession with this place. It's beyond imagination,' Massimo said as he gave her a hug.

'This is called *Sala degli Amanti* – the Room of Lovers,' called the Signor from the next room, and they rushed to follow him. 'The Marchese gave all the rooms a name. I can only tell you the more popular ones.'

'I would call this the Missoni Room. The zigzag pattern of the tiles looks just like a fabric the design family Missoni might create.'

'Perhaps they visited here once?' Massimo commented.

The Latin *Non Plus Ultra*, 'Nothing further beyond' was written above the door.

'I know where the Marchese took this from – it's Greek mythology. A warning that marked the edge of the flat world for explorers. I wonder why the Marchese wrote this?' Allegra directed her question at no one in particular.

'We have speculated that this was a statement the Marchese, as an architect, made to communicate to his visitors that the rooms they would see hereafter would be "beyond this world",' *Signor* Bazia quickly responded.

Massimo and Allegra smiled at his excellently phrased English expressions.

The next room was the Peacock Room. Allegra gasped when she saw it again.

'I can feel my grandpapa here. All those years, he kept at least one peacock feather somewhere about the house. It must have all stemmed from this magical room in some way.' Ignoring *Signor* Bazia, Allegra lay down on the cold tiled floor and gazed up.

It was exactly how she remembered; the drugs had done nothing to enhance the richness and beauty of the room. The elaborate ceiling tiles celebrating the shimmering colours of the male peacock, flourished in fan-like patterns and then ran down the walls in perfectly matching rows. It was like looking through a kaleidoscope. The lower parts of the walls and the floor repeated like feather upon feather, reminiscent of a gilded Indian palace.

Allegra's companions had the sense to stand aside quietly whilst she marvelled at the splendour and magic of the room. Even the garrulous *Signor* Bazia seemed aware that an epiphany of some sort was taking place. Once she had slowly risen to her feet again, both men waited for her to speak.

'I feel like I've learnt so much from a dream one man had one hundred and fifty years ago. He spent most of his life making it a reality, and now his legacy has been abandoned up here on this hill because people would rather look at paintings in a gallery. Surely his dream is just as important?' Allegra paused, as tears welled in her eyes.

'And to think that my great-grandpapa was a part of its creation. His hands might have laid these very tiles.'

Massimo placed his arm gently around her, as she struggled to control her tears.

Signor Bazia was fascinated. '*Signora* Allegra, tell me, who was your great-grandpapa?'

'His name was Alessandro Mancini.'

'Ah, yes. We have notes on your great-grandpapa. From what we understand, he was the Marchese's right-hand man and after the Marchese died, he was the official caretaker of the castle. Some rumours indicated he had stolen precious Florentine paintings after the Marchese died. But we assume the Marchese hid them somewhere. When Alessandro disappeared, the new owner, the Marchese's daughter, was very concerned. She gave a statement to a newspaper at the time saying she did not believe he had stolen anything; she just hoped he would be found. The Marchese may have sold the artworks, or they could still be hidden somewhere... He was a very secretive man.'

'Well, that gives me some consolation, I suppose. Until we have read Cosima's entire diary, we won't have any more clues.'

'*Scusami*, my excuse for coming here today was to check on a leak, so I will go down to the basement now. Will you both be all right here?' *Signor* Bazia asked.

'Absolutely!' Allegra almost kissed him.

'We can really only risk about half an hour more, so look where you must,' he said as he headed off.

'Can you believe this, Massimo? We are alone!'

The next room was what Allegra had called the purity room on her previous visit. The room consisted of different shapes that were all diverse shades of white. Above the mezzanine floor, the vaulted ceiling heightened a glow of infinity that seemed to inhabit the space.

They arrived at the small area that housed the chapel with the altar. Massimo wandered off, intrigued, into the next room. Allegra stood reverently, wondering if her grandpapa had been to Mass there. Enjoying the spiritual glow from the crucifix, she knelt and offered a silent prayer. She heard someone behind her and assumed Massimo had returned. But it wasn't him, and in the far corner of the room she saw the old man again. He wasn't as old as Allegra had first thought, it was just that his face stubble was grey and he looked as though he'd been wearing his clothes for a while.

'*Buongiorno, Signore,*' she said quietly. He said nothing. Then she heard steps on the tiled floor heading her way. She looked across to Massimo and as she did, the old man ducked out the door.

'Blast!' she said.

'Why? What happened?' Massimo asked as he came up beside her.

'I just saw the old man again. The one I thought was the gatekeeper. He must play cat-and-mouse with the Preservation Society people and be squatting up here,' Allegra said.

'I didn't see anyone.'

'Really? He was right there in that corner. He's actually not that old, just a bit scruffy. But I don't want him to be homeless on my account. Best we don't say anything to *Signor* Bazia.'

Twenty-Three

O nce they had left the castle and returned down the track to their cars, Allegra graciously attempted to express her thanks to *Signor* Bazia in Italian. He smiled and offered her his business card.

'I will have a closer look at anything directly related to your great-grandpapa and let you know,' he said before he shook their hands and drove off.

Later that afternoon, they sat side by side on a small sofa in the hotel sitting room, as Massimo continued to read from the diary. Allegra observed that since he had personally experienced the magic of the castle, he seemed more enthusiastic about the diary. Her great-grandmama's articulate script and the rhythm of Massimo's throaty reading transported her back in time.

'It is a very sad day today. Our dearest Marchese, who has suffered from paralysis for the past eight difficult years, has finally passed away. My Alessandro is beside himself with grief. Because the Marchese couldn't move about, Alessandro had been his eyes, ears, and legs all those years. Their mutual trust was a pleasure to witness. It was always with a taint of despair,

though, as his son Bandino, who has chosen such a debauched lifestyle, should have been at his side. The funeral is next week, and hopefully Bandino show some respect and attend. The Marchese's daughter, Marianna, has been in long talks with my Alessandro, as she values his opinion on some of the funeral details. The Marchese's wife died many years ago, but theirs was never a happy marriage.'

They had been reading for two solid hours. Allegra would have pushed for a bit more, but she thought better of it and offered to get them a drink.

'It must have been sad for the Marchese not to have his son at his side when he was so ill. It's very unusual for an Italian man to disrespect his father, but then the Marchese obviously didn't have any time for his wife. Perhaps the son was angry,' Massimo commented as he sipped his Prosecco.

'Possibly. But what amazes me is how articulate my great-grandmama was in her writing... Or are you putting an educated spin on the translation? Trying to impress me?' Allegra smiled and raised her eyebrows at her lover.

'Not at all, *Tesoro*. I am honest in what I read, word for word. She was an incredibly well-written woman. We know she was adopted, so she was probably illegitimate but well-born, which may explain her apparent education,' Massimo replied.

'So, I could be descended from anyone!'

'Well, you could change your flight and stay longer, and we could find out? I'll promise to read to you every evening.' Massimo squeezed her hand.

'I'm sorry. My first job is to be a mother, which means I need to be home tomorrow. There's a lot happening in my children's lives just now.'

Allegra was relieved to be interrupted by *Signora* Barbara who called them through to the dining room for dinner.

The following morning at the airport, Allegra sensed some discomfort in Massimo. He seemed to be struggling for words as they arrived at the departure gate.

'*Tesoro*. Please, tell me as soon as you feel confident about revealing our relationship to the children. Only then will I come to London for a weekend to see you again.' He held her tight, kissed her and then waved until she had disappeared through the departure gate.

Allegra carried a heavier heart as she arrived back at her London home. While she was looking forward to seeing the children, it was decision time. She had to tell them about Massimo... Or not.

'Well, dear, how was it all?' Maria greeted her, all smiles and hankering after the romantic details.

'Great, thanks. Let me just see the children and then I'll tell you everything.' Allegra shot her mother a look.

Once they were all around the table enjoying the soup Maria had prepared, and the children had updated her on their studies, Kirsty asked the leading question.

'So, how was Uncle Massimo, Mum?'

Allegra was prepared. 'Actually, he was very helpful. He accompanied me up to the castle and assisted with translation and volunteered a couple of hours reading great-grandmama's diary.'

She went on to tell them about the family involvement with Castle Sammezzano, and their newfound relative, the ugly old *Signora* Mancini.

After the children had gone up to their rooms, Maria poured them both a brandy.

'OK, now before I go home, I want the adult version please, Allegra.' Maria widened her eyes and flicked her hair back.

'Oh, Mum... I think I might be falling in love! He is so patient with me and now we have experienced the castle together, we are growing closer. I really want to spend time with him, but I just can't, I mean, what about the children?'

'My darling! I don't recall seeing such joy in your eyes since the day Harry was born, and I haven't witnessed such feisty curiosity and independence since you agreed to marry Hugo. Maybe it's time to give it a chance.' Maria leant over and affectionately caressed her daughter's hair.

'But... I have to warn you, Hugo has been in Harry's ear. Kirsty won't have a bar of it, but Hugo has been very manipulative with Harry,' Maria added as she put her glass on the bench and scooped up her bag and jacket.

'Thanks for the heads-up, Mum. I'd better prepare myself.'

Twenty-Four

Allegra was intrigued that as a sixteen-year-old male, Harry had really thought through his strategy and approach. He had risen a good thirty minutes earlier than usual to ensure he was at the breakfast table before Kirsty arrived.

'Mum…' Harry paused. Allegra looked up and raised her eyebrows. 'Dad and I were chatting about the family and we both thought it might be nice if the four of us got together for a meal, maybe once a month. What do you think?' He delivered his question with a smile reminiscent of Hugo in full flow.

'I'm sure we can manage that. Did you have a specific day and place in mind?' Allegra smiled back.

'Well, we used to always do a Sunday roast, so what do you think about that?'

'Yes, but that assumes I would be doing all the work, which I think is unbalanced somehow. So, if this is what you and your father would like, perhaps you could suggest he takes us all to a wonderful restaurant.' Allegra looked directly at her son.

'I guess so, but I think Dad thought it might be, you know, more personal here in our home.' As Harry spoke, Kirsty walked into the kitchen.

'What's this about Dad getting personal in our home?' Kirsty directed her question to her brother.

'You don't have to stir, Kirsty. Dad and I just thought it would be a good thing for us all to get together once a month.'

'Yeah, well, I may be busy that night!' She slapped her yogurt down on the table.

Harry abruptly stood up. 'He's our father, and I think we should forgive him and give him another chance!'

Allegra could see the distress on her son's face.

'Harry, you don't have to forgive your father for anything. He didn't hurt you. Having an affair was a slight on me as his wife, not on you as his children. And I have practically forgiven him,' Allegra added.

'So, does that mean you'll have him back?' Harry sat back down.

Kirsty went to say something and Allegra swiftly signalled for her to stop.

'No. Just because I have forgiven him doesn't mean I will go back to being his wife. After all the hurt, I've now moved on. I still love you both the same as I always have, but I don't feel the same way about your father anymore.'

As Allegra leant over to touch Harry's hand he quickly stood up, threw his spoon on the floor, and walked out.

'Well, that went down well, Mum!' Kirsty licked her yogurt spoon.

'I know, it wasn't perfect,' Allegra sighed and sat down again at the table. 'I'll be honest with you, Kirsty. I don't really know how to handle the situation.' Allegra twisted a strand of her hair.

'Yeah, it sucks. Dad has an affair, rubbishes you, and then he gets dumped so he wants you back. Pure chauvinism!'

'When did you get so wise! Well, anyway, you are eighteen, and you'll be leaving home soon. This is more of a battle for Harry. I'll think it through for a bit and see what I can come up with.' Allegra attempted to give her daughter a reassuring smile.

'Yeah, right, Mum. Well, I don't forgive him for the shit I've been through at college, like everyone knowing about slut-face Brooklyn. Please, don't tell me you would let him push you back into being his personal corporate wife.' She swigged down her tea, picked up her satchel, begrudgingly kissed her mother's cheek, and left.

Not long after, Harry stormed out the front door without saying goodbye. Allegra sent him a text: *I love you. x.* Just as she was hit by a massive guilt trip, the phone interrupted her thoughts.

'Hi, I want to hear all the details, please! I've got a property to visit in Fulham at 1:30 p.m., so I'll be over for lunch at midday,' Julia said before hanging up.

She quickly cleared her backlog of e-mails then cobbled together a salad, managed to find the herbal tea Julia favoured, and had the kettle on the boil as her friend arrived.

She updated Julia on the visit to the castle, layering on the descriptive prose about the colours and construction of the Peacock Room.

'Yes, yes, that's all amazing, but what's going on with you and Massimo? Is it going to be a long-term, long-distance kind of thing?' Julia cut to the chase.

'When I'm with him, it's like he takes up all my air. I feel totally in love. And totally in lust too... Then I arrive back in the UK, walk into my home, and discover my only son and my ex have conspired to get us back together. I have no idea what to do. And whatever I do will make me feel guilty anyway.'

'Tricky, I guess, but I don't have children… Let me ask you this: if you hadn't met Massimo and Hugo had wanted you back, would you have hesitated?' Julia took a bite of her salad.

'The thing is, I *did* meet Massimo, and I did go through a metamorphosis of sorts. I've had that discussion with myself, and I can see Hugo was controlling. He didn't want me to be me. Once the children have left home, if I do things his way, I know I will feel so lonely.' Allegra sighed.

'Have you heard any more about your interview at the museum?' Julia asked.

'No, not yet. But if I do decide to pursue my relationship with Massimo, and the investigation into my great-grandpapa's disappearance, I'm not sure I'll have time for a job.'

Julia frowned. 'So, in fact, you *have* given this a lot of consideration. I think you have your answer.'

Allegra nodded. 'Yes, probably. It's just exactly how to deliver it and keep all the important parties happy. That's what I have to figure out.'

Once Julia had left, Allegra was tidying the house when the landline rung. There was no caller ID, so she was surprised when Hugo's most charming voice sounded down the line.

'So, how was your research in Italy?'

'Great, thanks.'

'Did Harry have a chat with you?'

'Oh, for God's sake, Hugo, do stop playing games!'

'What do you mean? I just want our children to be happy.' Hugo struggled not to raise his voice.

'No, you're not. You are being your usual manipulative self and using our son's vulnerability as leverage,' Allegra said through gritted teeth.

'This doesn't sound like the Allegra I know. You usually respect my opinion of what's best for our children.'

'Bloody hell, look at yourself! You had an affair with a much younger woman, left your family to set up home with her, told me you were in love with her, and now that she's dumped you, you expect me to fall in line with your wishes. I don't respect you using Harry to get to me. If you have something to say, please say it directly to me. I'm hanging up now.' Allegra banged the phone down.

It was a rather tense supper with Harry and Kirsty not speaking to each other, in addition to Harry ignoring Allegra. She took her laptop up to her bedroom and noticed an e-mail had arrived from *Signor* Bazia.

Dear Signora Allegra,

After your visit you had me intrigued, as all matters of history with Castello di Sammezzano are my passion. I spent some time reading notes in our archives about matters that may relate to the disappearance of your great-grandpapa Alessandro Mancini. Various pieces of evidence suggest that before the Marchese died, he and Alessandro were involved in some secret affair that included the Marchese hiding valuable paintings from his son. His son, Bandino, was known to be a heavy drinker; he also had a gambling habit and apparently ran around with unsavoury women. The Marchese had disinherited him in favour of his daughter, but he wasn't sure if it would stand up in an Italian court after his death. So if we can establish what exactly was Alessandro's secret plan, we may get closer to the truth of his disappearance. Your great-grandmama's diary that you mentioned may hold the clue. Meanwhile, if you are agreeable, I will look closer into the history of the Marchese's daughter, Marianna, on your behalf, to see if that will reveal anything.

Mario Bazia

Allegra felt her pulse race. All manner of scenarios whizzed through her brain. Was Alessandro murdered? Was Bandino trying to get him out of the way? She needed to finish the translation as soon as possible, with or without Massimo.

Twenty-Five

'Harry! Enough of this silent treatment. We all have to live under the same roof. Just so you know, I have spoken with your father and as you requested we will sort out a monthly get-together.'

She handed him a glass of orange juice. As he took the glass, he offered her a smidgeon of a smile. She was relieved when he pecked her cheek on his way out.

Allegra's aim for the day was to find a quicker way of translating the diary so she could study it for clues. Her mother said she wasn't confident that any of her friends with Italian connections were fluent enough to be of any real help with the translation. She suggested what had already passed through Allegra's mind – that she may have to engage a professional translator. Allegra had started to work her way online through availability and pricing when she heard the mail plop through the door.

Amongst the junk mail, she noticed a proper letter in a smart cream linen envelope with an official-looking rubber stamp mark on it. As she walked up the hallway and studied it closer, she could see it was from the Victoria and Albert

Museum. She poured herself a coffee, then sat down and paid the smart letter the respect of slicing it open with a somewhat redundant antique silver letter opener. Her heart pounded in her chest.

Dear Mrs O'Brien,

I am writing to confirm that you have been successful in your application for the full-time, permanent position at the Victoria and Albert Museum as trainee assistant curator to Mr Desmond Tipple, in the department covering European art and architecture from the twelfth to the nineteenth century.

The salary we are offering is £35,000 PA and in addition to public holidays in the first year you are entitled to two weeks paid holiday. Your hours of work will be 9:00 a.m. to 5:00 p.m., Monday to Friday. The commencement date will be May 1st. We look forward to your acceptance which may be by way of e-mail directly to Mr Tipple, whose address is Dtipple@V&A.org.

Yours faithfully,
Mrs Jillayne Ennor

Allegra called her mother immediately, bursting with the news. 'Mum, it's me again. Guess what? I've been offered a job!'

'That's amazing, darling! I always had faith that you would find something. You are too talented not to.'

'Well, to be honest, I'm in a bit of a dilemma about whether to accept... But it certainly has boosted my confidence to think I'm actually employable!' Allegra went on to give her mother the details of the position.

'Just make the decision that's best for you and only you, Allegra. The children will be following their own passions soon. This is your time now. And if I might just add, please consider the money Grandpapa left you – it might make the decision a little easier,' Maria said, before she hung up the call.

Both children were home for dinner and Allegra was looking forward to telling them her news. They had started their meal and listened intently as she described the job. Kirsty wanted to know the salary and Harry was concerned that she wouldn't be home in time to cook dinner in the evenings.

'You are such a bloke, Harry! Your first concern is your stomach,' Allegra said. Kirsty laughed so hard she spat out some potato, which set them all off. Then the doorbell rang.

'Who could that be?' Allegra asked. Both children shrugged as she walked to the front door.

'Hi, I was passing so thought I'd just call in,' Hugo said as he walked past Allegra, carrying a bottle of wine and two Mars bars.

'You should have called,' Allegra said as she quickly followed him down the hall.

'I did. Before you hung up on me you clearly said I should speak to you direct. So here I am. Hi, you two. Brought your favourite chocolates.' Hugo placed the Mars bars down on the table.

'Ah, Dad! You're about two years out of touch!' Kirsty said, and shoved the chocolate bar towards her brother.

'Thanks, Dad, and Kirsty!' Harry grabbed both bars and proceeded to unwrap one at once.

Hugo opened the cupboard and took out two wine glasses.

Allegra bristled but held her tongue.

'So, Dad, what are you doing here? If this is the monthly "family" dinner, you're out of luck as we've just finished,' Kirsty said as she scraped her plate and placed it in the dishwasher. 'And I've got an essay to write,' she called as she left the kitchen.

Allegra was surprised when Hugo didn't shout about her manners. He took a large gulp of his wine and turned his attention to Harry. 'So, how is the new game going?'

Harry gave his father a comprehensive account of the expensive new computer game he had given him, most of which Allegra couldn't follow.

'Oh, by the way, Dad, Mum has been offered a really cool job at the museum,' Harry beamed.

Hugo looked at Allegra.

'Really?' he said.

'Yeah, good pay and everything. Look, guys, I've got an assignment, so I'd better go up and finish it,' Harry said as he left the room.

'You haven't touched your wine, Allegra.' Hugo said quietly and moved the glass closer to her on the table.

'I don't fancy any, thanks. Besides, why are you here, Hugo?' She pushed the glass away.

'Never mind that, tell me about your job. This could be just the thing to make you feel better.'

Allegra counted to ten under her breath; she so wanted to throw the glass of wine over his face.

'I do have a job offer I am considering, along with other options, none of which affect your life. I will e-mail you with suitable dates for our monthly family meal. You have seen your children now, so I would ask you to leave please.' She started to clear the table and load the dishwasher.

'Come on, Allegra! Let's talk this through. That probably came out the wrong way... I don't doubt your ability in your special field, and the job sounds great. I guess the kids are grown up enough now not to need you around as much, and if I come back, I am perfectly happy for you to have a job.' He knocked back the rest of his glass of wine.

Allegra grappled to keep her voice under control.

'You just don't get it. For a supposedly intelligent man who was married to me for twenty years, it's amazing that you just don't really know me at all. Leave before I do something I'll regret.'

'But wha...what about my wine?'

Allegra grabbed the discarded cork and jammed it in the wine bottle. She shoved it towards Hugo, then turned the kitchen light off and stood in the hall.

'Hugo, leave!'

She didn't move again until she heard the door snap shut in the darkness.

Twenty-Six

When Allegra woke the next morning and turned her mobile phone on, there were two texts from Massimo. She had to reply, but she still hadn't fathomed the right thing to do. She knew what she wanted... But she knew she was accountable for her children's needs as well.

It would have to wait until the children had left for the day. But he beat her to it. At 9:00 a.m., she answered the landline and it was him.

'So, *Tesoro*, what is wrong? You have not answered my last e-mail and you have ignored my texts.'

'I'm sorry, my phone was turned off last evening.'

'Ah, I know you well enough now to know you are not being entirely honest, Allegra. Just share with me, please!'

Allegra poured her heart out. First, she told him about the job. Massimo congratulated her and didn't seem to think it would pose a problem – after all there were long weekends and holidays. Then, with some editing, she told him about Hugo.

'So, are you telling me that you are considering taking him back?' She could hear the hurt in his voice.

'I just don't know. I don't love him anymore, but Harry needs us both and a part of me believes I am responsible for my son's happiness.' There was a prolonged silence before Massimo responded.

'Well, what can I say or do? I want to make you happy. I think I will finish this call now and leave the ball in your court, Allegra. You know where I am. Goodbye.' Then he hung up.

Allegra felt as if the breath had been ripped from her lungs. She hadn't expected such an abrupt answer.

The phone rang again. She quickly picked it up. 'Massimo?'

'No, sorry to disappoint you, it's just me,' Julia said. 'I got your message about the job and wanted to congratulate you.'

'Oh, Julia. Thanks,' Allegra replied.

'What's wrong? You sound a bit down.'

'Sorry, I'm a bit upset, yes... I think things might be shaky with Massimo.'

'Oh dear. I've got a client meeting now, but how about you meet me at that café near my office at midday and we can talk? Would that help?' Julia asked.

'Like you wouldn't believe,' Allegra replied, letting out the breath she didn't even realise she was holding.

Allegra was still feeling stunned about Massimo when she caught sight of Julia at a table in the far corner of the café.

She gave her friend the full, unabridged version of their conversation. Not that it lasted terribly long. Julia listened intently while managing a few forkfuls of her salad.

'If you are asking my opinion, what else would you expect a red-blooded Italian man to say? Did you really think he would just sit back and take it? It's not just because I have never really liked Hugo that I'm going to say this, Allegra. It's what I believe is right.' She took a sip of her water then continued. 'Your first responsibility is to yourself. Do you really think living with Hugo when you no longer love him will be at all enjoyable for any of you, including Harry? He will be off to university in a couple of years anyway. It's so obvious to me how much you are enjoying learning about your family's history and the Castle Sammezzano. No – don't interrupt – I cannot see Hugo allowing you both a full-time job and regular visits to Tuscany. You'll have to say goodbye to that part of your life if you take him back.'

Allegra nodded. 'I know, Julia. Thanks for your honesty. It pisses me off that I can't weigh this up so effectively. But the single thing I am absolutely sure of is that I want to find out what happened to my great-grandpapa.'

'When we were still at high school, I always thought it was a bit weird that your grandpapa did all the parenting. But he clearly adored you.' She smiled. 'Your great-grandmama's diary and all this assistance you are being offered is an excellent place to start. Follow the path that you are one hundred per cent sure of,' Julia counselled. Then in the next breath, she went on to tell Allegra that her affair with the chap she had gone off with in Florence was over.

It was a stunning London summer's day, so Allegra stopped in the park on her way home. It was the perfect place to contemplate. The fragrance of freshly-cut grass evoked memories of her childhood. There were very few people nearby, so she dropped down onto the grass and lay on her back to look up at the clouds.

She recalled the many times she had done just that alongside Grandpapa when she was little. He would hold her hand and they would gaze up to see different shapes within the white fluffy clouds: animals, funny people with odd noses, and always magical castles.

As Allegra momentarily closed her eyes she could almost smell Grandpapa's distinctive *Novella Melograno*. She could visualise him right beside her. As she opened her eyes and looked upwards, a rich, white fluffy mass of cloud appeared to morph into a castle turret and what resembled a line of the cypress trees that dotted the Tuscan landscape.

'Oh, Grandpapa, what should I do?' Allegra said out loud.

The words of his letter resonated. *Perhaps you can solve the mystery of my papa's disappearance.*

Yes.

Allegra suddenly felt the dampness of the grass on her bottom. She jumped up and rubbed the loose leaves from the back of her trousers. By the time she had crossed the road, unlocked her front door, and booted her laptop to life, she was confident of her decision.

Her first action was an articulate, considered e-mail to Mr Tipple at the museum. The second, an e-mail to Hugo.

Then, after counting the pages left to be read in the diary, she e-mailed two of the translator services she had identified and requested timings and quotes. And finally, she texted her mother and invited her to join them for dinner.

'Wow, Mum, roast beef on a weeknight. What are we celebrating?' Harry said as he cracked the crispy Yorkshire pudding on his plate.

'I have an announcement to make,' Allegra stated.

Three pairs of anxious eyes turned to give her their full attention.

'I have decided how I wish to live my life – well, for the next twelve months, anyway – and it may affect you three.'

'Neat! Are you getting back with Dad?' Harry smiled.

'Now, please just let me say all this without interrupting. First, I'm hoping that your gran will be able to assist.'

Maria raised her hands as if to agree, and allowed Allegra to proceed.

'I am not going to take the job at the museum. I'm going to follow my heart and Grandpapa's wishes and research where his papa disappeared – and hopefully find out why.' Allegra paused.

'Where does Gran fit in?' Kirsty asked.

'I imagine I will be away quite a bit in Tuscany, so I am hoping she will agree to make herself available to be here with you two.'

A scowl passed across Harry's face. 'So, what about Dad?'

'That's the next part. I'm so sorry, Harry, but I can't get back with your father just for your sake. I know how bad that must make you feel, but in a couple of years perhaps you'll understand a bit better. I hope you will.'

Allegra reached out to touch his hand but he snatched it away.

She continued. 'So, we will have to tighten our belts a bit, as Grandpapa's money will only go so far in addition to what your father gives us. But I have decided this is what's best.'

Maria smiled at her daughter and they all continued to eat in silence as the news sunk in. Harry let out a big sniff then wiped his wet eyes on his napkin. Once he had hoovered down his meal, he got up and abruptly left the room.

'Just leave him be, Allegra. Give him some time to digest it all.' Maria patted her daughter's arm.

'Yeah, he can't be too distressed, Mum. He still wolfed down all his roast beef,' Kirsty added.

'What about you, love? Do you have an opinion?' Allegra asked her daughter.

'For once, we actually agree on something. And as long as Gran doesn't try and tell me what to do…' She stopped and smiled, then said, 'God, maybe I am growing up after all!'

Maria grinned, and Allegra laughed loudly.

Harry appeared at the door, no sign of tears. 'I'm just here to have my pudding, but I'm not talking to any of you!'

Maria flicked her hair back and pressed her lips together. Allegra turned and suppressed a smile as she busied herself at the bench arranging the raspberries on the ice cream, while Kirsty openly sniggered. Harry kicked her under the table then tucked in to his dessert.

Later, when Maria was at the door ready to leave, she took Allegra by the arm. 'I'm happy you have invited me to be involved in looking after the family. I figure you will pre-book all your excursions, so providing you give me some notice I can stay over here while you're away. I won't ask about Massimo, since I figure you'll tell me about that when you're ready.'

Maria hugged her daughter tightly before heading home. 'Allegra, I'm very proud of you.'

Twenty-Seven

Allegra slept better than she had done in weeks. Once the children had left for the day, she started mapping out a plan of attack for her research. But it all hinged on how fast the diary could be translated.

At 10:00 a.m. she answered her first phone call of the day.

'Stuff your e-mail. You will regret this, Allegra, I promise you. And I'll get custody of our son and cut off all your money and make sure you suffer!' Hugo yelled in her ear.

After a few deep breaths, Allegra replied, 'Hugo, I respect you will do what you must. The children are old enough to choose where they live, and if you want to see them go without because you are angry with me, so be it. I have made my decision.' Then she couldn't help herself. 'I have to say you are really showing your true colours with all these threats. Such a shame.'

'Bitch!' was all she heard before the phone went dead.

Her laptop beeped with a reply from one of the translation services. Their quote seemed high, but they did say it could all be completed within a month.

Allegra's heart leapt when the landline rang again. 'Massimo?' she said.

'Hello, Mrs O'Brien, I hope you don't mind me calling you at home?' Allegra felt deflated as she recognised the distinct dulcet tones of Mr Tipple from the museum.

'No, Mr Tipple, I don't mind at all. Did you receive my e-mail?'

'Yes, I did, and that's why I'm calling. Look, I'm not great explaining things on the phone, and I'm not very good at meeting off the museum premises. Don't worry, I'm not going to try and bully you to change your mind. It's just I've been thinking about the *Castello di Sammezzano* you mentioned, and I think perhaps I may be able to assist...' He went quiet.

'Yes?' Allegra said.

'If you could manage it, perhaps you could visit me at the museum this afternoon?' he asked.

Intrigued, Allegra agreed to meet him at around 3:00 p.m at his office.

This time, as instructed, she entered around the back of the building at the staff entrance. She gave Mr Tipple's name to the uniformed man sitting in a booth inside the door and after a few words on the phone, he pointed her to the lift and said, 'Fourth floor.'

Mr Tipple greeted her timidly just outside the lift doors and she followed him to a small office with a large desk covered completely in folders and books. There was a silver tray set with a white china teapot, milk jug and two willow-patterned china cups next to a kettle on a shelf at the side of the room.

'I do hope you don't take sugar, as I don't have any,' Mr Tipple said as he made quite an exhibition of pouring the tea. Once he was seated back at his desk facing Allegra, he seemed a bit more confident.

'When you first mentioned the *Castello di Sammezzano* at your interview, I took the liberty of looking it up. Surprisingly, there is very little about it on Google and the other Internet search engines, so my curiosity got the better of me and I made a few inquiries in Florence. I have to say it was and still is quite a controversial renovation that your Marchese Ferdinando Panciatichi undertook back in the 1800s.'

'You pronounced the Marchese's name in perfect Italian,' Allegra observed.

'Thank you. Are you Italian, Mrs O'Brien?'

'My grandpapa was Italian, but sadly I didn't learn the language, which I deeply regret now. But please, Mr Tipple, do call me Allegra.' She smiled.

'Well now, I am fluent in both reading and writing the language. However, I'm not that confident speaking it,' he said, then paused. 'What I wanted to say to you was, after reading your explanation for not taking up our appointment, I can understand why you wish to pursue the mystery of what happened to your great-grandfather. If I was in your situation, I would do the same.' He took a delicate sip of his tea.

'I haven't yet discussed this with my employer, Mrs Ennor, who originally interviewed you. I thought I would run it past you first.'

'Run what past me?' Allegra willed him to go on, but he took another pause, and another sip of tea.

'I have a family friend who has a daughter. She is keen to do a one-year internship here with me, so I thought I could take her on for now, with the view to you reconsidering the position?'

'But why would you do that for me when you don't know me at all?' Allegra placed her cup on the desk with a clatter.

Without looking up he replied, 'In a way I'm envious of your mission, if I may call it that? I long to investigate things outside this office but sadly I am agoraphobic… It's all I can manage to get myself the few hundred metres from my flat in South Kensington to this office. So, to be honest, when I read your e-mail, I just thought I'd take a chance and see if there was anything I could do to assist and maybe…be involved in some small way.' He looked up and gave her an anxious glance.

'Mr Tipple, firstly let me say thank you for offering me the position. When I received the letter, it gave me such a confidence boost. Secondly, I would be delighted to involve you in my mission. I will graciously accept any help you are able to give. My challenge today is to decide on which Italian translation service to use, as I've never been in the position of needing to use one before.' Allegra tugged at a strand of her hair absentmindedly.

'I see. I don't use them in my department for Italian. As I mentioned, I'm fluent, so I do all the translating myself. We do use one for other more difficult languages like Russian, so I can check for you.' He shuffled a folder around on his desk, and then continued. 'Has your mother been helping you until now?'

'Oh, no, I wish! Her Italian is also limited. I had a friend in Florence basically reading it aloud to me, so I don't have anything written to review.' At the thought of Massimo, Allegra coloured a little.

'Oh! I didn't mean to pry.'

'Oh no, please don't worry, you're not prying. The friend is just a bit of a sensitive subject for me right now.' Allegra forced a smile.

'Well, I'd be delighted to offer you my translating services, and would feel privileged if you would accept. But I don't want to tread on anyone's toes.'

'What about your job?' Allegra asked.

'To be perfectly candid with you, Allegra, I don't go out in the evenings, so to be able to read and translate your great-grandmother's piece of history would be marvellous. I could probably manage about ten pages a night and could e-mail them to you daily?' He looked at her expectantly.

'Really? That would be so wonderful! I could pay you then instead of the service…'

'No, absolutely no money, please! It will be like my own social time… Meeting the Marchese and all these historical ghosts. A perfect excuse not to leave my apartment. I'm not only agoraphobic but still not quite out of the closet, either!' He smiled at his own witticism, and Allegra laughed.

'Why don't I tell you what I have found so far? It looks like the Marchese was a part of that group of the so-called elite Florentine art experts. That was until he fell out with them all by deciding to denounce the whole political scene and retreat to his inheritance, the *castello* in the countryside.'

He hesitated, pausing to see if he was boring her. She nodded enthusiastically for him to continue.

'Even though records seem to indicate he never left Europe, there is a suggestion that he attended the Great Exhibition in Paris. I mention this because to have designed such a foreign-looking interior, one would assume he must have visited Arabia or India.'

Allegra was used to his pauses by now, so she just sat quietly and waited for him to continue.

'But he could have observed these interior influences at the exhibition. Florentine cultured society was disgusted at the circus he had created at the castle. They completely side-lined him and, therefore, very little about him was officially documented.'

He handed her a piece of paper. 'I translated and wrote this down last night. You have probably seen it already but I managed to read it from the photo of the wall with the zigzag-patterned tiles.'

I am ashamed to say it, but it's true: Italy is in the hands of thieves, debt collectors, prostitutes, and brokers, who control and devour it. But I'm not ashamed of the fact that we deserve this.

'Thanks. I did see it, but I was so overwhelmed on my second visit to the castle that I didn't absorb everything *Signor* Bazia was saying. May I keep it?'

As Mr Tipple handed over the photo and Allegra said goodbye, she agreed to drop the diary off the following evening at his flat in Harrington Gardens. The translation of the diary could now begin in earnest.

Twenty-Eight

A week had passed and to Allegra's relief, Hugo had not called or appeared at her door. However, every day that passed without word from Massimo, the pain cut deeper.

On Friday morning, she had a welcome diversion as Mr Tipple's first translated pages arrived. She had told him it wasn't necessary to translate from the beginning and had given him the start point from where Massimo had last finished reading. But the wonderful gent had really pushed himself, and in four nights had translated and numbered each page up to that point, and the next ten pages beyond.

Allegra printed the pages and settled on her comfy chair with a notebook in hand. She started reading about the Marchese's funeral.

My Alessandro walked closer to the front of the funeral procession than me. I stayed holding little Luigi's hand at the back of the crowd, over on one side with the rest of the village women. The coffin was as I have never seen before – rich-coloured mahogany wood with ornate shining brass handles and the most beautiful flowers from the forest floor. I noticed a distinguished man walking close to the coffin. I think it was Bandino, the son we had heard all the rumours about… It is said the Marchese had disinherited him. He walked next to Marianna, the Marchese's daughter, but the bad blood was so obvious between them. I never saw them look, or even glance at each other.

He was buried near the castello. Just as the coffin was lowered into the ground, a large peacock wandered nearby. He didn't display his tail – it was as if he was showing reverence for the death of his owner. Alessandro assures me they only display their tails to attract the peahens, but I think they are like most males and like to show off their fine clothes.

Once the burial ceremony was complete, my Alessandro came to find us in the crowd. His face looked like it had aged ten years in just one week. He loved the Marchese and his heart was broken. For some reason, Bandino followed him and I looked up to see him in his striking black mourning clothes, studying my face. He smiled, then bent down and patted Luigi's head. Alessandro, of course, knew him and politely introduced us. Bandino repeated our little Luigi's name and gave him a big smile. As his sister approached he quickly hurried off and we never saw him again.

Allegra made notes of the son's and daughter's names and felt her first port of call would be to *Signor* Bazia in Florence. They were both titled in their own right, so there should be a record of what became of them. She spent the entire day setting up her research area in the mostly unused formal sitting room and looking through various search engines for anything on Bandino and Marianna Panciatichi. There was a lot of information on Marianna since she had married a titled man and become Marianna Paolucci.

Allegra was so engrossed in her work that it was only when Harry called out 'What's for dinner, Mum?' that she realised the time, and hurriedly threw a meal together.

Despite Hugo's threats, neither of her children had mentioned whether he had called or invited them to live with him. Once Harry had scoffed his steak and chips and gone back upstairs to his computer game, she broached the subject with Kirsty.

'Have you heard from your father at all?'

Kirsty went on alert. 'Why, what's he said now?'

'Nothing, that's why I'm asking, I just prefer early warnings so I have more time to prepare myself,' Allegra replied.

Kirsty looked a little sheepish and twiddled with the spoon in her tea cup. 'I didn't like to say but, you know the girl at school who is connected to Brooklyn? Well, she said something about Dad trying to get Brooklyn back. But Mum, really, they just say things to wind me up.'

'That doesn't bother me, love. I am more concerned with anything messing up Harry's life just now,' Allegra said as she offered a reassuring smile.

'Anyway, what's happening with "Uncle" Massimo? Still helping you with your research?' Kirsty gave a cheeky smile and tapped the table.

'Oh, I haven't heard from him this week. He must be busy.'

'You know, Mum, it *is* OK for the girl to text the boy first. It's not like the old days when you had to wait for the phone call.' Then she put her cup in the dishwasher, gave Allegra a peck on the cheek, and left the room.

Allegra looked at her watch. It would be 9:00 p.m. in Florence; maybe Massimo was out on a date. So, what? If she texted him, he could ignore it if he was busy. She took a deep breath, and typed into her phone.

176

Hi, just thought I'd let you know I didn't take the museum job and I'm going to divorce Hugo. Love, Allegra.

Then she turned the dishwasher on without pressing send. She still hadn't sent the message when she arrived up at her bathroom.

In her sanctuary, she put on a Mozart CD and took a long soak in the bath. Floating. Thinking. Finally, she emerged, wrinkled and prune-like. As she wafted back to her room, the peacock feather on the bedside table fluttered down to the floor.

She smiled. *It must be a sign.* She picked up her phone, pressed send, and then switched both the phone and the light off.

Twenty-Nine

It was Saturday morning, so with no alarm clocks going off, it was 8:00 a.m. before Allegra woke and turned her mobile on. It beeped three times.

The first text: *Why didn't you take the job? M x*

Second text: *Are you there Allegra? M xx*

Third text: *I am assuming after your bravery of sending a late-night text you have now turned your phone off. I will call you tomorrow. M xxx*

'So, you look happy this morning Mum, and you're all dressed up. Got a text back, did you? Or going somewhere nice?' Kirsty inquired with a silly grin on her face.

'I'm not going anywhere special, just taking your brother to buy some new trainers at Peter Jones.' As Allegra replied, Harry joined them at the table.

'No, not Peter Jones, Mum. That's so uncool. We'll get them in the Kings Road sporting club store.'

'Well, if Dad is forking out for trainers I need new jeans, so I'll join you,' Kirsty added.

Allegra heard the landline ring just as she had locked the front door. Then as she started the car, her mobile beeped in her handbag.

'That might be Gran. I'll text her back to say you'll call later. We're on an important mission just now!' Kirsty said as she opened the message on her mother's phone.

'Leave that, Kirsty!'

'Too late, Mum! I've read it. It's from you-know-who, but it's nothing private... He just wants to know when is a good time to call?' Before Allegra could grab her phone back, Kirsty had already typed an answer. 'Taking my amazing children shopping, call me after 4:00 p.m.'

As Allegra snatched the phone back and read the text sequence, she could see that thankfully Kirsty hadn't mentioned the 'x' at the end of Massimo's text.

The Kings Road had traffic backed up everywhere, and it took Allegra a full twenty minutes of driving around till she managed to secure a parking space. They found both the trainers and jeans in the same store, and Kirsty called her mother over to the fitting room where she was trying on a new top as well.

'Only the jeans, Kirsty!' Allegra said.

'But Mum, you don't want me to mention the kiss on the end of the text from "Uncle" Massimo to my brother, do you?'

'You devious thing! That's blackmail!'

'I'm just resourceful, that's all,' Kirsty said as she closed the fitting room curtain.

Allegra laughed as she queued to pay at the till.

'Excuse me, madam, but your credit card has been declined,' the shop assistant stated.

'That can't be right. Please would you try again?'

'I'm quite sure. Do you have another card, madam? There is a queue behind you.'

Allegra fumed as she took out her personal credit card.

'Shit!' She said it loud enough that both children arrived at her side.

'What's wrong, Mum?' Harry looked concerned.

'Your bloody father has cancelled the credit card, that's what's wrong!' Allegra then scrabbled in her wallet for her cash card and paid while Harry and Kirsty edged away with embarrassment.

No one spoke much on the journey home, and both children disappeared as soon as they arrived. Allegra figured the real fight with Hugo had just begun. She would have to call the lawyer first thing on Monday.

By 3:45 p.m. Allegra was in her bedroom hanging around near the landline phone. She longed to hear Massimo's voice, and only hoped he would forgive her. At 4:05 p.m. precisely, Allegra had to stop herself from immediately grabbing the ringing receiver. She inhaled and counted to ten before picking it up and saying hello.

'Allegra, it's wonderful to hear your voice. I was very happy to receive your text last evening.' Massimo paused.

'It's so good to hear your voice, as well.' Allegra was a bit lost for words.

'It's not really like us to be modest with our conversation, *Tesoro*.'

Allegra smiled with relief.

'Did I hear you give a little sigh?' Massimo laughed. 'Just because we have an argument, it doesn't mean all my feelings have changed. But you must understand when you said what you did about your ex, it momentarily blew my world apart. If the situation had been reversed, I'm sure you would have reacted the same way.'

'I guess that's right... I'm sorry, Massimo. It took me some time to come to the decision that I am going to divorce Hugo. I am also going to do all I can to solve the mystery of the disappearance of my great-grandpapa.' Allegra then went on to outline what she had organised so far. She attempted to be diplomatic as she mentioned the written translation Mr Tipple was working on.

'So, this museum man – is he single?' Massimo queried after her words had sunk in.

'Oh, yes, desperately handsome and single.' Allegra paused for effect. 'However, he also suffers from agoraphobia, not to mention the fact that he's gay...' Allegra trailed off and heard Massimo gave a little sigh of relief.

'In that case, he is the perfect person to help us solve the mystery.'

Allegra was thrilled that he used the word 'us'.

Thirty

When Allegra had first discovered Hugo's affair, she followed her mother's and Julia's advice and consulted a rather hard-nosed divorce lawyer. She had thought it all rather expensive and unnecessary. Hugo had convinced her he would be fair and they could work it all out between them. But now that he had cancelled the credit card with no warning, she was delighted to arrive at the sumptuous office of Saul Kramer; he would be a worthy adversary for Hugo.

Mr Kramer believed he could, at least, secure the use of the house for the period that the children remained at home. And of course, Hugo must cover the children's expenses. He assured her that once Hugo had received his letter they would work out an agreement that Hugo would, under law, be bound to honour.

Allegra returned home confident she had sufficient strength to weather a divorce battle with Mr Kramer in her corner. There were several e-mails waiting for her. She read Massimo's first, and in that moment, she was back to being a teenager, his wonderful words filling her with lust and anticipation.

The second was from *Signor* Bazia, who said if she could visit again, he would organise for her to meet an art historian who spoke English and could offer more information about the time at *Castello di Sammezzano* when her great-grandpapa worked there. He was also willing to take her for another visit to the castle, if that would help.

Allegra opened Mr Tipple's e-mail last, printed out the ten translated pages without reading them and collated them with the previous pages in her folder. She made a coffee then sat down in her special chair to return to her great-grandmama Cosima's life.

Alessandro has been acting rather strangely since the Marchese died and I know I should assume it is the loss and grief, but my heart tells me he is hiding something. I have asked him outright and he denies it, but I know my Alessandro so well. Even our little Luigi senses it. Alessandro seems distracted. When he is nervous, he has a habit of fingering the silver crucifix I gave him – if he keeps it up, he will rub off the inscription. I don't fear that it is another woman, but maybe I am deluded? We have never had a problem in that department, not one that he would need to seek solace elsewhere. After the behaviour of the Marchese's children at his funeral, I wonder if it has to do with that. Bandino, the son, acted in the strangest manner. Sometimes I wish my husband would give me more credit for being able to keep a secret. I had a formal education at Santa Maria private school and I'm not like the other women in the village, who thrive on gossip.

Cosima went on to describe the fresh pumpkin and ricotta cheese pie, a favourite she liked to cook for her husband, and the local nature walks she took Luigi on. It intrigued Allegra to know that back then, the mothers got together for informal playgroups just like she had when the children were young.

That evening, Allegra chatted to Massimo at length about where someone could just disappear to in 1914 Italy. They both agreed it had to have been foul play, or an accident somewhere where his body would not be found.

'I agree with you, but as a policeman, I'd consider other factors, as well. You don't know both sides of the relationship – we are only getting the wife's view. Alessandro's perception may have been quite different. Men do run off if they are shamed, or have lost their money or committed a crime; and there is still the rumour of the missing paintings,' Massimo said.

'I'm hoping I can learn more about the paintings when I meet with the historian *Signor* Bazia has lined up,' Allegra commented.

'And when will that be, *Tesoro*?'

'Well, I wanted to get further along with the diary and have as much information as possible so I can maximise *Signor* Bazia's kind offer.'

'I'd like you to consider the really important reason – that your lover needs to see you!' Massimo interjected.

As he spoke, Allegra caught herself blushing in the bedroom mirror. She agreed to check with her mother and look at flights in the morning.

Allegra realised she hadn't had a catch-up with her mother for some time, even though she usually called most days. She decided to pop in for a visit instead of using the phone.

'Hi, Mum, I hoped I'd catch you,' Allegra called as she let herself in the front door of her mother's house.

She heard her mother blow her nose then call out, 'Just in the loo, darling. Out in a mo.'

Allegra went into the kitchen and turned the kettle on. Maria appeared from the cloakroom with fresh lipstick but reddened eyes.

'Mum, what is it?'

'Nothing, my eyes are irritated, that's all,' she said, and quickly turned to make the coffee. Allegra went over and stood beside her.

'No, Mum, I know when you've been crying. What is going on?'

'Oh, it's just that I do miss Papa so much,' Maria replied, as she scooped up an opened envelope and shoved it quickly in her handbag.

'Mum! What's that?' Allegra grabbed the envelope; it had a Royal Marsden Hospital stamp on it. 'Oh, my God, what's wrong?'

Maria turned to face her daughter. 'I didn't want you to know. Well, not until I have all the facts. You have enough to deal with just now.'

They sat facing each other across the kitchen table, cradling their coffee cups.

'I want to know. You are my mother, and I am your only child!'

'OK, OK, calm down.' Maria let out a small sigh then continued. 'I went for my routine breast scan last month, and they called me back two weeks ago and did a small biopsy. Now, they have confirmed I have cancer and will need to have a course of chemotherapy, which I commence next week.'

Allegra sat silently as she attempted to absorb what her mother had said. 'Oh, my God, Mum, I've been so selfish. I didn't even notice anything. Have you been suffering? Or in pain?' A tear escaped.

'Hush, you silly girl. No dramatics, please. I've not been out of sorts and haven't had any pain at all. Your job is to look after your kids and make me happy. Even though I may not have expressed it, I have a high expectation on my papa's behalf that you solve the mystery of his papa's disappearance. A part of me wishes I had done what you have chosen to do. But seeing you so enthused and happy makes me happy.' Maria reached out and hugged her daughter. 'Now, what did you call round for, anyway?'

'That doesn't matter now. When is the chemo session? I'll come with you.'

'Well, only to the first one. Then, once I know how it all works, I'd rather go with my chum Sue. You know she has nothing better to do, and she has juicier gossip than you!' Maria smiled. 'I'm going to change my diet, as most of what I've read seems to indicate that alternative therapies supplement the chemical treatment. Over 50 per cent of women who get breast cancer survive to live normal lives, so no terminal discussions, OK?'

They chatted on about the various breast cancer theories, and then Maria deftly led the conversation back to Allegra's life.

'So, I'm guessing you were going to ask me to stay over with the children so you could go to Florence?' she asked.

'Yes, but I won't be going now till I know you're all right,' Allegra replied.

'That will be after next Thursday, when I have the treatment. I don't want to be made to feel like an invalid, Allegra. I'm going to beat this, and live to see a resolution to my grandpapa's disappearance, and maybe even the birth of a great-grandchild, so book the tickets for the following week. When I'm at your place, if I feel unwell, I can just do nothing all day, other than check in on the children after school. I need to feel useful.'

Allegra agreed she would think about it. Reluctantly.

Once she arrived home, Allegra texted Massimo and asked if he was free to chat. She was up in her bedroom when the landline rang.

'I can talk, *Tesoro*. Did you just want to hear my voice?' he crooned.

'Oh, Massimo, I need to tell you something. It's awful… My mother has cancer!' Allegra burst into tears.

'Hush now, just let the tears flow. I will wait, and then tell me all.'

After a few sobs, Allegra blew her nose; he listened intently without interruption as she told him everything.

'I agree with your mamma. The survival rate is very good with early diagnosis, and she needs to feel you are positive about this. Take a few days to grasp it all, then we can discuss going forward with your visit.'

Over dinner, Kirsty seemed more concerned than Harry when Allegra gave them the news, questioning Allegra about the treatment. 'She'll be OK, Mum. You know Gran. As Dad always says, she's a tough old bird.'

Allegra retreated up to her bedroom after dinner.

She stroked the peacock feather then held it to her face, hoping to feel Grandpapa's presence. 'Please, Grandpapa, let my mother be OK, please!' she whispered in desperation before she turned out the light.

Thirty-One

In a bid to distract Maria, Allegra called her daily and read out interesting parts of the diary to her. Mother and daughter marvelled at how many similar thoughts the three women shared, even though there was over a hundred years time difference.

Thursday seemed to arrive very quickly, and Allegra drove Maria the short distance up Fulham Road to the Royal Marsden Hospital.

The specialist invited Allegra to sit in as he explained the treatment. Her mother had dressed impeccably in a knee-length pencil skirt, turquoise silk shirt, and kitten heels. As he spoke, she widened her eyes, flicked her hair back, and flashed him a smile. Allegra repressed a grin – even in the worst situation her mother managed to flirt.

When the doctor had finished his chat, a nurse ushered them to a sitting room where several other patients sat in large extended armchairs with lines dripping into their arms. After the nurse had implanted the shunt and connected the drip, Maria took a copy of *Vogue* from her bag, put her feet up, and started to read.

Allegra went off to where she had been directed to get herself a cup of tea. Maria had been instructed to wait until after the treatment for any refreshment. She looked up when Allegra arrived back.

'Look at that lot, jeans and tracksuits. No matter how sick I may feel, I'm never going to turn up dressed like that!' she whispered.

'Mum, shush, they'll hear you. Besides, their cancer could be worse than yours and their treatment more intense, so don't judge!' Allegra whispered back.

'I guess you're right, but darling, she is reading *Heat* magazine!' Allegra let out a giggle as she marvelled at her mother's attempt at humour in such adversity. She was thankful when Maria squeezed her hand and eventually drifted off to sleep as the potent solution slowly dripped into her body. Allegra shuddered as she imagined it flowing through her mother's veins and killing all the cells, good and bad.

Initially, Maria looked quite pale and a bit unsteady on her feet after the drip was removed. But once she had a cup of tea and Allegra had gently escorted her to the car, her mother's optimism returned.

'I guess one good thing about all this is I won't have to worry about my weight for a while. I certainly don't feel at all hungry,' Maria said with a smile as they arrived at her house. She walked into the living room and plopped down on the large, soft sofa.

'You get off home and read the latest translation please, so you can read it out to me tomorrow.'

As Allegra began to object, her mother raised her hand. 'No, Allegra, do as I ask. I just fancy having a nap now, alone. Also, my next chemo session isn't for another two weeks, so I would like you to book your tickets and get over to Florence next week. I'm looking forward to luxuriating in your sacred bathroom.'

Back at home, as Allegra printed out the translated pages from Mr Tipple's e-mail, she felt twinges of guilt for leaving her mother alone. But her mother was not used to losing arguments. It was not like she could have stayed even if she had wanted to.

Instead she turned her attention to the diary.

What a month we have had. It's been that long since I had the time or the inspiration to write anything. It's much more difficult for me to write when awful things are happening around me; I only truly feel comfortable about putting my thoughts to paper when they are happy. As I write, I wonder if anyone will ever read this. Consciously, that is not my intention; it is really a record for me to look back upon and reminisce when I'm old.

Things have deteriorated with Alessandro's state of mind. I am trying to be patient, but he is at the castle more than ever, even though Marianna is still away. She has honoured her papa's wishes and made him guardian until the will is settled. I'm pretty sure it's all to do with some paintings the Marchese bought not long before he died. I managed a glance at some papers Alessandro had, but didn't see the name of the artist.

The peacock feathers Alessandro keeps in a vase are his pride and joy, but I was always told it was bad luck to keep them in the house. He tells me it's a stupid superstition but with the way he is now, I am beginning to believe they are bringing us bad luck.

My little Luigi is always a delight, but he is hardly little anymore. He is two-and-a-half years old and plays with the village children now. He is so clever, and he loves to make pictures with Alessandro's paints. I'm sure one day he will be a famous artist.

Allegra made a few notes. She googled the artwork in the castle, wishing to be prepared and display some knowledge when she visited the historian.

As before, there was plenty of information on the Marchese's daughter, Marianna. She had become Marchesa Paolucci delle Roncole when she married. There was an impressive portrait painting of her online, but no mention of any missing paintings.

Admitting defeat, and in response to her mother's encouragement, Allegra booked her Florence flights for the following Thursday. She sent an e-mail to Massimo, and e-mailed *Signor* Bazia to make a time to visit the historian. At the end of the email she put in a polite request for any information on the Marchese's son, Bandini.

Up until that point, Allegra had only been communicating with Mr Tipple via e-mail, but it felt more appropriate to phone him and discuss the trip to Florence.

'Ah, Allegra, I'm happy to hear from you. If you are agreeable, I would be keen to see what information I can find on the school Cosima mentions. I'm thinking if it was one where there were fees paid, there may be some written records about her birth parents.'

'Please, be my guest. I'd be honoured to have your help.' She then told him about the paintings and her trip. 'So, if you want to have a break from the translating next week, I probably won't get to read much from Thursday onwards,' she said.

'I will continue regardless. For me, it's so much better than a DVD or novel. I am totally engrossed in Cosima Mancini's life. She is so real. It is such a privilege to read something that no one other than the writer has ever read before.' Mr Tipple sounded the most animated she had ever heard him.

'I hadn't thought of it like that before.'

'You do realise there is only about a week's worth of manuscript left. When I peeked at the final page, I could see she came to an abrupt halt in her writing,' he added. 'So however, it ends, I am not sure it is going to offer any resolution.'

Thirty-Two

The week had flown by. There had been no update from Allegra's divorce lawyer, but he had said it would take some time for a line of negotiation to be established. Maria continued to be upbeat, and Massimo brought light to her life with his daily texts and calls.

In the diary entries Cosima continued to dwell on her angst over her husband's secretiveness. Allegra dreaded arriving at the last page, sensing that it might all come to a tortuous end.

Signor Bazia confirmed a meeting for Saturday afternoon with the historian *Signora* Katarina Piacenti at her home in Leccio. He also offered Allegra a discreet visit to the castle on Sunday morning.

Massimo had suggested she stay with him at his apartment on Thursday and Friday evening, then at the *Villa al Vento* on Saturday evening. Then perhaps, if she was agreeable, they could have lunch at his mamma's home after the castle visit.

The day before she left, Allegra met up with Julia for a spot of shopping, and to ask a favour. 'I'm worried about Mum. Can you call her from time to time, to keep an eye on things?'

'Of course I will, but try not to worry. She's not having another chemo treatment till you're back. And she wants you to do this. So, along with all your investigating, don't forget to have fun with that wonderful policeman!' Julia pressed her fingers to her lips and gave a cheeky grin. 'Now come on, let's go to that Beatrice von Tresckow boutique on Portobello Road and buy you one of those glorious jackets. It will look so glamorous in Florence.'

Both children were unusually affectionate before they left for school, and even Harry told her to have a good time. Allegra figured it was her twenty pound note that was the motivation for his demonstrative outburst.

Once Maria had dropped her off at Victoria Station and she was nestled in her seat on the Gatwick Express, she finally relaxed for the first time since hearing of her mother's diagnosis.

Allegra's heart filled with joy as she spotted Massimo across the airport arrivals hall. He was easy to spot as he was holding an impossibly large bouquet of white roses.

She was conscious of people staring as she approached him, and was pleased she had invested in the new cobalt-blue silk jacket from the Beatrice von Tresckow shop. It made her feel fabulous.

Massimo appeared to be in agreement.

His eyes never left hers as he strode purposefully towards her. He carefully placed the bouquet on top of her wheelie bag. Then he took her in his arms and kissed her, handing over the white roses. '*Bianca*, for peace between us, *Tesoro*,' he said as he took the wheelie bag and led her out to the car.

As soon as they arrived at Massimo's apartment, he put the flowers on the hall table, dropped the bag and kissed her again. Allegra was instantly aroused and in a blink of an eye, he had manoeuvred her to the bedroom. In the time it took for her heart to skip a few beats, her strong Italian policeman was making exquisite love to her on his neatly made bed.

'Sorry if I was too fast, *Tesoro*, but I missed you so much,' he whispered as he stroked her hair.

'Me, too,' Allegra responded.

'Shall I pour us a drink? Then we can have a bath. I have a wonderful date planned for this evening,' he said as he gently kissed her nose.

'I'm all yours tonight, Massimo. It's been a terrible two weeks, so tonight, whatever you wish.' Allegra's eyes lingered on his taut bottom as he walked out to the fridge to get the champagne.

They sat naked on the bed, sipping the Beau Joie Champagne in Massimo's best goblets.

'I'm impressed. Real silver, and chilled in advance!'

'Out of everyone I know, Allegra, you are the only person who would notice the vintage and appreciate they should be chilled before the champagne is poured.' They clinked the goblets and took another sip. 'They were my grandpapa's,' he added.

'I'm honoured.' Allegra reached out and swept her fingers through his thick black hair.

Massimo had poured some luscious-smelling bath oil into the large iron bath and filled it with hot water. They both managed to squash into the tub and sat face-to-face, sipping the Beau Joie Champagne and blowing the froth at each other. In those watery moments, the frightening thoughts about her mother, her soon-to-be-ex-husband, even the pull of her grandpapa's quest, all slipped to the back of her mind as she lost herself in Massimo's warmth.

After some hilarity at the procedure of getting out of the overflowing bath, and drying each other's backs with the giant towels, Massimo left, giving Allegra some space to get dressed. She slipped into a simple black, knee-length dress and low court heels, punctuated with a bright orange pashmina around her shoulders, and they stepped out into the crisp Florentine evening. Holding hands, they strolled the familiar cobbled streets for a ten-minute sojourn to the restaurant that had been the venue of their first official date. They were greeted with the same enthusiasm as Allegra's previous visit, but this time were ushered to an upstairs table where the welcoming owner made sure the attractive lovers were the focus of his establishment.

The first course of antipasto included zucchini flowers expertly stuffed with an aromatic blend of mint and mincemeat. They had been so delicately cooked in a light coating of breadcrumbs that the flowers remained intact.

'You like?' the hovering owner asked as Allegra took her first bite. She swallowed then placed her fingers to her pursed lips and blew him a kiss of delight. Massimo beamed.

Then the next dish was placed in front of them, a miniature creamy pumpkin pie. As Allegra tasted it, she recalled Cosima's description in the diary. The pie had a subtle touch of nutmeg that complemented the pumpkin mix perfectly under the soft, homemade pastry.

'I don't think I can eat any more, Massimo,' Allegra whispered, once the antipasto ritual had abated.

'Well, that is impossible, *Tesoro*. We will have a rest then you will be having the main course regardless. I have said we'll forgo the pasta course, so you have some reprieve.' He reached over and touched her cheek before topping up her glass with the excellent Chianti.

Allegra could smell the main course as the waiter came from behind her, the fragrance of rosemary and chargrilled meat filling the air. He placed a huge T-bone steak on a wooden board on the table.

'Don't panic. I have explained that you need a lady's portion, and they have agreed to slice it for us,' Massimo said.

The waiter took out a razor-sharp knife and expertly sliced the juicy steak, *carne alla griglia,* into manageable pieces. He placed them on their plates alongside hot roasted potatoes that had been tossed perfectly in fresh basil and crunchy salt.

Much to the host's disappointment, they both refused dessert and only managed to leave after accepting a second glass of limoncello. With lovemaking satiated from their pre-dinner tryst, the couple fell into dreamland entwined in each other's arms.

Thirty-Three

Massimo had reluctantly agreed that Allegra should meet with the art historian and *Signor* Bazia on her own. Instead he said that he would visit his mamma alone, for some quality time. Allegra didn't wish to overwhelm the older woman and besides, *Signor* Bazia had told her the *signora* spoke excellent English.

When they arrived to check in at *Villa al Vento*, the wolfhounds ran enthusiastically up to the car, wagging their feathery tails and Barbara greeted them both as old friends. By the time they returned to reception, *Signor* Bazia was waiting for them. Allegra momentarily felt guilty leaving Massimo, but as soon as she was in the car with *Signor* Bazia and chatting about the castle, it quickly passed.

Allegra updated him on the diary contents, and he nodded along, listening attentively to her as he navigated the winding road to *Signora* Piacenti's. They drove up a long shingle driveway and parked in a courtyard outside a rambling old villa. The courtyard was edged with beautifully groomed small trees and shrubs that stood to attention in large ornate terracotta pots.

As Allegra opened the car door, a tall, slim woman in an immaculate navy trouser suit appeared at the door of the villa. She seemed to be steadying herself on a dark wooden cane. *Signor* Bazia called out a greeting as the woman walked towards them. An Indian man resplendent in white tunic and trousers topped with a red turban, materialised directly behind her.

'Good afternoon, you must be Allegra. I am Katarina Piacenti. Please, call me Katarina. I am delighted to meet you.' She extended her hand to Allegra.

'I am honoured to be here, thank you for agreeing to see me,' Allegra replied, noticing that the older woman's weathered hands belied her more youthful face.

'This is Raj. He is my main companion now that my husband has passed,' Katarina said as Raj nodded to her, offering a jaunty smile with massive white teeth. Allegra was slightly surprised to hear that Katarina spoke with a clipped upper-class English accent.

The entrance room in the villa was filled with the most impressive range of both Chinese and Indian antique furniture. Although she was bursting with curiosity, Allegra felt it wasn't the right time to ask questions. Raj led them through to an even more impressive room. Half the walls were covered by floor-to-ceiling bookcases holding predominantly leather-bound books. On the remaining whitewashed walls hung several large Italian oil paintings that looked as if they belonged in a Renaissance museum.

Allegra and *Signor* Bazia sat side by side on a feather-filled, chenille-covered sofa whilst Katarina sat opposite on a carved upright armchair. She explained that she was born eighty-seven years ago to Danish parents in India, and educated at boarding school in England. When she was twenty and on a tour of Europe, she met her Italian husband and had lived in the area ever since. She studied art history at Florence University and had become an advisor to many different organisations over the years. Once she had finished her introduction, she then asked Allegra questions about herself. Allegra happily obliged and finally explained her quest.

'My challenge to date is that we know nothing of the paintings. The Marchese was quite secretive about what art he bought, and my great-grandmama's diary suggests her husband was complicit in many of these secrets.' As Allegra spoke, Raj appeared with a large Indian beaten-silver tray carrying a delicate Chinese teapot with four cups and saucers, and a plate of molten brown, aromatic cakes.

The conversation halted briefly as Katarina introduced the Ceylon tea, explaining that she had it sent out especially, along with the Italian cake, *pan di spagna*, which was made with local chestnuts. Once the tea was poured and cake eaten, Katarina finally responded.

'When *Signor* Bazia briefly told me about your interest, I referred back to notes that were documented around 1820. There was a rumour that a work by Fra Filippo, who you will know better as the artist Lippi, that was lost in the fifteenth century, had surfaced and passed through private hands. The Marchese Ferndinando Panciatichi Ximenes d'Agraona's name was mentioned as someone who had the power and funds to purchase it.' Her pronunciation was perfect.

'So, is there any record of it in the Marchese's estate that you know of?' Allegra asked.

'No, definitely not. If it were found, it would be claimed as a national treasure. When the assets of the Marchese's estate were sold, there was a comprehensive inventory made of all the valuable artworks, and there was no mention of Lippi,' Katarina said, pausing as she ate a small forkful of cake.

'We still don't believe we have discovered all the small secret rooms of the castle, so there is a slim chance that there may be paintings hidden in there somewhere. What would be the Lippi's value today?' *Signor* Bazia asked.

'Ah, well, that's not for me to say with any expertise, as I do not value paintings. It depends on many different circumstances in the complex art world, and whether provenance could be proved... But if the lost Lippi, which was actually a piece of a church altar panel called *The Adoration of the Child*, ever came to light, I would say many millions of euros would be at stake.'

Allegra and *Signor* Bazia took a minute to absorb her statement.

'So, that much money would be a good reason for someone to steal it?' Allegra queried.

'Yes, I'm sure it would, but in most cases of stolen art they often appear back on the market by the next generation. Greed takes over I'm afraid. However, the Lippi has never resurfaced.'

She told them which galleries and museums held Lippi paintings. She also talked about how sad it was that, even in the present day, the Marchese was not really given the credit she felt he was due for creating the spectacular artistic architecture of *Castello di Sammezzano*.

'Florence is still full of art snobs, but I, like *Signor* Bazia, believe *Castello di Sammezzano* needs to be bought by the government and made a museum that preserves this great man's contribution to the art of Tuscany.'

The conversation then turned to the fact that while Allegra's great-grandmama Cosima was adopted, she was clearly well-educated.

'An education for an illegitimate child of that time would normally be because one of the parents was titled or well-bred. The Marchese was apparently quite a lad, and he was estranged from his wife. So, you may wish to pursue that line of enquiry?' Katarina said.

'I did think about that when Allegra first e-mailed me, but the dates just don't fit,' *Signor* Bazia added before Allegra could say anything.

Once they had said their goodbyes and driven a fair distance down the driveway, Allegra asked *Signor* Bazia to stop for a minute. He pulled over to the side of the road.

'Sorry, but the last part of the conversation in there floored me. Is there any possibility Cosima could have been the Marchese's daughter?' Allegra's eyes widened as she pulled at a strand of her hair.

'He was in his sixties when your great-grandmama was born, and from the Preservation Society research letters and documents of the time—.' He paused for a moment then exclaimed, '*Mamma mia!* I don't know how to say this very well in English, but he was having no sex.' *Signor* Bazia blushed.

Allegra laughed and shrugged her shoulders. 'Well, that's pretty definitive. So, the mystery deepens.'

For the rest of the journey, they speculated about Cosima's heritage. *Signor* Bazia agreed with Mr Tipple that they should search her school records. The school was prestigious, and still in existence in Florence.

Massimo was waiting on the terrace with a glass of wine when they arrived back at the villa.

'Thank you, *signore*, and tomorrow I will be joining your visit to the castle,' Massimo said as he waved off Allegra's afternoon companion.

'That was a bit abrupt, Massimo. If I didn't know better, I would say you were jealous!'

'Well, you *do* know better – I am jealous!'

Allegra laughed. 'I was away for three hours altogether. As we say in England, get a grip.'

Massimo scowled, then let out a laugh. 'I like that. "Get a grip." I will use that in future.'

Thirty-Four

The lovers enjoyed a wonderful supper of crumbed veal escalope accompanied by fresh porcini that Barbara's chef prepared for them. This was followed by the lightest tiramisu that had ever graced Allegra's palate, and washed down with a glass of dry, crisp Prosecco. They declined the coffee and just managed to keep their hands off each other as they walked upstairs to the room. Unlike the urgency of their first night back together in Massimo's apartment, this time their lovemaking was more leisurely.

Signor Bazia was waiting at the base of the castle gardens when they arrived the following morning. As they walked up the track in the shadows of the gigantic sequoia trees, they chatted about the real possibility of an unknown hiding place for paintings.

'I have to tell you, *Signora* Allegra, hearing your story has piqued my interest in a different way. My focus has always been on the building itself. The original *castello* was built in Roman times and quite different to what is here now. But your descriptions from the diary make Cosima so real… the human connection now seems more important than the architectural one.'

Before Allegra could respond, Massimo interjected. 'I was under the impression you were limited as to the amount of time you could spend in the castle, given it is under private ownership.'

'Well, that is true, and I am a little uncomfortable that you are a *poliziotto*. But given *Signora* Allegra's desire to research her own history, I hope you will avert your eyes to our small trespass?' *Signor* Bazia winked at Allegra and walked off, brandishing the key to the large castle door.

Allegra shot Massimo a look.

'I know, *Tesoro*, I should "get a grip," but remember, I can't be seen to be breaking the law,' he whispered as they entered the castle.

They decided to split up so that they could cover more ground in searching for secret doors or recesses.

Allegra volunteered to take the mezzanine floor that overlooked the largest room. Even though this was her third visit to *Castello di Sammezzano*, the emotional impact of the maniacal colours and the detail of the interior architecture still had a profound effect on her. She found it hard to stay focused. If she were to express it in spiritual terms, it offered a sensation of harmony in her soul.

The mezzanine level gave a fresh perspective of the room below and a clear view of the unruly, stately gardens. As she ran her hands along the tiles, she studied the exquisite colours and visualised her great-grandpapa there with his toddler son, her grandpapa, Luigi. The brilliantly coloured lead-light windows enabled the sunlight to diffuse and flicker remarkable shards of light into the room, creating a magical kaleidoscope of colour. She had covered the whole area and could find no obvious hidden panels or openings when she heard a noise below, no doubt from Massimo or *Signor* Bazia.

'Hi, I'm coming down,' Allegra called as she descended the darkened staircase to the ground floor. She arrived in the room with the large stone bath. 'Massimo, don't you jump out and scare me. Where are you hiding?'

He didn't emerge, so she followed the sound of faint footsteps down the hall. 'I know it's you because you're tiptoeing!' she said, following the hollow sound through to the side of the building, and passing through the Peacock Room.

'Allegra! Where are you going?' *Signor* Bazia called out from behind her.

'Oh! You gave me a fright. Massimo must be messing about. I think he has gone out that side door,' she replied.

'Really? I only just saw him on the first floor examining the wall, like only a *poliziotto* would.'

Signor Bazia pushed the side door, which swung open, and they walked out onto the overgrown path.

'Where does this lead?' Allegra asked.

'There may have been a building, or feature of some kind at the end of the path a long time ago, but it's gone now.'

About five minutes along the overgrown track, they arrived at an abandoned piece of wrought-iron fencing which looked as if it had been knocked over. It lay next to a mossy mound.

'Allegra, where are you?' They both turned to look back down the track.

'We're over here!' Allegra called back, as Massimo appeared from the direction of the castle.

'I saw the side door open and assumed you had come this way. Find anything?' he asked.

'I swear I heard you sneaking up on me in there,' Allegra said.

'No, it wasn't me, *Tesoro*. I was diligently looking for the lost paintings, like you asked.'

'Perhaps it was that homeless man again.' Allegra tugged at her hair and frowned.

'What man?' *Signor* Bazia raised his eyebrows.

'Oops! I didn't really mean to tell you. I thought at first he may have been a caretaker, but then the second time I realised he was probably sleeping rough in here. But what does it matter? He's not doing any harm.' She felt a pang of disloyalty for letting it slip out.

'That is very strange… I come up here regularly, authorised and unauthorised,' he gave Massimo a quick glance, 'but I have never seen any sign of a vagrant.' *Signor* Bazia frowned.

'I guess he suspected I wouldn't dob him in and now I have,' Allegra sighed.

'What is "dob" him in?' The *signore* looked at Massimo.

'It doesn't matter now. Anyway, what is this place?'

'We're not entirely sure. We think the Marchese was about to build a new folly or outbuilding before he died. There are no plans or documentation on it. But we have records of an earthquake around that time that disturbed a few unsafe buildings in this area. By the look of this lopsided fence we assumed any construction was damaged then, and probably halted as a result.' He looked at his watch.

'I realise we have taken up much of your time. I so greatly appreciate it, *Signor*,' she said as they walked back towards the castle.

Once they arrived back at their cars, Allegra felt sufficiently relaxed to give *Signor* Bazia a hug as she thanked him again.

The man beamed. 'Please, keep me updated on the diary and any new information you find. I feel involved in your "mission" now. I will do what I can to help.'

Massimo drove them back into Florence as they had agreed to stay in the apartment for their last evening together. Allegra would catch the 10:00 a.m. flight back to London the next morning.

'I'll just print out my boarding pass, if that's OK?' she called as she hit the button on her laptop to connect with the printer in Massimo's office.

'Sure, *Tesoro*, help yourself. I am going to take a shower.'

Once Allegra heard the water running, she went to the printer to collect her pass. She cast a quick glance up to the shelf where the certificates in the frames had been. But nothing... They had completely disappeared, but she felt too guilty to open any of his desk drawers.

Hearing the shower finish, she switched off the printer and went into the bedroom to repack her case.

That evening, they walked the few metres to Massimo's favourite pizza restaurant. Along the way he gave Allegra a detailed explanation as to why the establishment did the best thin, crispy pizzas in the whole of Italy.

Once they had been through the ritual Italian greetings from the owner and his chubby wife, and were seated on the hard-wooden chairs, Allegra could only agree with Massimo. Her taste buds were alerted to the warm, smoky aroma that only a wood-fuelled fire could bestow. As she bit into the wafer-thin base, Allegra had to concede it was the best tomato, mozzarella, and ham pizza she had ever tasted.

'You see, *Tesoro*? I am never wrong – especially when it comes to Italian food.'

Thirty-Five

The house was very quiet when Allegra arrived back in London the next day. Harry and Kirsty were at school, and Maria must have decided not to wait for her and gone home. After she had unpacked Allegra sorted through the post which her mother had left in a neat pile on the kitchen bench.

Amongst the usual bills there was a very formal-looking letter in a crisp, white envelope. As she opened it, she could see it was from Hugo's lawyer, and her hands began to tremble. She was on the brink of tears reading it when the phone shrilled.

'Yes?' she snapped.

'Allegra, it's me. What on earth's wrong?'

'Sorry, Mum, but Hugo has just informed me through a bloody letter from his solicitor, that he wants Harry to live with him. Oh, and he will also reduce my allowance.' Allegra was all choked up.

'What an arse! To play the children card like that.'

'The letter says he has done all in his power to attempt a reconciliation, if you please, as if it's my fault!' she added.

Maria tried to console Allegra, and then brought her up to date on the household comings and goings.

Allegra eventually cut the conversation short. She needed to deal with the Hugo situation.

She scanned and e-mailed the letter to her lawyer, and then immediately phoned him.

'Don't panic, all this can be resolved. I advise you to be very tactful with your son on the matter – and don't mention it unless he does. If he *does* bring it up, just try to assess what his father has told him and remain as calm as you can. I will get back to you tomorrow with a proposed response.' He then apologised, saying he had to go as he was due in court that afternoon.

Allegra sat at the kitchen table with her head in her hands. She felt wretched. Hugo had successfully blown away all the happiness she had brought back with her from the weekend. She switched on her laptop and scrolled through the e-mails until she spotted Mr Tipple's latest diary translation. While the pages were printing she made a coffee. Then, in a bid to divert the effects of her ex-husband's venom, she settled back in her chair to lose herself in the distant past of her great-grandmama Cosima.

My heart is almost torn to pieces. My Alessandro has disappeared. As I write this, it has been ten days since anyone has seen him, and no one seems to care as they should. With no extended family to talk to, my writing is the only way I can express myself. The staff at the castle last saw him in the morning, walking towards the forest. The police have scoured every ravine and valley and friends are still searching, but they can't go on forever. Marchesa Marianna has been to visit me; she said she was due to meet with Alessandro this week for an update of affairs at the castle. She asked if there was any reason for him to run away. I was horrified to think she would even ask, but now I am having doubts. Is there another woman?

In my heart, I harbour no fear that I have upset him. The evening before he disappeared, I prepared his favourite meal of pasta with fresh fine asparagus, and we laughed together making a personal joke about it. Once our little Luigi was asleep, we sat outside in the moonlight and Alessandro told me he was looking forward to his meeting with the Marchesa. He said he had something important to tell her, and felt sure that she would be happy with the way he had arranged everything. He always treated the late Marchese's secrets with respect. Then after we chatted and had inhaled the perfume of the gardenias in the cool night air, he led me to our soft bed and gently made love to me. That night he made me feel like a young woman again, like before I became a mamma. I know in my heart my Alessandro wouldn't do that if there was another woman in his life. I want him back. He is my world. My heart is too cold. I need his warmth.

The morning of the day he went missing, I remember sitting in my special chair and feeling the room shake. We often have earthquakes, but that one sent a shiver down my spine. Now I think it was a sign. But a sign of what? The peacock feathers fell from the shelf. I just know they are bad luck. What can I do?

An involuntary tear escaped down Allegra's cheek, creating a blotch on the paper. She thought about how Cosima must have felt… To lose the man she loved without explanation would be a terrible thing.

Back at her computer, she noticed a second e-mail from Mr Tipple, inviting her for a cup of tea and a chat over some details that might prove helpful. She replied and they agreed to meet the following day, late afternoon, at his office.

Allegra felt anxious as she listened out for Harry's arrival. Kirsty appeared first, and Harry came in just as Kirsty was giving her mother a detailed description of a new boy she fancied.

'Hi, Mum, I'm glad you're back. Gran's cooking wasn't up to much. What's for dinner?' Harry asked as he plopped his iPad on the table and opened the fridge.

'Do you mind? I was having a serious conversation with Mum!' Kirsty snapped at him.

'Oh yeah? About that latest dickhead you fancy, no doubt. Another druggie, is he?' Harry replied, then quickly grabbed his iPad, and scooted out of the kitchen with a cold chicken leg before his sister could get at him.

'Spaghetti and meatballs in an hour, Harry,' Allegra called out behind him.

'He's the dickhead, you know. Mum, he spent all of Saturday over at Dad's and that Brooklyn bitch was there. I don't know how he can stand her. But he did score a new computer game from Dad.'

'Don't be too hard on him, love. Hugo is his father, and I think boys need a male influence in their life at that age. I appreciate your loyalty, but you must also be respectful,' Allegra replied.

'I notice you're talking through gritted teeth, Mum!' Kirsty laughed and Allegra returned to the mince balls she had begun making on the bench.

Over dinner it didn't appear as though Harry was going to say anything about his father so, while Allegra was on tenterhooks, she decided to take the lawyer's advice and say nothing. Whilst Harry showed no interest, Kirsty was intrigued as Allegra spoke about her trip to the castle and the latest diary translation.

'But that's so sad, Mum! Do you mean she never found out what happened to her husband?'

'Yes, it looks that way', said Allegra, 'but I'm going to figure it out. For Cosima, and Grandpapa too.'

Thirty-Six

The following morning, after the children had left for the day, Julia appeared at the back door.

'Well, this is a surprise,' Allegra said.

'I have a viewing in the next street with a client in an hour's time, so I thought I'd come here for a chat first.'

Julia looked immaculate, as usual. She was wearing a soft blue suit that Allegra surmised was from Hobbs' new collection, and the latest neutral classic high heels.

Julia was particularly keen to hear all about Massimo. Allegra attempted to sidestep the sexual questions, but it wasn't much use. After all, it was Julia's specialist subject.

'Look, I don't know whether to tell you this or not, but I was at Colbert in Sloane Square for lunch on Friday and Hugo was there with the child bride. He couldn't see me, as he had his back to me. I was actually close enough to hear some of the conversation.' Julia paused and looked at her friend.

Allegra nodded. 'Go on.'

'Well, I noted that she drank a fair bit of wine and she was shouting at one point. He seemed uncomfortable and patted her hand several times to try and quieten her down. From what I could hear, it was all about her wanting to move to a new apartment,' Julia said.

'Well, he sent a lawyer's letter saying he wants Harry to live with him and that he intends to reduce the payments he makes for the children. When he first left, he assured me he would always look after us. I guess he didn't bargain on her being such a demanding young woman when they were having the affair,' Allegra sighed.

'He spotted me when he stood up, I'm afraid. He was so embarrassed, then angry when it dawned on him that I might have overheard. He ushered her out of there double quick,' Julia added.

'It's amazing… A couple of months ago hearing this would have really affected me. But now, I don't really care, other than the effect it has on my children.' Allegra took a sip of her tea then added, 'Mum mentioned you popped over here on Sunday to check on her. Thanks Julia, I really appreciate it.'

'I didn't think she looked all that well, but then I guess she has only just started the chemo. She seemed very tired, but that's to be expected. However, she told me how delighted she is about your family quest – and about your romance.' Julia beamed then reached out and squeezed Allegra's hand.

Once Julia had gone, Allegra phoned her mother with the intention of going around to her place for lunch. Maria put her off, though, saying she was tired and to leave it till Thursday when she would accompany her to the chemo treatment. Allegra felt uneasy but knew her mother's ways well enough to respect her wishes.

At 4:00 p.m., Allegra arrived at Mr Tipple's office. The fragrance of vanilla tickled her nose, and she could see there were two large Paris-Brest cream cakes sitting on a china plate beside the teapot.

'My favourite pastries, from the new French bakery in South Kensington. My new intern is happy to shop for me; in that sense she is very useful,' he said, indicating for Allegra to sit down as he closed the door. She was impressed with the old-fashioned formality as he gracefully poured the tea. He placed the abundant cream cake on a delicate china plate along with a small, exquisitely engraved silver fork and a napkin, and handed it to her.

'The forks are sterling silver and were used by Queen Victoria. I reserve them for my special friends.' He smiled and popped a bite-sized piece of cake into his mouth.

Once they had finished eating and discussing antique china, he shuffled some papers on his desk and cleared his throat. 'Now, you know how you gave me permission to delve a little further into your great-grandmama's heritage? Well, I have managed to find out that it was the Marchese Ferdinando Panciatichi's trust that paid for her education.' He paused.

'Wow. Do you think that means he was her father after all?' Allegra was wide-eyed.

'Well, no. I managed to smooth talk an archivist and he revealed there was a letter in the accounts books at the Santa Maria private school. He wouldn't scan and send it to me, but he did agree to read it out over the phone. The letter stated that the funds were included and that Cosima should not have anything less than the other girls at the school. Also, it said that her adoptive parents would be regularly reporting back to him, as he was moving to America. The letter was signed Bandino Panciatichi.'

It took a minute for the words to sink in. 'So, you're telling me my great-grandmama was the illegitimate granddaughter of the Marchese Ferdinando Panciatich?'

'It looks that way. He was only eighteen at the time and his father must have known as he wouldn't have had access to that sort of money otherwise.' Mr Tipple took the final sip of his tea and sat back in his chair.

'It explains how Cosima came to be so literate. But I'm not sure how it's connected with Alessandro's disappearance,' Allegra frowned. 'This time when I visited the castle, I gained some insight into the Marchese. I feel he was making a statement with his architecture, and the placement of the room where he built the altar was where he wished his material and spiritual worlds to connect.' Allegra paused. 'Sorry, I hope I'm not boring you.'

'Not in the least. I'm sure he would be proud to hear you speak so powerfully about his vision – especially since it seems you are related. I only have one more session with the diary before it's complete, so I should have it to you by the end of this week. I feel sad to say goodbye to Cosima, as it's been wonderful being an observer in her life.'

Allegra couldn't help herself; she leant over and gave him a kiss on the cheek.

Thirty-Seven

There was an e-mail from Saul Cohen, the lawyer, waiting for Allegra when she arrived back from the museum.

He said he had considered Hugo's threats, and as Harry was almost seventeen, he was confident that any judge would agree it was for Harry to choose where he lived. He reiterated that if Harry brought up the subject, Allegra should keep her emotions in check; in his experience, children in these situations usually ended up returning to the mother once the novelty and gifts of inducement had worn off.

However, on the matter of finances, he requested that Allegra send him all she had on their joint assets and liabilities, and that he would need about two weeks to draft up a suitable proposed settlement. He added that these cases usually took a long time to settle and 70 per cent of them ended up before a judge.

Harry appeared quieter than usual during dinner and once Kirsty had left the table to Skype her new boyfriend, he lingered over his dessert.

'Mum, can I talk to you about something without you getting upset?'

'Yes, of course, love. What's on your mind?'

'You know how you've always said that a boy needs a father? Well, I think it may be a good thing for me to go and live with Dad for a while.' He paused and pushed a spoonful of ice cream into his mouth.

'OK. I get that. If it's what you want… But what about getting to school each day? It will take two buses travelling each way and at least a half hour longer. Also, what about your dinner each evening?' Allegra said, struggling to keep an even voice.

'Well, Dad said he will give Brooklyn a list of my favourite foods, or I can order take-out.'

'Does Brooklyn cook, then?' Allegra couldn't help herself.

'No, not yet, but a part of the deal with them is that she learns to cook and agrees to have me live with them. In return, he'll consider taking the posh flat she wants in Notting Hill, as Pimlico isn't really the right area.'

As Allegra tugged at her hair, she could feel the beat of her pulse in her neck. 'So, I'm assuming in the new flat, you will have your own bathroom and be allowed mates to stay over?'

'Yes, Dad has promised me a big room with a TV and DVD player and a new Mac, so it will be really cool.' He noticed his mother's eyes, and added, 'But I can come home here and visit most weekends.'

In a bid to conceal her emotions, Allegra turned and pretended to busy herself at the sink. 'If it makes you happy, Harry, then I give you my blessing,' she said without turning around.

'Cool, thanks, Mum,' he called as he went out the door.

Allegra left the kitchen without cleaning any pots, turning off her mobile and her computer. Grabbing a Randy Crawford CD from the lounge, she went upstairs to her bathroom and closed the door. She turned the stereo up to full volume, and then, as she ran the hot water, the tears finally erupted. She slunk down onto the tiled floor and clutched the bath as she wept.

After unsuccessfully attempting to calm herself down in the hot bath, Allegra rummaged through the medicine cabinet under the sink till she found some old sleeping pills Hugo used when he travelled long haul. She downed two of the pills and crawled into her bed.

Somewhere far off, hours later, she could hear Kirsty's voice. 'Wake up, Mum! Are you sick? Shall I call Gran?'

'No, it's OK. I just had a rough night, I'm fine,' Allegra managed to respond in a medicated haze.

'Harry's already left for the day. I'll see you tonight,' Kirsty called as Allegra heard her run down the stairs.

Allegra struggled to lift her head from the pillow. It felt as if she had been left behind in a dream. Slowly, she forced herself to wake up. She could recover from her husband's infidelity, she could accept her mum's cancer, but how the hell could she deal with the loss of her own son?

When she had dressed she made a very strong pot of coffee in a bid to counteract the effects of the sleeping pills, then picked up her mobile and opened her laptop. A text immediately appeared from Massimo. *Are you OK? Love M xx.*

She took a deep breath and texted back. *No. A xx.*

He must have been in a meeting, as the phone didn't ring for two more hours. During that time she managed to pull herself together and was about to print out the final translation of the diary.

'*Tesoro*, I just received your text. Tell me?'

As soon as she heard his voice, she fought back the tears. 'Sorry if I blub, Massimo. I took a couple of sleeping pills last

221

night, and it appears drugs just don't sit well with me. I can't seem to get my emotions under control at all.'

It all came out – along with the tears – as she told him about Hugo and Harry and what the lawyer had advised.

Massimo listened patiently until she had finished.

'Allegra, first, please listen to this one important thing: you have not lost your son. He will only be across London. It's not as if he has died. You will see him every week. A lot of young men his age are off at boarding school or have left home after conflict. Think back to being sixteen. We were all selfish and self-centred. He will return soon enough.' He paused to let his words sink in. 'Just take one day at a time. I need to go into a meeting now, but will call you tonight again, OK?'

Allegra felt a little better after hearing Massimo's reassurances, and adjusted her focus back to the diary translation. The date in the diary entry was two years later than the last one she had read.

It has been a long time since I have expressed myself on these pages. Life has been hell for the past two years. But I forced myself to read back over the previous pages of when my Alessandro was here and as I read the words, it resurrected the essence of the love we had.

If I had his body, a corpse, even a disfigured one, anything, it would be easier than this nothing. He has completely disappeared off the face of the earth and now, after two years, nobody cares but me. Luigi has grown and no longer looks for his papa. He seems much happier being at school with the other children than he is at home with me.

It's so obvious that the other women avoid me. I was distressed when I inadvertently overheard one of them saying that bitterness had devastated my beauty. Why would a woman who was supposed to be my friend say that? What did I ever do to her? How would she feel if her husband disappeared? I try to distract myself but nothing works; Alessandro is always in my thoughts. I sleep very little and feel so tired during the day. In my dreams I hear him calling, but I can never quite hear what he says. Then I wake up in a sweat.

Marchesa Marianna has been so kind. She has ensured I have an adequate pension; apparently her father organised it for Alessandro as part of his will. Why is it these aristocrats are so kind and yet my own village people treat me like a leper? The marchesa told me I am still young and could marry again. But how can I ever marry again or be with anyone when I don't know whether my husband is dead or alive? I pray that God will reveal to me where Alessandro is, but God ignores my plea. From now on, I shall ignore Him also.

Allegra put the pages down and poured herself a glass of chilled water. When she resumed, she could see the date had skipped forward thirteen years.

I vowed I would never write any words here again unless I knew where my Alessandro had gone. But I rediscovered this diary of thoughts and with my current crisis, I feel the need to pen a few more.

I have forgiven God, as after several years I missed the comfort and familiarity of the Mass. Then about five years ago, the Marchesa invited me to a special Mass at the castle. It was the anniversary of the Marchese's death. She said nothing about Alessandro on that visit; it was as if she respected my grief. I took Luigi with me, who was thirteen by then and awkward, with pimples on his chin.

As we walked across the path towards the castle, I heard the terrible noise that peacocks make – cawing and cackling. There across the lawn was a huge peacock spreading his tail like an arrogant playboy, and not a peahen in sight. Luigi was transfixed and walked over towards the bird. It didn't move – it just stood and looked at him. Once we were inside the castle, we were ushered to a room like a small chapel; there was an altar with a crucifix on it but no seats, so we all stood. Although I was very nervous, as the priest recited Mass I felt a sense of calm. It was probably only wishful thinking on my part, but I felt the presence of Alessandro all around me. I know the castle was his favourite place in the entire world.

When the Mass was over, I noticed an older man at the back of the church who had not gone up to receive communion. He stared at me intently and smiled at Luigi. I thought I recognised him. It was only once we had left and were walking down the path to the village that I recalled his eyes, as his face had aged since I had last seen him. It was the marchesa's brother, Bandino, who lived in America; he must have returned for the anniversary. When we arrived back home, Luigi went to the cupboard where I keep all of Alessandro's things. He pulled out the peacock feathers and reinstated them in a vase in his room.

I feel as though the feathers have brought back the bad luck… Perhaps it never left. My worries are for my son who is now a man of eighteen. Well, he thinks he is a man. He has fallen head-over-heels in love, which is normal at his age, but she is English and she is not polite to me. She came on a trip to Tuscany to learn some Italian and further her education. She is twenty, and more worldly wise than my innocent Luigi, but what can I do? My world is shattered by his announcement that he is to marry her in England. He has invited me to go over for the wedding, but I will not go.

224

I must accept some blame for his radical decision. I am what they say I am, bitter and ruined. No matter how hard I tried I couldn't protect my son from my sadness, so why wouldn't he want to get as far away as possible?

Apart from that one day I visited Castello di Sammezzano, I have become adept at avoiding anything that provokes memories of Alessandro, for instance, the food he enjoyed (even the aromas are too much for me) and the music we listened to together. I have waited too long. Now that God and I are on speaking terms again, I pray my Luigi will be happy despite my dislike of his choice of wife and country. In my heart, I hope he builds a new life and family for himself, and that the legacy of Alessandro's disappearance will not blight his life as it has blighted mine.

Thirty-Eight

When Allegra arrived at her mother's house the following morning, she was shocked to see how thin she looked. The chemo treatment was due at 11:00 a.m., so she arrived at 9:00 a.m. allowing time for a chat and a pot of coffee.

Allegra tried to hide her shock, and instead shared her angst about Harry going to live with Hugo. Her mother listened intently without interrupting. Allegra then continued with the latest from Cosima's diary; as she spoke she could see her mother struggle to curb her tears.

Maria reached out a hand. Allegra didn't ever recall seeing her mother's hands void of a colourful nail varnish; right now they were colourless, unmasking her age.

'My darling girl, you are going through a lot of change and I only wish I could help you. It's ironic that I am hearing both my grandmama's and my daughter's emotional journeys with their sons at the same time.' She sighed and continued, 'Allegra, we don't own our children. They just come through us – they will always leave and choose their own path.' She leant back in her chair as if to catch her breath. 'Forgive me, I am just so tired. I guess having cancer is forcing me to slow down and act like a senior person…' She smiled.

'Yes, you certainly sound very wise!' Allegra tried to return the smile.

'I feel for my papa, too. It would have been hard nearly a hundred years ago, growing up in a fairly small village with a sad mamma, no papa, and surrounded by ignorance.'

'That's true, Mum. Look, we had better get going since you're due at the hospital in half an hour.' Gathering her bag and her mother's basket, Allegra guided her towards the door.

The treatment room at the Royal Marsden seemed more morbid than their first visit, but Allegra held her tongue. There was a whole new bunch of patients this time, already hooked up to their plastic tubes and ensconced in the unattractive brown velour armchairs.

Maria had brought along her new Kindle. Once the nurse had inserted the chemo drip, she showed Allegra how she had downloaded her upmarket magazines and the latest bestseller, *The Silent Village*, onto the amazing tablet. But her enthusiasm waned quickly, and she showed obvious signs of discomfort before she finally managed to close her eyes. Allegra gently took the Kindle from her hands, turned it off and placed it in her basket. Then went off in search of another coffee.

When Allegra returned, she sat beside Maria and watched over her as she drifted in and out of sleep. A feeling of nausea settled itself in the pit of her stomach as she scrutinised the last of the potent drug dripping stealthily into her mother's distressed-looking vein. The nurse appeared beside them and offered Maria a cup of tea as she removed the drip.

'Yes, please. My lips and tongue feel so dry, much worse than the last time.'

'That's because the dose has been stronger this time,' the nurse replied. She bustled off to make the tea, carrying the empty chemo bag.

After Maria had sipped the tea, Allegra helped her to her feet. Taking her arm and carrying her basket, she slowly walked her out into the hallway. Suddenly, she felt her mother slipping. She dropped her handbag and her mother's basket in a bid to hold her upright, but Maria slipped to the floor and vomited all over herself. A young man in a white coat appeared immediately beside them.

'It's OK, I can deal with this,' he said as he lay Maria on her side in the recovery position and pressed a button on his pager, requesting assistance. Within a minute, two nurses had arrived and gently lifted the unconscious Maria onto a trolley bed. Allegra, in blind panic, followed them to a small treatment room.

'Please, just give us some time to look up her notes and examine her. You can wait there.' The young doctor spoke briskly as he pointed to some chairs along the corridor.

Allegra did as she was instructed, her heart pounding. It was the longest hour of her life. Finally, the doctor appeared.

'Sorry, in all the commotion I didn't introduce myself.' He extended his hand. 'I'm Dr Grant Dockery. Be assured I am a qualified oncologist, I'm just in the process of completing my internship here. Your mother is conscious now. She suffered a bad reaction to the chemo dose so the team will assess her blood tests and adjust the next session accordingly. She is perhaps more frail than we realised. She is also anaemic so we are going to keep her in for a day or two, just to keep an eye on things. She'll be on ward four, so you are welcome to go up in, say, about half an hour?' He gave a half smile as he stroked his chin.

Eventually, Allegra was allowed at her mother's bedside. Maria was deathly pale but smiling as Allegra walked over to the bed and pulled up a chair.

'Now, don't look so distressed, Allegra, I'm not dead! It's just I've no make-up on and apparently I'm temporarily lacking in those darling little blood cells that help give me my usual youthful looks.'

Allegra gently held her mother's hand as she forced back her tears.

'Well, you are lucky to have your own room,' she managed to get out, forcing a smile.

'No, not luck, darling, private health insurance. Initially, they had me in the ward with a rather motley crew, so I upgraded.' She offered Allegra another warm smile and squeezed her hand.

After Maria had mentioned a few necessities that she wanted Allegra to bring in the morning, she said that the doctor had prescribed her a mild sedative and that she must sleep.

'Oh, Allegra, if it's possible, would you bring me the printed translation of the diary tomorrow? I'm finding the print on the Kindle a bit difficult to read,' she added as Allegra left the room.

Thirty-Nine

When Allegra arrived back home, Harry immediately appeared, asking when dinner would be ready. Allegra instinctively knew the wrong thing would come out of her mouth so she said nothing and quickly went upstairs to her room.

'Are you going deaf, Mum?' Harry called after her.

She splashed her face in the bathroom, said a silent prayer, then went back downstairs. Kirsty was sitting at the kitchen table.

'Where have you been? The creature who is apparently my brother has had a couple of rants about not being fed!' As Kirsty spoke, she looked up from her magazine and registered the look on her mother's face.

'Mum, what's wrong? Shit, it's Gran, isn't it? It was her treatment day today.'

'Yes, it's Gran. She is very unwell and collapsed at the hospital after she had the chemo. They are keeping her in for a couple of days.' Allegra sat down at the table.

'So, when is dinner?' Harry barked as he appeared at the kitchen door.

'Bloody hell, you selfish little shit! Can't you think about anything other than being fed and being given money for your bloody computer games? Look, will you! Mum is upset. Our gran is in hospital with cancer!' Kirsty was on her feet and eyeballing her brother.

'Kirsty, please don't swear,' Allegra said. 'But I agree with the rest of what you just said.' She looked over at Harry who stood bewildered at the door. 'You seem to be going through a very selfish period just now and I'm almost over it, so it would be best if you have some time with your father. I believe it will do you both a lot of good!'

'Why are you both ganging up on me? All I asked about was my dinner.'

'For God's sake, Harry, just dial a pizza or whatever it is you do!' Allegra said as she strode out of the room, not waiting for the ramifications of her outburst.

She ran the water for a bath and then, desperate for a drink, nipped back down to the sitting room cocktail cabinet to pour an extremely strong gin and tonic.

The edge of her anguish slipped away as the hot, scented water embraced her body, the music of Mozart's Fifth filled her ears, and the gin hit her relax button. She was disturbed by a gentle knock at the door.

'Yes?' she called out.

'Sorry, Mum. I know you don't want to be disturbed, but I don't have enough cash to pay the pizza man,' Kirsty called through the door.

'In my wallet in the bag on the bed. Oh, and Kirsty, don't worry. I'll be OK. I'll come down and chat in a little while.'

She topped up the hot water. The double gin was doing its work. Her thoughts drifted away to the huge stone bath at *Castello di Sammezzano*. Did her great-great-grandpapa Bandino once bathe in it she wondered?

The gin took its toll. She enlarged the print so it would be easier for her mother to read, but it took Allegra almost an hour to print out a second version of the diary translation. Then, aware of the time difference in Italy, she texted Massimo to see if he was still up. The phone beside her bed rang within a few minutes.

After she had filled Massimo in on her mother's condition, she asked him about his day. He sounded hesitant, but mentioned he might be seconded for a while to a Rome-based division.

'It's not ideal, but they say they require my skills, so I guess I'm going to have to consider it if I want promotion here in Florence. But let's not talk about that now. I'll call you tomorrow evening to see how your mamma is,' Massimo said, as they finished the call.

In the morning, Harry was a little more contrite, even telling Allegra to say hi to Gran from him.

Being in a private room at the hospital meant that Maria was allowed free rein with visitors. When they arrived, Kirsty was clearly shaken at the sight of the very sick patients in the ward, so Allegra quickly closed the door. Maria, although still very pale, was propped up with cushions and was especially pleased to see her granddaughter.

'It's my first time ever in a hospital. Are you going to be all right, Gran?' she asked.

'If you mean am I dying, well, no, not immediately. I have breast cancer that I'm being treated for. I also seem to have developed a temporary anaemic condition, and the specialists need to adjust the chemo dose to accommodate my individual tolerance, but once that is all sorted, my darling Kirsty, I will be back at yoga and may even join you clubbing!'

Kirsty visibly relaxed to see her gran's old humour emerge, albeit from a hardly recognisable, pale face.

Allegra placed the weighty printed manuscript on the bedside table, and Maria smiled as she saw a peacock feather photocopied onto the cover. They began chatting about Cosima's birth father as Kirsty listened, intrigued.

'Mum, you didn't tell me any of this! You mean this Cosima, who was, let me see, my three times great-grandmama, was the illegitimate daughter of an Italian Marchese? That practically makes me royalty!'

'I haven't told you simply because there has been so much going on. All the facts we can find point to that being highly probable, but unless we do a DNA test, we may never know for sure. The Marchese was the grandpapa of great-grandmama Cosima. Her apparent papa, his son Bandino, was disinherited in favour of his more stable sister.' Allegra was interrupted as Dr Dockery opened the door.

'Oh, sorry, I didn't mean to disturb you. Just checking how you feel this morning, Mrs Mancini-Soames.'

'Much better, thanks, doctor. When can I go home?' Maria spoke with a smile as she flicked her hair and sucked in her cheeks.

'I will let you know later when the blood tests are back from the lab. See you later.' He winked as he left.

'Gran! Even without your make-up I think he fancies you.' Kirsty laughed, then proceeded to ask lots of questions about the missing Alessandro.

'I have been thinking that perhaps he was murdered after someone discovered and stole the hidden paintings. They would have been easier to sell if there was no record of them,' Allegra offered.

'Or he may have run off with another woman, like Dad did!' Kirsty chipped in.

'Somehow, I doubt that. It wasn't as easy back then to take off and leave your family, especially with a restricted income. And remember, the Catholic Church ruled over all morality issues. You couldn't just set up home somewhere, unmarried. Anyway, I'm sure Papa meant us to uncover the mystery and God will help us. We will figure it out,' Maria said as she pushed herself up on the pillows.

'Is that your Kabbalah, Buddhist, or Catholic side speaking, Gran?' Maria grinned and Allegra chuckled.

'Well, I may have to be hospitalised more often if it brings us three generations of girls together like this.'

After an hour of chat, Allegra could see her mother was fading, so she gave Kirsty a nod and they said their goodbyes.

'Allegra, I want to be firm about this. Don't you avoid returning to Italy because of me! I will be up and about in a few days. If you discover you have new information to pursue, get yourself back to Florence and follow all leads,' Maria said before they left the room.

Allegra dropped Kirsty at her college and, once home, opened her computer and sifted through her e-mails.

She opened the one from *Signor* Bazia first. He said that *Signora* Katarina had phoned him, and asked him to pass on some information.

She said she had sourced and studied some records of the six-month period before the Marchese passed away. There appeared to be two lesser-known paintings by the artist Raphael Sanzio, known simply as Raphael, which had been sold in Florence around that time. However, their provenance had

been the subject of some debate. Raphael was a prolific painter.
His early work included many religious paintings, mainly of the
Madonna, and then his later works moved on to portraits. He
died a young man in his thirties and his students completed
several of his works. These paintings were always under a
shadow as to their authenticity, so they couldn't command
the high prices that his other work did. They may have been
purchased by the Marchese. Katrina found a record of a private
auction at which they were sold about four months prior to
the Marchese's death. The payment appeared to bear the name
Panciatichi and, what was more interesting, the signature on
the collection slip, although not clear enough to read in its
entirety, appeared to end in the letters 'ni'.

Allegra immediately googled Raphael, whose work she
knew well from her studies. If the Marchese had purchased
any paintings, they weren't Raphael's most famous ones as
most hung in galleries and museums throughout the world.
But her heart beat faster as she noted the prices that private
collectors had paid for the paintings his students had likely
completed. They brought the price range right down, possibly
to what the Marchese could afford.

Next, she phoned Mr Tipple at the V&A Museum. He
listened intently as she read *Signor* Bazia's e-mail to him.

'If the last two letters were "ni", it may have been Mancini.
If my great-grandpapa had purchased them it may help us
discover what happened,' she added.

'Leave it with me for a day or two, Allegra. I know
someone who may have more information on the paintings
that Raphael never completed.' Mr Tipple's enthusiasm gave
Allegra a boost.

Forty

Allegra was relieved when two days later, Maria was discharged from the hospital, having been given an effective dosage of iron. Dr Dockery was also confident that Maria would be better able to cope with the adjusted dosage in the next chemo treatment.

'You look so much better, Mum. The make-up certainly helps!' Allegra commented as she arrived at Maria's house to check on her.

'Yes, Estée Lauder and I have a wonderful ongoing relationship. Now look, Allegra, I don't want you tipping up here every day treating me like an old invalid. I have friends my own age to play with, and you need to be focusing on your life, which is far more exciting,' Maria said as she tidied up her small herb garden.

Allegra took the hint and, after a quick coffee, returned home.

There was an e-mail from Saul Cohen waiting for her. He requested she read it then give him a call. He was recommending that Hugo admit his adultery was the cause of the separation so that she could have the family home unencumbered by any mortgage, plus an annual allowance to support her and Kirsty, and also Harry, should he choose to live with her. The allowance for the children would last until they had completed their education. If Allegra didn't remarry, she would also receive a portion of Hugo's pension.

Allegra felt numb. This was the real thing – divorce. She picked up the phone and called Mr Cohen.

'Allegra. I'm sure Hugo's lawyer will come back with a counter-offer – it's what we expect. There is a mortgage on the house but I can see in the documents you sent me that he has two life insurance policies, so he can always cash one in to pay that off. The next step is to get this proposal in an official form, off to Hugo and his lawyer.'

Once she had agreed, she made a mental affirmation not to allow this divorce process to take over her life. Instead, she returned her focus to her Alessandro 'theory', that he had been killed and the paintings he purchased on the Marchese's behalf had been stolen. But then where on earth was his body? She would talk to Massimo about it this evening, but in the meantime, she sent Signor Bazia an e-mail.

With your invaluable grasp of historic details, would it be possible, if I came to Florence, to look up any old records of criminal art dealers operating in Florence around 1890 to 1920? And possibly any unsolved murders or recovered bodies that weren't identified in the same era?

He replied promptly.

I believe there are archived police records for these dates, which, as sufficient time has passed, we should be able to access. It would be helpful if you could ask for Signor Massimo's help to clear the way for us? I would be willing to spend the time searching with you as a translator if this would be of some assistance.

Allegra considered another trip to Florence and the joy of being with Massimo. But first she needed to sort things out with her son and ensure she had backup in case Maria took ill again.

She prepared Harry's favourite roast chicken with her special stuffing, and parboiled the potatoes ready to throw them in a hot oven dish with ground rosemary and salt; Harry always said her extra-crispy roast spuds were the best.

He smiled as he entered the kitchen and dropped his computer bag on the table. 'Yum! What time are we eating?'

'Six-thirty, if that suits. Do you have much homework?'

'Yep, a bit. I'll just grab an apple and go and get it done,' he said as he opened the fridge. He picked up his bag as he left.

An hour later, Kirsty appeared in the kitchen sporting a unique outfit; her jeans had big rips in the knees and her fingernails were painted brown.

'Something smells good, Mum! Are you testing the theory that the way to a boy's heart is through his stomach?'

'Not quite, but it sure helps get things on an even keel.'

'So, are you going to try and persuade him to stay?'

'I just want to have everything OK between us all before he goes,' Allegra replied sadly.

Both children reappeared in the kitchen punctually at 6:30 p.m. After they had offered some conversation on subjects as varied as the new Xbox 360 computer game and Beyoncé's bum, Allegra discussed the Alessandro theory and her possible investigation.

'Which brings me to the timing of when you intend to move in with your dad,' she said to Harry, then paused. 'It's not that I want rid of you, it's just that if I am going to be in Florence for a bit, I need to have you two sorted out.'

Harry shoved another potato in before he responded.

'Well, the deal is I don't move in until they have moved into the bigger apartment… But I know Dad won't mind me staying at the old one for a week or two. I'll ask him, if you want.'

'What about Bitch-Face? Won't she mind sharing the bathroom with another teenager?' Kirsty asked.

'Nah, doesn't matter if she does. Dad is the boss, since he pays the rent,' Harry said as he swiped the last potato from Kirsty's plate and popped it in his mouth.

Allegra frowned and raised her finger at Kirsty so she did not respond. Once Harry had completed his obligatory duty of clearing the plates from the table, he returned upstairs.

'He really doesn't give a shit, Mum. Why don't you pull him up when he sounds like the chauvinist his father is?'

'It's not worth getting upset about. It's his age, his hormones, and his DNA,' Allegra replied, managing to raise a laugh from her daughter.

Later that evening, during their regular phone chat, Allegra broached the subject of her trip to Florence with Massimo. She knew he would be happy to have her to stay, but she omitted to mention that *Signor* Bazia had offered to assist her.

'I can talk to the historic records office and encourage them to help you. But you may have to ask *Signor* Bazia to translate for you. I'll assigned to this new squad and won't be able to take time out during the weekdays.'

'That's one problem solved then,' she muttered under her breath after she'd put down the receiver.

Forty-One

Maria's next chemo session went as smoothly as it could, given the circumstances. Allegra felt reasonably secure about stepping back and letting her attend the following session in the company of an old friend. And Maria had sounded enthusiastic about spending some quality time with Kirsty at Allegra's house while she was away in Florence.

She had managed to pin down a time to meet up with Julia, and they were enjoying a long lunch amidst the buzz and gossip of the Botanist brasserie in Sloane Square. Julia had willingly agreed to keep an eye on Allegra's mother and daughter while she was away and to be available in case of emergency.

Julia looked fantastic wrapped in a black short shift dress that displayed her slim legs and a pair of killer heels. The women shared a laugh as they noticed two middle-aged men giving them the once-over from across the room.

'So, Detective O'Brien, enough of this flirting with those old boys! Tell me, if your great-grandpapa was murdered, how do you propose to find his body?' Julia asked.

'Well, before I can start the search, I need to find out if any bodies or skeletons were found in the wider area of *Castello di Sammezzano* in the ten-year period after he disappeared.

Communications weren't great back then, and my great-grandmama wasn't anyone important, so she couldn't force issues with the police of the time. If there were any male bodies recorded, I'll try to find out where they were buried, then take it from there. It's a long shot, but I'm hoping another visit to *Castello di Sammezzano* may throw up some more clues.'

'On the subject of policemen, it's also *primo* that you'll get to spend a whole week of lust with your lover!' Julia gently tapped Allegra's shoe under the table.

'Well, evenings, anyway. He's on some new squad and will be fairly busy, apparently.'

When Allegra returned home an e-mail from *Signor* Bazia had arrived, confirming he would be able to offer her two half days in Florence for research and translation. The only confirmation she didn't have before she bought her flights was Harry's living arrangements.

She tactfully attempted to bring the subject up with Harry that evening.

'Dad says of course he will have me, but why can't you put the trip off till they move apartments? That would suit Dad and me better,' he quipped.

'It's not always about you and your father. I have my life, as well.' Allegra's moderate responses were beginning to fray around the edges.

'Yeah, well, Dad reckons you've got some bloke over there, and I've worked it out that it's probably that cop!' Harry raised his voice as he began to walk away from his mother.

'Harry! Don't you turn your back on me. Come back here and sit down,' Allegra fumed.

Harry stood facing her with his hands on his hips.

'Look, I don't want to argue with you, and yes, I have developed feelings for Massimo, just as your father has feelings for Brooklyn. It doesn't mean we love you children any less. The whole situation in the beginning was not my choice, but I am moving on now. Despite what you might think, I am still young enough to have another relationship.' Allegra felt terrible as she watched her son force back his tears.

'But if you didn't have anyone else, there... there would be a chance Dad would come home and we could all go back to how things were!' Without waiting for a response, and with tears streaming down his face, he stormed out of the room, slamming the door behind him.

'Shit!' Allegra said aloud as Kirsty walked in.

'What was all that about?'

'Your brother is under the delusion that if I didn't have a relationship with anyone, it would leave the door open for a reunion with your father.' Allegra sighed and poured herself a glass of wine.

'So, does this mean you're coming clean with both of us about "Uncle" Massimo?' Kirsty smiled and raised her eyebrows.

'I guess it does. Are you upset about it?' Allegra asked.

'No, not really. I just think it's weird to imagine my mother having sex!' Kirsty put her fingers in her mouth and pretended to vomit.

'Well, you and me both, because I hate to think about my daughter having sex, as well! Let's both not dwell on it.' Allegra offered a grin that was more like a grimace.

Harry seemed calmer the following morning and Allegra didn't raise the subject of his father again. Whilst he tried to slip out without giving her a kiss goodbye, she forced the issue with a hug at the front door.

Saul Cohen had advised her to put as little as possible into writing or e-mailing Hugo; anything that may have been written in the heat of an emotional moment could be misconstrued and twisted by a skilful lawyer somewhere in the future. So, after a strong coffee and a clear head, she carefully constructed an e-mail to Hugo.

Dear Hugo,

Harry tells me you are moving apartments soon and that is when he will officially move in with you. But I would be grateful in the meantime if he could stay with you for a week while I am away. My mother has been ill, so it would be less of a strain on her to have only Kirsty to look after. Also, as Harry seems to be relating to you so well, I believe it would be better for him to be around his dad. I intend to fly out next Wednesday.

Many thanks,
Allegra

She inhaled before she hit the send button. Then she spotted a new e-mail from Mr Tipple.

Allegra,

I did a bit of digging with my contact in Florence who works at the L'Archivio di Stato, which is where your Signora Katarina found her information. He recommends you call in to see the records for yourself when you are there, just to confirm the name and perhaps get a closer look at the signature on the sales record. My contact will be very happy to meet with you.

243

Allegra decided she would re-read Cosima's diary, this time searching specifically for any clues that might give more information about Alessandro's disappearance. As she went along, she wrote down a list of key points that she considered could be of relevance. It was a laborious process. She was still reading it two days later, considering each paragraph carefully.

Twenty-four hours had passed and Allegra hadn't had a reply from Hugo, so that evening she broached the subject with Harry.

'Has your father agreed that you can stay?'

'Oh. Yes. He's picking me up on Thursday morning before work. He said to make sure you had all my stuff ready as he doesn't want to be hanging around.'

Allegra was fuming at Hugo for not replying directly, but she paused and thought better of admonishing Harry for not volunteering the information. She had her answer; she now just had to learn to accept the limitations of any communication with her ex-husband.

Forty-Two

On the evening before Allegra left, her mother arrived with a large case and moved into the downstairs spare bedroom.

'It's a little on the small side for a woman of my standing. However, in your absence, I shall avail myself of the sanctuary that is your bathroom!' Maria said with a laugh. She kissed Allegra then excused herself, heading for bed.

Amidst Allegra's chaotic packing, Kirsty appeared at her bedroom door in shorty pyjamas printed with neon pink sheep.

'Come in,' Allegra beckoned and Kirsty flopped down on the super king-sized bed.

'Mum, I don't want you to dwell on this, but I thought I should tell you.' Kirsty hesitated.

'Tell me what? Out with it.' Allegra stopped her packing and hopped on the bed beside her daughter.

'Well, I overheard Harry yaking to that friend Sam he had over yesterday. He was saying he wanted to stay with Dad as he figured he'd get more money for things and that Dad isn't as strict as you. But he also said that Dad and Brooklyn fight a lot, which pisses him off. So, when Sam left, I pulled Harry up on it, and he said that during a really bad row Brooklyn said, "You don't really love me, you only agreed to everything I want because your wife doesn't want you back and you're scared of being on your own".' Kirsty stretched out on the bed and let out a sigh.

'Oh dear. No wonder Harry doesn't like Massimo. But Hugo and Brooklyn are not my problem anymore...' She pulled her daughter in for a hug.

'I don't want you to go back to Dad, but some days it all makes me feel a bit sad. It's such a mess,' Kirsty said as she cuddled back into her mother.

After Kirsty had returned to her own room, Allegra flickered with guilt. Once she had completed packing, she ran her bath, put Mozart's Fifth in the CD player and immersed herself in the hot, fragrant water, her thoughts veering between Massimo and *Castello di Sammezzano*. By the time she was out of the bath and dry, her guilt had floated away with the steam.

When Allegra arrived downstairs with her suitcase the following morning, Maria was already in the kitchen. Kirsty and Harry appeared ten minutes later; Kirsty was in her usual rush but gave her mum a big hug.

'Don't worry, I'll take responsibility for Gran!' she said as she winked at her grandmother.

Just after Kirsty left there was a knock at the door.

'That'll be Dad!' Harry gave his mother a quick kiss and ran to the door. He appeared back in the kitchen with Hugo.

'Can I please have a word, Allegra?' Hugo asked.

'Yes, of course.'

'Not with an audience – in the living room. I don't think our son and your mother need to hear what I have to tell you.' He glared at Maria.

He closed the living room door and stood facing Allegra.

'I've received the proposal from your solicitor – it's a joke! I know for a fact you inherited from your grandfather and, from what I hear, the old girl has cancer. You'll get her house when she goes, so why go for everything of mine?'

Allegra was gobsmacked, but she stood her ground.

'Not that I have to defend myself, but for your information, I inherited a small amount from my grandpapa, and my mother is not dying! And *you* have a responsibility to your children.' She steadied her shaking hands.

'Also, it has come to my attention that you are shagging the Italian. I've done some research on him and he's not who you think he is. He may call himself Massimo Rossi, however when he was on the force here in the UK, he was Massimo Ross. And you – for someone who's always been anti-war and anti-guns – well, that's a joke too! This Massimo murdered a man! How do you feel about that? Shagging a murderer and exposing my children to a criminal like that!' He spat the words at her.

Allegra was stunned.

'You are a liar!' She opened the door. 'Just get out of my home,' she said loud enough for only Hugo to hear before she walked back to the kitchen. She forced a smile then kissed her son.

'You'll text or e-mail if you need me, won't you?' she said as Harry walked out to the car with his father.

'What was that all about?' Maria asked.

'Just Hugo being the arsehole we both know he is,' Allegra replied.

'Ah. Well you have more important things to think about now. Good luck with the search. My grandmama's diary has stirred so many emotions in me. Now I see so much of my papa's life through fresh eyes. I wish I had listened to him more. We could have done this for him when he was alive…' Maria shrugged and opened her hands, in true Italian style. 'One day, I will just be a memory, and I pray to God you and Kirsty keep my spirit alive the way we are doing now with my papa.' The sound of a horn disturbed them.

'That will be my cab, Mum. I love you, take care, and I'll e-mail you as soon as I arrive.' Allegra hugged her mother then wheeled her case to the front door.

Whilst preoccupied by her mother's newfound insights, it was the word 'murderer' that kept spinning around in her brain. *Massimo is a common Italian name, Hugo will have it wrong*, Allegra thought as the taxi made its way to Victoria Station. Once she was on the Gatwick Express, she tried to google Massimo Ross but she had no signal as the train ducked in and out of tunnels and valleys.

This was the first time she had taken a checked-in case with her and she had not banked on the massive queue at the easyJet counter. It took her twenty minutes of queuing followed by another twenty minutes at security. She had planned to buy *Signor* Bazia a thank-you gift at the Duty Free, so she rushed into the slick, well-lit store. There she was confronted by a stunning woman dressed in black and white.

'ZV2 refreshes and rejuvenates the skin for men, one product for day and one for night,' she relayed her obviously rehearsed script. Allegra was in a rush as the gate had already been called so she grabbed the ZV2 bottles from the stand next to the promo woman and quickly paid for them. She was last to board the flight.

Once the plane had taken off and they announced that devices could be turned back on, Allegra attempted to access Google again. She could not get Hugo's words about Massimo out of her mind. But the Internet required all sorts of sign-ups and fees. She would just have to wait till they landed and ask Massimo in person.

But there was no sign of Massimo when she stepped into the arrivals hall. A tall man in a peaked hat holding a sign with 'Allegra O'Brien' written on it caught her attention.

'*Signora* O'Brien? Massimo asked me to collect you. He is so very sorry; he has had to go to Rome on important *polizia* work and instructed me to take you to his apartment. He will phone you this evening.' The tall man spoke in English with a strong Italian accent.

Her heart sank an inch or two as she attempted to get her head around the situation. She had been so looking forward to seeing her lover, to being enveloped in his arms and made to feel special. Her thoughts were flooded with doubt.

She followed the chauffeur outside the airport to a late-model sleek, black Mercedes. He put on his aviator sunglasses and offered no more conversation as he skilfully manoeuvred the large car through the busy Florentine lunchtime traffic.

Allegra's mood lifted a little as she looked out the window at the familiar monuments, the busy piazzas and the well-dressed Italians enjoying their lunch. If she was reasonable, Massimo had to work, she could accept that. And he had warned her... She just needed to 'get a grip'. She smiled to herself, remembering how he sounded when he'd first borrowed that expression from her.

But what if any of what Hugo had said was true? Could she accept that?

The driver carried her case up to Massimo's apartment, handed her the keys and nodded goodbye. She felt strange being in his apartment alone. She caught a subtle whiff of his fragrance, a mixture of Hugo Boss and something more personal. After she put her case in his bedroom, she made her way to the kitchen to see if she could operate the coffee machine. The aroma of fresh basil enveloped the small space; there was a prolific pot of the herb sitting next to a bowl of deep red tomatoes on the bench. A folded piece of paper leant against it with *'Tesoro'* written in capitals on the front.

Tesoro, my dearest Allegra,

I feel so bad. I tried to ring you this morning, but you must have been on the plane by then. An emergency situation has arisen with the case I am working on, and I have had to go to Rome immediately. I am so sorry. I trust the car company collected you OK? I bought you some wonderful mozzarella cheese for lunch (it is in the fridge), to have with the best Italian tomatoes in the world. Rip up lots of the fresh basil and throw that on the tomatoes before you drizzle it all with my best olive oil. I won't be able to speak to you till later this evening. My home is your home.

All my love,
Massimo xxx

Allegra smiled and picked a leaf of the basil. She rubbed it in her hand, enjoying the fresh aroma and savouring Massimo's words. After she had mastered the coffee machine, as instructed, she enjoyed the tomato and mozzarella salad.

Next, she made some space in Massimo's wardrobe and hung up her clothes. She took her laptop out of her case, turned it on and managed to find the code for the Wi-Fi on the wall by Massimo's desk.

Sitting at his desk, she typed 'Massimo Ross UK police force' in the search box. After trawling a couple of pages, she spotted an article from the *News of the World* newspaper.

An officer with the Metropolitan Police today shot a man dead, supposedly in the line of duty. It was during a planned raid of the victim's home. The police spokesperson said due to the nature of the raid, under the new terrorism laws, there would be no further comment on either the shooter or the victim until the police had conducted an inquiry. The officer is believed to be a Massimo Ross.

There was nothing else Allegra could find under that name, but the date was right – 1995 was when Massimo had said he was in the force in the UK. She found similar articles in the *Times* and the *Mail*, but none mentioned the name Massimo Ross.

Sitting at his desk was a bit too tempting; she hesitated and then opened one of the drawers. It contained only a file with his utility bills, and there was nothing of note in any of the open drawers. The framed certificates were nowhere to be seen.

I'll just have to do the right thing, and ask him when we speak.

It was early evening and Allegra felt hungry. Recalling the route Massimo had taken to the special pizza restaurant, she walked the short distance and ordered a take-out pizza. On her return journey, the air was filled with the sounds of a city at dusk as she gazed along the Arno River with the Ponto Vecchio providing its famous backdrop.

It was 9:00 p.m. before her mobile buzzed with a text: *I will call you on the landline. Love M x.* She heard the apartment phone ring.

Massimo explained he was working on a case that he couldn't speak about. He told her how sorry he was and how he would do all he could to be back in Florence by Friday.

'*Tesoro*, you are very quiet. Please don't be angry with me, this is the nature of my job,' Massimo explained.

'It's not that. I understand about your job; it's just that I wanted to ask you something and it's tricky over the phone.'

'Ask me what?'

'Did you use the name "Massimo Ross" when you were on the force in the UK?'

There was a long pause.

'Allegra, this is a conversation we should be having face-to-face, for personal reasons,' Massimo finally replied.

At the same time, her mobile buzzed with another text. *I'm not sure how secure the phones are. I will tell you all when I see you. M x*

They continued their conversation in a somewhat contrived manner. Allegra didn't know what to say and for the first time felt the threat of danger. Why would his phones not be secure? Finally, he instructed her on the best route to get to her meeting at the offices where the police archives were located, before saying goodbye.

She felt strange slipping into Massimo's bed on her own and left the shutters open, allowing the moon to cast a golden ray of light into the room. It was a struggle to get off to sleep as she began to consider a thread of deceit. Was anything Massimo was involved in of any risk to her?

Forty-Three

When Allegra lazily awoke the next morning, the sun had replaced the moon streaming through the window. She took it as an optimistic sign for a fruitful day.

She suddenly realised when she saw Massimo's bedside clock that she had forgotten to put her watch forward, so she had only an hour to get dressed and reach the archive building. She had the Google Maps app on her phone programmed to take her from the apartment to the meeting place, but felt a little cheated at having to concentrate on where she was going rather than taking in the ambience of a Florence morning.

Signor Bazia was waiting outside the majestic government building with his small, worn-looking leather satchel slung over his shoulder. Once the greetings were over, the *signore* got right down to business.

'I've been through the list you sent and had a conversation with the man in charge of the archives, so I am hopeful he will have what we want ready for us,' *Signor* Bazia informed her as they walked through the large glass doors into the eighteenth-century building. The office they were looking for was located on the fourth floor. Allegra noted the musty smell of leather-bound books as they were ushered into a room with a large wooden table surrounded by floor-to-ceiling shelves.

Their contact seemed very pleasant. When he showed them in, he smiled at Allegra and spoke in rapid Italian; she just about caught Massimo's name. Then he pointed to four large books he had laid at the end of the table, with yellow bookmarks poking out from several of the pages.

'He said that you must be someone special. In addition to my phone call, an important police officer, Massimo Rossi, also called and requested you be given the highest courtesy and assistance,' *Signor* Bazia translated for Allegra once the man had left.

Allegra blushed.

The first bookmark in the initial book was dated 1914. As *Signor* Bazia translated, it revealed that there were five unidentified bodies found in the surrounding area around that time. Only one was close to Leccio, and there was a comment that the body was of a man over the age of sixty. The records had only identifying features to rely on, in the absence of later technological breakthroughs such as DNA testing. Another was described as being bald, the third had a missing thumb and the fourth was recorded as having no front upper teeth. The fifth body was that of a woman, and the comment beside her was 'prostitute'. As *Signor* Bazia translated, he looked across at Allegra.

'I guess they wouldn't have bothered trying to locate her relations back then.'

Allegra made notes of what she would have to check out. Was Alessandro bald? Did he have a missing thumb or front top teeth?

The next book of records *Signor* Bazia had requested concerned any known art thieves or art thefts around the same period. There was quite a lot of information on an art forger who had been caught, but they both agreed none of that seemed relevant.

It was midday by the time they had read all the pertinent files, so Allegra invited *Signor* Bazia to join her for lunch.

'I am not sure any of that will move your investigation forward,' he said as they waited for their lasagne.

'I daresay you're right... I need to go through the diary again and see if Cosima made any reference to Alessandro's distinguishing features. I'll also call my mother; she may know more than I do.'

'Tomorrow morning I will need to meet with you a little earlier, if that is OK? I need to be at my work in the afternoon. When I phoned the curator who oversees the records of historic art sales at the L'Archivio di Stato, he said he knew who you were as he had a colleague at the Victoria and Albert Museum in London.' Allegra smiled. 'You have many influential admirers, *Signora* Allegra!'

Allegra took her time returning to the apartment; she had a whole day and a half before she would see Massimo. She wandered into a couple of boutiques but wasn't in the mood to shop.

The first thing she did when she arrived back at the apartment was call her mother.

'No, love, I can't say I ever heard anything about grandpapa's teeth. As you know, Papa had a great head of hair right up till he died aged at almost one hundred, so I somehow doubt Alessandro was bald. Perhaps we should locate a photograph of Bandino and establish whether he was bald, since baldness is usually hereditary?' Maria suggested.

'Do you have any photos that Grandpapa brought with him from Italy?' Allegra asked.

'I think there is a box of things up in the attic that he brought back from his mamma's house when she died. I'll see if Kirsty will go over with me this evening; she can get up there and have a forage around.'

Next, Allegra googled Bandino Panciatichi. There were many men with that name from the fourteenth century onwards, probably all associated with her Panciatichi family, but none of them in the nineteenth century.

She took her copy of the translated diary out of her case, along with a yellow marker pen, and began rereading it to see what mention there was of her great-grandpapa's physical appearance.

Her concentration was broken by the buzz of a text coming through from Massimo. Glancing at her watch, she was surprised to see it was 6:30 p.m. already; she had been reading for four hours.

Involved in police activity, impossible to call tonight. Will see you tomorrow evening. Love M x

The plot thickens, Allegra mused as she replied to the text with a kiss. She decided she was still full from lunch so would just finish off the rest of the mozzarella and tomatoes for her supper.

The next morning, she awoke early and hungry, so she allowed time on route to the *L'Archivio di Stato* to have breakfast. She took an outdoor seat at a small *trattoria* and wolfed down a ham panino and large cappuccino. She found a taxi stand nearby and during the relaxed journey took in some of the wonderful Florentine sights.

Allegra had come to understand that *Signor* Bazia was exacting and punctual. That morning was no exception and at ten minutes to nine, he was waiting on the steps at the entrance to the modern research buildings. The *L'Archivio di Stato* was reputed to house over seventy kilometres of shelved documents. After asking for directions a couple of times, they managed to arrive on time at the Historic Art Transactions office.

Allegra smiled as they introduced themselves to *Signor* Sarno, Mr Tipple's contact. He wore very conservative olive-green corduroy trousers and a lighter green shirt. A small set of dark-framed Harry Potter glasses sat low on his nose, and he looked over them as he offered his hand to Allegra. His hair was parted on the side and appeared glued to his head. As he led them through to the records room, the way he walked with such a distinct, affected tone, fascinated her.

With expert precision, *Signor* Sarno pulled on a pair of pristine white silk gloves. Then he opened the book that he had carefully placed on the large desk in the side room. It was similar to the books they had viewed the previous day, double A4 size. However, its heavy leather still had a trace of a gold leaf decoration; art records were a cut above criminal records in Italy. *Signor* Sarno judiciously turned to the page where he had placed a soft leather bookmark.

'This is the book of records from the art auction house that *Signor* Tipple told you about,' *Signor* Sarno began as he beckoned for Allegra to join him, offering her the horn-handled magnifying glass.

The page was divided into five columns: date, name of painting, painter, price and the last was for the name and signature of the person who paid for and took possession of the painting. The record the *signore* showed her was from 1910, for a painting called *Madonna Santa Maria*, painted by Raphael and sold for 30000 lire. The name Ferdinando Panciatichi was written neatly, but in a completely different hand there was a scrawled signature. Allegra put the magnifying glass close to the page and leant back until the signature appeared clearer. She asked *Signor* Bazia to look with her.

'It does look like "A Mancini". If only we had some of his handwriting to compare,' Signor Bazia commented as he peered through the glass.

The second painting was just entitled 'portrait' and was also by Raphael; it had sold for approximately the same amount on the same day with the same name, as well as the rough signature.

'We would value your opinion, *Signor* Sarno,' Allegra stated as she placed the magnifying glass down on the table.

'Well, I do not believe either painting was completed by Raphael Sanzio. He may have started them, but one of his students probably completed them. Apparently the signature on the paintings was not quite right. Nevertheless, even though Raphael may have only had a hand in these works, they are still very valuable.'

'Would you permit me to take a photo of what I think might be my great-grandpapa's signature?' Allegra asked as she nervously tugged a strand of her hair.

'Normally I would not, but as you are *Signor* Tipple's valued friend, I will allow it. But please let me take the photo.' As Allegra reached into her bag for her camera, *Signor* Sarno ceremonially removed his gloves and placed them in their purpose-made box.

After a protracted display of gratitude to their host, Allegra, and *Signor* Bazia made their way outside and sat down on a street bench.

'My goodness! He was something, wasn't he? So, what do you think? Is it Alessandro's signature?' Allegra asked her companion.

'I do believe the signature read "Mancini", but does this prove anything? Where are the paintings now? Did Alessandro steal them? Were they stolen from him and he was harmed? I am not sure what to make of it, Allegra.' *Signor* Bazia shrugged.

'Well, I was wondering if before I leave, you could perhaps arrange another visit to the castle for me?' She offered a shy smile.

'I'm not sure I can... I've been informed that some of the directors of the hotel company who officially own it are due to visit, and I don't want to be caught taking unofficial guided tours.' He shook his head. 'But I will call you tomorrow and let you know if I can sneak in one more for you.'

Allegra smiled broadly. 'Thank you.'

She felt she might have just sealed the deal as she proffered him a goodbye hug. *Signor* Bazia beamed and walked off towards his car, swinging his little leather bag.

As she opened the door to the apartment, her phone buzzed with a text. *Where are you? Open your e-mails! Love Mum x*

Allegra hurriedly opened her laptop and scrolled through to her mother's email.

Hi, Kirsty had fun up in the attic, apart from a rodent or two that crossed her path! She wrestled the box down, which was bigger than we thought and yes, there were photos in there that I had never seen. Kirsty used her superior computer skills to scan and enlarge the small black and white photos we thought might be relevant. Good luck. Love Mum x

Allegra texted back immediately. *Huge thanks to both of you. I'm just back from my archives visit. I'll open and print them now. Love A x*

Allegra took her laptop into Massimo's office, plugged it in to the printer and opened the attachment. She was flooded with emotion as the first photo appeared on her screen. It was Cosima and Alessandro standing side by side with the toddler Luigi at their feet; he looked about two, so it must have been taken not long before Alessandro went missing. Cosima's hair was tied back, but Allegra could see she had dark curls like her own. She had a distinct face with a strong Italian nose and seemed a little nervous of whoever was behind the camera. Little Luigi looked as if he had just been thrust into a clean romper suit especially for the photo, and Alessandro was smiling broadly with a full set of white teeth and a head of thick, greying hair. As she looked more closely at him, she could see in the hand dropped at his side he was holding a peacock feather. At the bottom of the photo, Kirsty had typed, *1915 was written on the back of the photo, Kx*

Forty-Four

Allegra condensed her investigation hit list down to fifteen points; she hoped at least one of them would bear fruit. She trusted *Signor* Bazia would break the rules for her one more time, as she really needed to visit the castle. Now late afternoon, she put her folder away and went out in search of some fresh food to prepare an impressive meal for Massimo's arrival home.

She had bathed and spent time getting dressed into her fitted jeans and a crisp white, V-neck T-shirt when she heard the heavy key unlocking the door.

'Oh, Allegra, I'm so pleased to see you!' Massimo dropped his bag, opened his arms, and enveloped her. Hugging her tight, he then gently kissed her lips. 'You smell beautiful, and so does something from the kitchen. Let me have a quick shower then you must tell me all.'

Allegra had made one of her specialties, a traditional English cottage pie using Italian veal mince, and a fresh salad presented on a flat white platter. She had opened a bottle of Chianti to let it breathe, and set the table with all Massimo's best silverware.

'This is wonderful. Now, tell me about your research,' Massimo said, kissing her again.

Allegra updated him with all the latest news, and showed him the photo of her great-grandparents before sitting down to eat.

'So, it's your turn now. I have to say, I lost some sleep over the "secure line" comment and the covert text.'

Allegra noticed that for the first time since she'd met him, Massimo was showing signs of discomfort. He put a forkful of pie into his mouth and murmured, 'Oh, this is delicious!'

'Massimo! Tell me what's going on.' Allegra placed her hands on the table.

Massimo put down his knife and fork, took a sip of his wine, and leant back in his chair. 'There is something in my past I would have preferred you not to know. It is something I wish I never had to talk about again.' He took another sip of wine.

'I thought this was an adult relationship?' Allegra said.

'What I am going to tell you is highly confidential, so it's in your best interests that I leave out some of the details. When I joined the force in London, I was still only a lad. I wanted to be just like the cops in the movies; I had a fantasy about guns and catching bad men. I just happened to be an excellent shot so quite quickly I was picked as a marksman for the special armed-defenders squad. Terrorism was beginning to rear its ugly head back then in the UK, and I was attached to a unit that was investigating a terrorist ring in South London. We had intelligence that they were going to attack a government building and were armed, so we were ordered to shoot to kill if necessary. We raided a South London property and there were several men with weapons. I did as I was ordered – and shot to kill. The perpetrator had a gun pointed at another policeman, so I did not hesitate.' He sighed.

Allegra was silent.

'For security reasons we could only give the public and the press a little information. However, they were unable to stop the *News of the World* reporting my name – that is, the anglicised name I used in the UK.' He took another sip of wine. 'Then there was the usual fallout; accusations that it was a racist killing and that the perpetrator's gun wasn't loaded.'

'And the scars on your back?' Allegra asked.

'A few months after the court case, I was attacked late one night in the street by what I can only assume were radicals from the same group. They knifed me and left me for dead, but as you can see, it didn't work!' He smiled tightly. 'I suffered what they call post-traumatic stress, so I decided that was the end of the UK for me. I took a demotion and managed to get myself a position here in Florence. Tell me, how did you find out?' Massimo asked.

'Hugo told me. Harry has been playing us against each other. He is hurt, and he's a teenager, so I must ride along with his behaviour till he grows up a bit more. But Harry must have given Hugo details about you and somehow, he found out the rest... He took great enjoyment telling me I was dating a murderer.' As Allegra got up to put clean plates on the table for the salad, she stiffened. 'I worry about you carrying a gun. What's this current case all about? Does it involve you needing a weapon?' she asked as she handed him the plate.

'I'm sorry, Allegra, but I am not allowed to speak about it. I can tell you it's related to a terror group and I'm as far away as I can be from the live action. I've been seconded for my UK experience and because of my fluent English, but I'm working primarily on intelligence gathering.'

'And the phone tapping?' Allegra asked.

'We are tapping their phones. And they have the means to do the same. Maybe I am being paranoid but in this highly technical age, better safe than sorry.'

Once they had finished their salad, Massimo stood up and took her hand.

'Come with me, my beautiful Allegra. I would prefer my dessert in my bed.'

Allegra was hesitant, struggling to come to terms with what he had just told her. But lust swiftly overcame her. Their first coupling was urgent, but after cuddles and laughter, Massimo skilfully seduced her again, this time with prolonged lovemaking.

As they lay on the bed, Massimo returned the conversation to her quest. 'I am worried you will be disappointed, Allegra. These "cold" cases, as they are known in the force, are very difficult to solve, especially after a hundred years. But on the positive side, you have found out some great facts, one being that you are a direct descendant of the colourful Marchese Ferdinando Panciatichi.'

'Well, an illegitimate descendant!'

'Still, it explains a lot. If you can discover what happened to those two missing paintings, you may be a step closer. Once my own case is over, I will schmooze a couple of detectives I know in art fraud and see if they can be of any help.'

They were awakened at 8:00 a.m. by Massimo's mobile phone ringing from somewhere in the apartment. He stumbled out of bed and grabbed it just in time.

'Shit!' he said as he returned to the bedroom.

Allegra sat up. 'What's wrong?'

'Something has come up and I have to be back at the station for the rest of the day. Look, why don't you go to *Villa al Vento* for the night? I'll join you tomorrow evening as I know for certain they have another translator signed on for then, and we can stay there till you leave on Tuesday. I'm sure the tame *Signor* Bazia will manage to sneak you in one more time to your Peacock Room.' Massimo attempted to sound upbeat.

'I guess so.' Allegra sighed.

'Oh, *Tesoro*, please don't look at me like that! This situation is totally out of my control.'

'I'm trying to be understanding, but I worry about you getting hurt. This mysterious case sounds so dangerous,' Allegra said.

'I'm going to make us some coffee and give Barbara at *Villa al Vento* a call before I go. We can talk this through tomorrow.'

When Massimo returned with the coffee, Allegra had dressed and was brushing her hair.

'Please, Allegra, you knew I was a policeman from the first time I met you. I haven't been untruthful,' he said as he sat beside her on the bed with his arm around her shoulders. He gently kissed her cheek.

Once he had gone, Allegra felt stupid. What if something happened to him and she had given him the cold shoulder? She was determined to make it up to him.

Barbara said she had no other guests that weekend so would welcome Allegra's company. Massimo had called a taxi service before he left which gave a reasonable quote to take Allegra the thirty-five minute drive out of Florence. She gathered up her research papers, her laptop, the present for *Signor* Bazia, and an overnight bag. She hadn't as yet heard from him but decided she wouldn't hassle him till after she arrived in Reggello.

Forty-Five

A llegra smiled at the macho taxi driver who remained firmly in his seat with the door closed when he spotted the two large wolfhounds running towards the car. They instantly recognised Allegra and with their tails wagging madly, brushed up against her as she took her bag from the trunk of the car. Barbara was pleased to see her and once Allegra had taken her bag up to her room, they sat together in the garden with a pot of fresh mint tea.

Barbara's English seemed much better now that she was on her own with no one to translate. Allegra shared the photo of her great-grandparents and explained that she hoped for another visit to the castle.

Back in her room, Allegra went through her list. She couldn't see any more clues and the reading was becoming frustrating. Massimo was probably right; it was all such a long time ago, perhaps she would have to give up and just be happy that she had uncovered her own family history. And yet she could almost sense her grandpapa sitting close by, with his mamma Cosima, urging her onwards.

She called Massimo, but there was no answer and she didn't think she should leave a message. It didn't help that Signor *Bazia* hadn't called. Finally, she crumbled and dialled his number on her mobile phone.

'*Signora* Allegra, I am so sorry I haven't called you but I am still waiting to hear from the hotel director. As much as I want to help you, it would not be appropriate for me to take you up to the castle until I know for certain he won't arrive without warning. Let's give it another day or two.' He was clearly uncomfortable. Allegra had no choice but to agree.

She had accepted Barbara's invitation to join her for dinner as they were the only two people in the villa. After a couple of glasses of wine, Allegra shared her frustrations with her dinner companion.

'I don't speak English very well, but I feel your pain. I am the same, I believe we must go where the feelings deep inside take us. The *Castello di Sammezzano* is your birth right, the Marchese and Alessandro, your blood family. My great-grandparents also worked at the castle; my great-grandmama worked in the kitchen and her husband in the garden. The castle provided for so many families here in these two villages. It is part of who we are. The rich hotel men may own it now, but they don't care about its heritage. It's all about money to them.' Even though Barbara's English was stilted, her passion was obvious.

'Barbara, I have been so tied up with my own investigations, I never even considered that your family would be connected to the castle too. I'm so sorry.'

'No need for sorry, it takes time for different people to trust one other. Now you are here in my villa alone, I believe it is meant to be.' Barbara raised her wine glass in a salute and smiled.

Allegra tossed in her bed all night. Eventually she was awakened by the same dream she'd had when her grandpapa died: a magnificent male peacock walking up the track beside the castle, its tail flourished. But the peacock's presence seemed to symbolise something more than pride – it almost felt like a challenge.

Since it was 5.00 a.m. she gave up trying to get back to sleep and instead turned the TV on to CNN. A breaking news item flashed on the screen. In a city called Christchurch in New Zealand there had just been a massive earthquake, 7.5 on the Richter scale. They were showing footage of a collapsed stone cathedral and people running from crumbling buildings; it was horrific. She thought about Zara, one of Kirsty's school friends, who had just left for New Zealand to do her gap year. Thank God Kirsty hadn't gone.

Allegra had no knowledge of earthquakes in New Zealand, but somehow she didn't expect to see devastation on that magnitude in a country that so closely resembled England. The picture froze on the screen and formed the background as a reporter with a distinctly Kiwi accent, spoke to the camera.

Allegra stopped listening to the reporter; she couldn't take her eyes off the photo being projected behind her. It was of wrought-iron spiked railings tipped on their sides next to a pile of rubble and dust by the collapsed church. She had a sudden flash of revelation. An earthquake destroyed instantly. Why hadn't she thought of it before?

She tiptoed downstairs to quietly make a cup of coffee in Barbara's kitchen. She was just pouring the milk when Barbara appeared at the door in her dressing gown.

'Oh, I'm sorry if I woke you,' Allegra said.

'No, I couldn't sleep. I was coming for coffee, too,' Barbara replied, and Allegra poured her a cup from the pot.

Allegra told her about the earthquake. 'Cosima mentioned an earthquake in her diary around the time Alessandro disappeared. She didn't mention any damage in her house, but the grounds at the castle may have been disturbed.' Allegra let out a small sigh.

After a protracted pause, Barbara looked directly at her across the table.

'Allegra, there are often small earthquakes in this area, but I've never heard about a big one in the past. Look, I have an idea. Perhaps you should take my hounds for a long walk this morning. It is early and a Sunday, so not many people will be around. If your walk should take you near the discount shopping mall and one of the dogs gets off his lead in the direction of the castle, you will have to chase him.' She smiled.

Allegra responded with a wink. 'Aha. I understand. How long will it take me to walk to the shopping mall?'

'Well, for me, about thirty minutes to the mall, and then you know how long after that.'

Allegra rushed upstairs. She put her camera and her phone in her small shoulder bag, pulled on her trainers, and when she appeared at the villa entrance, Barbara was waiting. She had already attached the leads to the two hounds. They were wagging their tails like crazy, and Barbara was attempting to calm them down.

'They will behave once you get walking as they are used to the leads. I always walk them together.' She handed Allegra two bottles of water which she just managed to fit in her bag.

'The mall doesn't open till 10:00 a.m. on a Sunday. It's only 7:00 a.m. now, so there will be very little traffic on the road, but the dogs will lead you along the track that goes most of the way.'

It took Allegra the first kilometre before she felt she had the hounds under control; they were following the well-trodden pathway that ran along the side of the fields beside the road. It was a fresh, crisp morning, and her thoughts were interspersed with the vision of the peacock from her dream and the CNN piece on the New Zealand earthquake.

As she strode out close to the road, her curly hair wafted around her face with the slight breeze. She was unable to push it back as she needed both hands on the dog leads. She smiled as a man in a white van tooted and waved at her. The dogs did look magnificent as they trotted on either side of her. She could understand why wolfhounds had been the pets of kings; they moved with all the grace and pomp of aristocrats. It was like they belonged to the castle already.

Forty-Six

As she rounded the final corner, the ugly but familiar mall was directly in her sight line. It stood in brutal contrast to its surroundings, with no cars, buses or tourists to give it credence. It was as she first viewed it, an eyesore and a stain of commercialism on an historic landscape.

The hounds sensed her change of mood and stepped up their pace. When she arrived at the gate to the path up to *Castello di Sammezzano* she stopped and, after having a few gulps of water herself, poured some into her hand for both dogs.

Allegra looked at her watch. It was 7:40 a.m. and there was no sign of life anywhere, just the distant pealing of bells.

Picking up the dog leads, she made her way up the path beneath the tall sequoia trees. The hounds slowed down as the path grew steeper. Their confidence waned slightly in the unfamiliar territory; the leads loosened as they both walked closer to her side. The sun had only just reached this side of the hill, and the overgrown bushes created shadows between the trees.

As she passed the gatehouse, the hounds stopped and had a good sniff around. 'I bet you can smell that vagrant, can't you?' She gave them both an encouraging pat.

Allegra stood at the end of the grassy area in front of the castle, marvelling at how plain the exterior architecture appeared in comparison to the beauty and magic that lay inside. Knowing the front door was locked, she went around to the door she had first entered in her drugged-out state. She pushed hard. The door opened. Both dogs whimpered and sat down.

'Come on, don't be scared. There's nothing in here except perhaps one poor homeless man and he is more afraid of us than we are of him.' She yanked their leads and the dogs reluctantly followed her up the stairs.

The sun had begun to colour the castle as Allegra walked up the second flight of stairs and made her way to the Peacock Room. Both dogs stopped in their tracks and whimpered, refusing to budge. 'Don't be silly. It only looks strange because the sunlight is hitting all those coloured glass panels,' she said as she tugged their leads.

Allegra stood admiring the room that had been so important to her family. The dogs straining on the leads finally broke her from her reverie. She'd better get them back outside.

They quickly descended the stairs and, once on the ground floor, made their way through the multiple sets of doors and rooms to the side exit on the opposite side of the building. As she pushed the final door, she caught a glimpse of the homeless man up ahead. He looked strange, like he was disappearing into the light. A haze hovered around him. The hounds pulled on their leads and without thinking, she let go. They galloped forward up the path.

Shit, I shouldn't have done that! He'll be terrified.

When she caught up with them at the wrought-iron fence, both dogs were sitting on the small raised mound of mossy ground panting, with their tongues hanging out. Allegra was relieved the man was not in sight. She trailed her hand over the heavy wrought-iron spikes and sat down beside the hounds to have another drink.

The moss felt very soft beneath her; when she pushed her hand down, her fingers slid easily into the loose earth. She pushed again and scooped up a handful of slack, damp earth. The dogs' ears perked up. One of them began digging furiously, then the other one joined in. 'Oh, you two, this game could get us into trouble!' she said, laughing at the hounds' enthusiastic antics. Then her hand hit something. Assuming it was a rock, she pushed in further to pick it up. She could see it was the corner of a large, square stone – like a building block. Allegra shushed the dogs and they sat back down. She carefully knocked all the soil off the block, and then brushed it with a tissue.

It was embedded in the ground at a precarious angle, probably for the same reason the wrought-iron spiked fence was on its side. The structure must have been disturbed in an earthquake.

Allegra was compelled to dig deeper, but she needed a shovel or something similar to help her. She walked briskly back towards the rear of the castle where she had noticed some old sheds. The dogs followed her and were sniffing around one of the shed doors. She pushed the door and was greeted with the stench of what appeared to be the remains of a dead rat. However, beyond its nauseating corpse was an old pickaxe. She shooed the dogs away from the corpse, reached over and collected the pickaxe. She made her way back to the mound with the heavy tool slung over her shoulder.

The hounds moved away and settled in the shade of a tree as Allegra swung at the ground and began to break up the moss and loose earth beneath. After she had shifted a large amount of earth, she was forced to stop for a breather and heard her phone ringing from her handbag.

'Allegra! Where the bloody hell are you? I'm at *Villa al Vento* and Barbara tells me you left to walk the dogs nearly two hours ago,' Massimo bristled.

'Calm down, I'm OK. I'm up at the castle, and I think I'm on to something. I'm digging around what I think may be the ruins of a building of some sort.'

'What! Is *Signor* Bazia with you? It's private property, you can't do that.'

'No, he's not here. And for God's sake, Massimo, nobody has bothered with this part of the grounds for over a hundred years, so why would it upset anyone now? If you are coming up, borrow a shovel, and bring it with you, please.' She clicked off her phone, took a gulp of water, and returned to her labour.

Once she had broken up the earth, she used her hands and shoved away the loose soil to expose a few larger blocks. Then she heard her phone ring again.

'Massimo, stop calling me, just get up here!' she barked into the phone.

'Eh, *Signora* Allegra, this is not Massimo. It's me, *Signor* Bazia. I am calling to tell you the hotel man is now not coming, so perhaps tomorrow I can take you to the castle.'

Allegra deliberated for a moment, and then came clean. 'Look, I'm sorry but I came up here to the grounds this morning. I had an idea and now I am down the path on the far side digging, as I think there is a forgotten building of some sort here.'

'Oh, please, no. Be careful. Wait till I get there, I will come now!'

'Then bring a shovel for digging,' she said, for the second time that day, and hung up.

As she dug in to the soil like a mad woman, the sight of the old vagrant niggled at her. This time she was straight and sober but he had looked as though he was literally fading away. It struck her that perhaps something supernatural had taken place. She heard Massimo calling her name. She was stripped down to her camisole, her jeans rolled up and covered in soil when she spotted him coming along the track. The dogs were up in a flash and rushed to greet him.

'Don't worry, *Signor* Bazia is on his way as well,' Allegra said, smiling at the sight of her immaculately dressed lover holding an old weather-beaten, rusty shovel.

'I can see this is now a hands-on investigation!' Massimo laughed. He took off his jacket and shirt and kissed Allegra's dirty face.

'Please, Allegra, just stop and listen to me for a minute. Once I left you yesterday, I realised I wasn't clear in my explanation. Then I saw your missed call and no message. Allegra, I need to tell you that I am not allowed to aim a gun anymore. In the terrorism case, I only listen in on phone conversations. I do all the translations if they are speaking in English. I don't go anywhere near the action.'

'Thank you for telling me that.' She smiled.

'I had to. I care about you, and I know that means I will have to compromise on less pleasant aspects of my job.'

'I guess we will both have to compromise.'

'Good. Now, let's just hope neither of us gets arrested, as I have no excuse…'

'Well, in that case, stop talking and start digging!' Allegra pointed to the shovel.

After Massimo had been swinging his shovel for some time, Allegra took a break and watched how his body gleamed, his scars glinting like ivory in the sunlight. Then he hit something that sounded like wood. He hit the area again. 'Perhaps it's a door or a window frame?' he said as he started digging towards it.

'*Buongiorno*, here I am!' *Signor* Bazia called as he walked briskly towards them carrying a pristine new shovel. The dogs rushed up to him before Allegra could give him any warning.

'It's OK, they don't bite,' she said as he held up his arms in surrender.

Massimo stopped digging and found it difficult to suppress a smile. 'And I won't shoot you either, so you can put your arms down.'

'These dogs are giants! Also, I must say, this is not a legal situation,' *Signor* Bazia stammered, still looking warily at the hounds even though they had lost interest and resumed their positions in the shade.

'I will take full responsibility, but I am sure this is an undiscovered building belonging to the Marchese. It has something to do with the *castello*,' Allegra said.

Massimo kept digging around what they now could see was a door that appeared to be lying on its side. *Signor* Bazia eventually took off his jacket, then carefully rolled up his trousers to the knee, picked up his shiny silver shovel, and after a hesitant start, began assisting Massimo in clearing away the soil. The two men had worked up quite a sweat, so Allegra suggested a break and offered them a sip from her second water bottle.

'I think you are correct, Allegra. This building must have been destroyed in one of the earthquakes,' Massimo commented.

'It might even have been built underground – the Marchese had a lot of secrets after all,' Allegra replied.

'I remember thinking when I first saw the wrought-iron fence that it could have been the beginning of a structure the Marchese never completed. But now I can see you are probably correct. He certainly enjoyed his secret designs,' *Signor* Bazia added.

Allegra began to speak, then halted. Both men looked at her expectantly.

'What did you want to add?' Massimo said as he stroked her arm.

'You will think I am even crazier than you do already,' she replied as she tugged at a strand of her hair.

'Please *Signora*?' *Signor* Bazia asked.

'I saw the old man again; he was fuzzy all around the edges. He led me here but it was as if he was disappearing into the light, like a ghost...'

There was an expectant pause in the conversation. Eventually *Signor* Bazia broke the silence.

'It is possible. I for one believe in lost spirits.'

They continued shovelling the soil away from the door. Once it was fully exposed, they could see the large iron ring that would have been used to pull it open. Massimo bent down and lifted it. Although it was a bit stiff, the ring still had some movement. Then it slipped from his hand and banged back down against the door, making a hollow sound as it hit the wood.

'Did you hear that? I'm sure there is a space under it. Come on, let's see if we can pull it open,' Massimo said.

Signor Bazia and Massimo both pulled on the door ring together, but it barely moved.

'There's years of soil imbedded in the doorjamb. We will have to remove it first,' Allegra said as she started scraping at the packed soil around the edge of the door with a sharp branch.

'This should work better.' Massimo pulled out a Swiss Army knife from his trouser pocket and began gouging out the soil. It took him ages but once he had removed all he could, the two men pulled again at the heavy iron ring. This time, the door moved.

'Allegra, get the shovel and this time when we pull, try and wedge it in the crack we make at the side,' Massimo said.

She did as instructed then swapped places with Massimo. He levered the shovel further into the door as she and *Signor* Bazia pulled at the door ring. Once Massimo had the shovel head fully jammed in, he resumed his position next to the other two.

'On the count of three, pull with all your might. One, two, three!'

Allegra's hands were blistered from the pickaxe and hurt like hell, but she wasn't giving up. As they pulled, the door began to open, and they all stepped backwards. Allegra tripped and let go, but the men hung on and once they had it at a certain angle, managed to flick it open, before falling down too.

Allegra was already looking inside by the time the two men were back on their feet. There were wide dusty stone steps leading underground. Allegra stepped inside.

'No, stop, Allegra. It may not be safe.' Massimo put his hand firmly on her shoulder.

'I don't care. I've come this far, I'm not stopping now.'

'OK, OK, I can see there's no stopping you. I'll go first, though. You follow me.'

He moved to the front and Allegra placed her hands on his hips with *Signor* Bazia directly behind her. They descended the steps into the pitch black. A strong musty smell filled their lungs.

'Wait! I have a small pen torch in my jacket pocket,' *Signor* Bazia exclaimed, and rushed back up to retrieve it.

The small torch gave out adequate light and after going down only a few steps, they were in a room of some sort. With Allegra and Massimo standing beside him, *Signor* Bazia scanned the space with the torch. It was about six metres square and they could see in the corner that the wall had collapsed. As they moved closer in, Allegra saw what looked like the outline of several large frames stacked against the wall, the front one covered in a thick blanket of dust. She gently rubbed it with the sleeve of her shirt and began to reveal the outline of a painting. Massimo stepped in to assist with his handkerchief, while *Signor* Bazia continued to hold the torch. As the years of dust were brushed away, the *Madonna Santa Maria* came into view in all her splendour. Massimo carefully lifted it to one side; the next painting was relatively free of dust and appeared to be the partner of the first. It all tallied with what they had seen described in the register at the L'Archivio di Stato. Several other paintings were stacked behind it.

Massimo was using the light from his mobile phone to look further around the room. Allegra heard him gasp. *Signor* Bazia immediately shone the torch in the same direction towards the pile of rubble and they all approached it.

'Oh, no!' Allegra clasped her hand to her mouth.

'It's OK.' Massimo put his arm around Allegra's shoulder. There was a skull attached to a broken skeleton poking out from under the fallen rubble.

Massimo cautiously edged towards it, closely followed by the others. It was obvious the person had been crushed by the collapsed wall but the skull was still intact. Allegra pushed past and reached it first. There were remnants of rotted clothes stuck to the skeleton, and a pair of old leather boots at its base. As she bent down, Allegra caught the shimmer of something shiny against the neck. Massimo was immediately beside her, shining his mobile. As she bent down and fingered the crucifix, a current of energy shot through her body. She instantly recognised it – it was identical to her own. She turned it over and rubbed away the grime with her fingers; Massimo held the light closer so they could read the inscription. *Ti amo per sempre. Cosima.*

Allegra was overwhelmed, and tears ran down her cheeks. The two men instinctively stood back, giving her space to digest what had just been revealed. Wiping her eyes, she turned towards Massimo and saw the old man in the far corner of the room. It was the closest they'd ever been to each other, and the first time she had seen his face up close. She was transfixed by its familiarity. He appeared to smile directly at her, nodding his head before fading away into the darkness.

'Goodbye Alessandro; rest in peace with your wife and son,' she whispered as she fingered the silver cross.

Alessandro had not been unfaithful… He was not a thief, and he hadn't been murdered. She had fulfilled her promise. She had found her great-grandpapa.

Epilogue

Twelve months later

The discovery of the body of Alessandro Mancini would not have been newsworthy without the discovery of two famous paintings.

The headline in the Reggello weekly paper revealed that in fact Allegra was the illegitimate great-great-granddaughter of Marchese Ferdinando Panciatichi Ximenes D'Aragona. This had been confirmed when she had tracked down his descendants in America from her great-grandpapa Bandino, and they had happily agreed to submit a sample for DNA testing.

The CEO of the UK hotel group that owned *Castello di Sammezzano* had officially allowed the full excavation of the underground room, and Alessandro was finally laid to rest in the small crypt in the cemetery at Reggello alongside his beloved wife, Cosima. Alessandro's three-times-great-grandson Harry had commented at the funeral that it looked a bit small for two people, but his gran Maria had assured him after all those years apart, they would be very happy lying on top of each other.

The provenance of the paintings was established and the court ruled their ownership lay with the trust of the legitimate heirs of the Marchese. They were in remarkably good condition given the length of time they had been in the underground chamber, thanks to the quality of construction of the room and an ingenious natural ventilation system built into the walls – no doubt by Alessandro himself.

The hotel group had no finance available to develop *Castello di Sammezzano* and, desperate for positive publicity with the local council, they agreed to formalise *Signor* Bazia as temporary custodian. They also commissioned Allegra to compile a full photographic history of the castle over the past hundred-and-fifty years in English.

Kirsty commenced her degree in Florentine history at Cambridge University, the second year of which would be undertaken at the University of Florence. Harry looked forward to his school holidays in Florence, as he had met a hot Italian girl who was excellent on the Xbox 360 and as geeky as him. Maria visited regularly on pensioner-friendly flights from London. In addition to writing her book, the rest of Allegra's time was taken up with her doting new husband and their demanding baby son, Alessandro Luigi Rossi.

Author's note

My first experience of the Peacock Room was a hypnotic photograph posted on Facebook by my brother Andy. When I tracked it online I found it was a room within Sammezzano Castle in Italy – only four hours by car from our home of Menton on the French Riviera.

The castle is not open to the public, remains unoccupied and is currently for sale. It is watched over and protected by a local preservation society.

We first visited on the one open day a year that the current owners allow. There was no electricity so our visit was illuminated by the sun through cleverly positioned stained-glass windows. The castle gave out a special beauty and was pervaded by a mysterious ambience of the past.

The richness of colour and the intricate design of the luxurious internal architecture was a genuine feast for our eyes.

From the time we first arrived at the base of the hill my creative juices were pumping, and by the end of the day, my story had a beginning and an end.

The research has been a delightful journey; Florence offers such an abundance of history and romance, from its food, wine and architecture to its inhabitants' zest for life.

The nearby Tuscany countryside is a visual symphony of perfectly sculpted hilltop castles and villas offering any visitor a taste of the Italian dream.

Every step of writing this story, from onset to completion, has been a sheer pleasure for me. I trust you will enjoy reading it as much as I have writing it.

Acknowledgements

I offer my sincere thanks to all those who helped and encouraged me with this book.

To my brother, Andrew Rennie, for the very first seed of an idea when he posted a photograph of the magical castle of Sammezzano on Facebook. This initiated the journey that culminated in this story.

To Massimo Sottani, the gate keeper of Castle Sammezzano, for his assistance and support.

To my editor, Philippa Donavan, for her persistence and tolerance.

To the special friends who shared their time to read for me: Dame Pieter Stewart, Mary Ciurlionis, Wendy Newman and especially the late Michelle Amass – a kindred spirit and a wonderful friend.

To Sue Winston and Sue Howard for their constant support.

To the talented Robin Anderson and Anneke Stewart for their inspiration for the cover.

Many thanks to RedDoor Publishing for your belief in my story.

With all my love, I thank my daughter Emily and her husband Marc for their support and the gift of my adorable granddaughter Poppy. Most of all, I thank my extraordinary husband Tim, whom is always there for me.

Also by Merryn Corcoran

The Silent Village

Chapter 1

What were those girls up to now?

Their giggles sounded as noisy as a flock of seagulls. Hopscotch was meant to tire them out, not stretch their vocal cords. Allessia rested back on the park bench. She closed her eyes to avoid squinting into the low Mediterranean sun and seized the moment to selfishly indulge in her own thoughts. Old Jean Claude was perched on the adjoining bench, watching the pétanque game that his friends played close to the young girls' hopscotch. He mumbled something.

'What did you say, Jean Claude? I can't quite hear you!'

Edging across so he was right next to Allessia, Jean Claude pushed his white, garlic-scented, moustache close to her ear.

'If I were you I'd be very wary of that Marseilles farmer who's taken over the property in front of yours. They say he bribed officials to get it at that price. He'll be looking at yours next.'

'Thanks, Jean Claude, but don't worry – my Joseph has been keeping an eye on him.'

Attempting to mask her anxiety, she gave the old man a goodbye peck on his ruddy, wrinkled cheek then quickly moved over to wind up the hopscotch game.

'Mama, Mama, please can I have a gelato? Please, please?'

Allessia's daughter Sylvie jumped up and down like an excited kitten as they left the pétanque terrain. Sylvie was eight years old, an only child with dark, curly hair and large, brown eyes. Happiness and curiosity radiated from her perfectly oval face. She clutched her mother's hand tightly, but quickly dropped it once they were in sight of Giovanni's Gelato Parlour.

Giovanni's had been selling ice cream in Menton since Allessia first visited nearly twenty years ago. Like Giovanni, Allessia was born and raised in Italy, just across the border from Menton. She had met her French husband, Joseph Reiss, at the border market when she was just fifteen years old and for her, it was love at first sight. Joseph and his family were Jewish and it had taken two years of family arguments before both sets of parents had eventually conceded to the couple's marriage.

It used to be so simple. The border was just a formality. While the French believed their wine was the best, there was no doubt the Italians made the best gelato. Why should it all have to change because those fascists in Berlin and Rome said so?

'Buongiorno, Giovanni. The usual for my little one, please.'

'Ah! Allessia, you look as beautiful as always.'

'And you, Giovanni, are as charming as always. And, before you ask, just one scoop!'

As Allessia followed Sylvie out of the parlour, Giovanni lifted the counter lid and sidled up beside her, his kind, wrinkled eyes full of concern.

'My dearest friend, things are not looking good. Many of our Jewish friends have left town – you should all be on your way.'

Allessia prickled defensively. 'My Joseph takes the view that most of what they're saying is just hearsay or rumour.'

'I pray to the Blessed Virgin that is true,' he replied, sadly.

Allessia forced a smile at Giovanni's parting comment and then took her daughter's free hand as they walked briskly up the street.

Allessia looked like a typical northern Italian woman. She stood at a mere five-feet-two inches, her long black hair was loosely braided and her deep brown eyes complemented her sun-tinted, glossy, olive complexion. She'd spent the first seventeen years of her life cocooned with her close-knit family in the medieval, hilltop village of Castel Vittorio. Since then, her husband Joseph had influenced every part of her life, down to the Rubinstein red lipstick which accentuated her full, sensual lips. The last nine years under his influence had added a veneer of French chic to her natural, striking appearance.

The family villa was only a ten-minute walk from Giovanni's. It nestled in the midst of a large garden, up a gentle slope, with colourful views across Menton to the sea. Sylvie had finished her ice cream and skipped ahead, arriving first at the ornate wrought-iron gate. It creaked loudly as she struggled to push it open, using the full force of her small frame.

The fragrant path that led from the gate to the family villa and their small hotel was Allessia's pride and joy; her contribution to her husband's family home and business was to design and plant a welcoming perfumed approach. The small eight-room hotel shared the pathway and sat just behind their villa. The grounds had been neat and tidy when she first arrived but the gardens had lacked structure. Placing tubs of lavender and citronella, interspersed with exotic flowering succulents bordering the path, Allessia had managed to create a rather grand first impression – more than the property itself delivered. Climbing jasmine clung to the fence beside the path, emitting its delicious fragrance, whilst neatly clipped boxed hedging gave a feeling of structure to the borders of the property.

'Happy Birthday, Allessia.' Ruth, Allessia's mother-in-law, greeted her with a big hug.

'Thank you', she replied, 'I didn't expect anyone to remember considering what's going on.'

'On that note, where's the little one?'

'In the back garden in her secret hiding place, with her baby.' Both women smiled.

'I think it best to wait 'till after dinner to give her the bad news. Let her enjoy the cake first.'

'Oh Ruth, you shouldn't have gone to any trouble. But, seeing as you have, did you use the last of the sacred chocolate?'

Ruth was happy to see a brief flash of her daughter-in-law's dry sense of humour. Allessia adored Ruth. She was a matronly woman who inspired confidence, who always stood tall and self-assured. Her pure-white hair never left the constraints of a severe bun, tied at the nape of her neck. In contrast, her faded eyes radiated a relaxed happiness from behind the wire-rimmed spectacles, and her soft mouth was rarely without the warmth of her generous smile.

The door flew open and Sylvie held up her bedraggled-looking doll.

'I kept the secret, Grandmama! I never told Mama – and look, my baby is all dressed for the birthday party. I can't wait for the cake. Please say it's chocolate. Are Gramps and Gran Orengo going to bring Mario with them? I can't wait to play with him again.' Her words spilled over themselves.

'I'm sorry, little one, Mario won't be coming this time. Gramps is coming alone and will be leaving early in the morning. Please go up and have your bath, then you can put your special party dress on.'

'It's not fair!' Sylvie stamped her small foot and stormed off.

The Reiss villa wasn't as grand as some of its neighbours. But the rooms were large enough and stylishly decorated, predominantly in pastel blue and soft shades of lemon – the favoured colours of neighbouring Provence. Downstairs was a salon, a large kitchen and a washing room. Upstairs there was a bathroom and four large bedrooms, three of which enjoyed sea views.

The villa had always basked in loving family warmth, but divided opinions now soured the once comfortable atmosphere and Allessia's dread of the following day dampened the joy she normally would have felt on her birthday.

'Happy birthday, beautiful girl.' Allessia's father-in-law Daniel joined them. He handed her a bunch of tiny white and lemon daisies tied with some old string.

At six-foot-two inches Daniel towered over Allessia. He was extremely tall for a French man and completely bald, with a perfectly-shaped, bronzed head that shone above a deeply-furrowed brow. His eyebrows were grey and bushy like two fat furry caterpillars that were the butt of many family jokes.

'Oh, Daniel, thank you, I'm going to miss you both so much.'

He took the posy from her hands, laid it on the table and pulled her towards him in a tight hug. The three of them then sat together as Ruth poured out the hot chicory essence they drank in place of coffee. As he absent-mindedly stroked his eyebrows, Daniel asked Allessia about her day and how she thought Sylvie would react to the news.

'Come on, Daniel, what are you getting at? I know you well enough to recognise the signs of father-in-law diplomacy.'

'Well, my dear, I would like to say something now as there may not be another chance after tonight. When Joseph first wanted to marry you it wasn't that we didn't like you, or that we were particularly religious – our hesitation was that mixed marriages can be so difficult. Not so much with you being Italian, more with us being Jewish. But Ruth and I want you to know that you are the best addition to the family we could have wished for. Whatever happens, please know how much we love you.'

Humbled by his words, Allessia took their hands in hers and gave them an affectionate squeeze.

'You didn't need to say that, I know you love me. But thank you – it means a lot. Let's just get through our last night together as happily as we can.'

Allessia excused herself so that she could freshen up before dinner. She sat in front of the dressing table and brushed her hair, feigning enthusiasm by dressing up a little. As she scrutinised her face in the mirror she felt a sense of loss of her youth. A few more laughter lines had made an appearance around her eyes and the dimples on either side of her smile had deepened, well on their way to becoming wrinkles. She regularly found herself plucking out the odd grey hair but at least she hadn't put on any weight. Having applied her signature red lipstick, she felt a little more confident. She offered herself a brief smile in the mirror before heading back downstairs.

'Sylvie, you may get the special cutlery set out tonight and give each piece a shine before you place it down.' Allessia had tried to keep things as normal as possible. They'd all gathered in the kitchen, the true heart of their home, as the mouth-watering smell of fresh baking pervaded the room.

'Yes, Mama. What icing is Gran going to put on the cake?' Sylvie was now washed and dressed in a pretty pink pinafore dress that was saved for special occasions.

'The birthday cake only comes out when we've eaten our main meal. You'll see the icing then. So you'd better be hungry.'

'Where's the birthday girl?' Joseph called out as he walked in with a huge bunch of lilies. 'Happy birthday, my darling.' He laid the flowers on the sideboard and kissed his wife passionately.

'That's yukky, Papa. You're being so soppy,' Sylvie shouted as she squeezed in between her parents' embrace.

'OK, a big kiss for you too, my angel in pink.' Joseph swung her up and gently planted a kiss on her nose. Allessia's husband was tall, handsome and rugged and his rapidly receding hairline made him look like his father. But the similarity ended there. Joseph was like an ostrich with his head in the sand – he didn't want to believe the German propaganda and was reluctant to leave his family home and business.

At around 6 p.m. the old Orengo truck pulled up outside. Allessia quickly slipped out of the kitchen so she could have a few words in private with her father.

'Papa, is everything organised for the morning?'

He embraced her with both arms, whispering his reply to her in Italian. 'Allessia, you don't have to do everything your husband says. You and the little one can come tomorrow as well. Your Mama and I only want you to be safe.'

As Allessia inhaled the familiar tobacco fragrance that clung to her father's clothes and heard the soothing lilt of her native tongue, she relaxed a little.

'Papa, I've been over it a hundred times in my mind and I've decided we must stay together. I think Joseph will be safer if he's with a Catholic wife.'

Her father, Luigi Orengo, was only forty-eight years old, but hours spent working outdoors coupled with the stress of the war had emphasised his bad posture and aged him prematurely; but while he stood only two inches taller than Allessia, he still had a full head of rich brown hair.

The rest of the extended Reiss family greeted Luigi at the door. He wearily took a seat at the table, and then took a large envelope out of his tatty satchel. He kissed his granddaughter and passed it to her.

'Look Mama, look! Mario has drawn me a picture, and written me my very own letter.' Sylvie's smile was infectious enough to lift the sombre mood, albeit momentarily. 'Don't you read it, Mama, I can do it by myself, I can read Italian very well.' She proudly read out the few simple words from her ten-year-old cousin and then basked in the applause that followed the demonstration of her linguistic skills.

When the first course was finished, Daniel stood up and tapped his glass to gain everyone's attention.

'Oh no, Grandpapa, not another of your long speeches? We need to eat up so we can have the birthday cake!'

'Sylvie, I want you to sit quietly and listen very carefully.' At the sound of Grandpapa's serious voice, Sylvie was wide-eyed and sat perfectly still.

'Terrible things are happening to Jewish people because of this war. We don't know if everything we hear is true, but we must protect ourselves, so Grandmama and I will be leaving Menton in the morning. But we must all keep it a secret, especially you, Sylvie, as we don't want to get anyone else into trouble for helping us. You can't even tell your very best friends. OK?'

Allessia pulled up her chair close to her daughter; she could sense the child's fear as the adult's sombre mood enveloped the room.

'Where are you going? How long will you be away?' Sylvie's baffled questions sounded small and fragile.

'Gramps Orengo will take us with him early in the morning. We'll stay up in Castel Vittorio with him and Gran.' Daniel maintained his authoritative stance.

'But Grandpapa, that's all the way to Italy.' Sylvie was on the verge of tears.

'Nonsense, it's just across the border. You can come and visit us, dear child, when we all agree it's safe.' He shot a questioning glance at his son.

The two women retreated out to the cooking area.

'Allessia, please reconsider; please keep the pressure on Joseph to see sense.' The tears glistened in Ruth's eyes as she whispered to her daughter-in-law.

'I've tried,' Allessia replied, 'but he just won't believe the Germans will oust the Italians and occupy this part of France. You know how passionate he is about this hotel. What more can I do?'

They wrestled to contain their emotions as they finished icing the birthday cake, but at least it created a distraction and put a smile back on Sylvie's little face. The family sang a subdued 'Happy Birthday' before mother and daughter blew out the candles.

'Grandpapa, I have an idea. As I'm not allowed to go to proper school now, why don't I come with you and Grandmama – just for a holiday?' Sylvie asked as she started on her second piece of chocolate cake.

Allessia immediately interjected. 'Sylvie, you're only half Jewish on your father's side. I'm Roman Catholic which is what you are as well, so you'll be safe here with us, and besides, you're our little girl and we want you here with us.'

'Sylvie,' Joseph continued, 'it is very important you say you are a Catholic to anyone who may ask questions. You remember taking your First Holy Communion with the other children? Well, that makes you Catholic.'

The five grownups hadn't touched their cake. Each sat quietly, their strained faces betraying their inner turmoil.

*

Once Allessia had finally tucked her daughter into bed, the adults huddled closer around the table and spoke in hushed voices.

'Joseph, please reconsider coming with us tomorrow. Allessia and Sylvie may be Catholic but with a name like Reiss you're obviously Jewish.' Daniel was clearly desperate.

'Papa, I just don't believe it will be as bad here in Menton as in other parts of the country. I'm sure a lot of it is exaggerated. Besides, you built up this business and I'm damn well not leaving it for the Germans or any of the Mussolini henchmen to take. The minute we show weakness, we'll lose it all.'

Allessia had listened to this same conversation in many different forms over the past few weeks. The question continually gnawed away at her like a nagging pain: were her in-laws right? She now feared her husband was allowing his wishful thinking and pride to cloud his judgement.

Despite the tension and the strong differences of opinion, they all shared a tender kiss as they finally said goodnight. Ruth placed her arm around her husband as they sat together on the large bed they had shared for over thirty years, their careworn faces softened by the glow of the single burning candle.

'Daniel, we just have to accept this situation. We don't want to part with bad feelings tomorrow. Joseph hasn't experienced the same anti-Semitic sentiments you did before you moved here. I guess it's because we've been more or less accepted by the extended family and community. He just can't believe the worst of them.' She rested her head on his shoulder.

'This may be our last night in this bed, in this house,' said Daniel anxiously. 'Oh Ruth! I'm so frightened for our son. But he's his own man. You're right… tomorrow our goodbyes must all be without judgement, regret or blame.'

About the Author

Merryn Corcoran was born in New Zealand and has enjoyed success in the business world. In addition to writing, Merryn is the London ambassador for Beau Joie champagne. She also works for London-based **Cork Films** as executive producer and publicist, with its most recent movie *The Stolen* released in UK cinemas in October 2017. Merryn has been a keen supporter of **UNICEF** for the past 14 years, chaired and organised an annual celebrity Gala Ball in London and raised approximately £1,000,000 for the charity. She was made a UNICEF Honorary Fellow (UK) in 2002.

Find out more about RedDoor Publishing and sign up to our newsletter to hear about our **latest releases, author events,** exciting **competitions** and more at

reddoorpublishing.com

YOU CAN ALSO FOLLOW US:

 @RedDoorBooks

 RedDoorPublishing

 @RedDoorBooks